THE TRANSFER

THE TRANSFER

SILVANO CECCHERINI

Translated from the Italian by Isabel Quigly

GEORGE BRAZILLER

NEW YORK

87325

"*And they know nothing,*
they do not want to know,
And they feel no pity"

TOLSTOY, *Ivan Ilyitch*

PART I

I

THE GUARD CALLED HIM. OLGI PICKED UP HIS
haversack, with all his things stowed in it, and went out. He
had already said goodbye to the others. The guard shut the cell
door again.

The courtyard glared white in the sunshine. Unused to it,
Olgi blinked. His chest and the nape of his neck hurt. Huge flies
circled dizzily in the heat, frantically round the dustbins.

A few steps down a passage, and there was no longer any sun
and summer light, but a grey unchanging season. The kingdom
of dusty records.

"Prisoner leaving," said the guard.

"Searched him?" asked the sergeant in the records office.

"Not yet."

"Do so then," said the sergeant, acting the sergeant.

Olgi, who remained passive – not hostile, merely passive –
was searched, and so was the haversack, revealing its miserable
contents: two books, an exercise book, a bagful of olives, a
loaf of bread, some old linen.

Meanwhile the sergeant was hunched over a large register,
writing. His face lacked nobility, but looked calm and contented
and had something of the beauty and dignity of a priest saying
mass.

"Come along," he said gently, without looking at Olgi. He
opened a small door at the end of the passage. "In here. The
carabinieri will be along soon."

And, professionally diligent, he locked the door behind him.

It was a small, bare room, with a bench fixed to the wall. On
it were scrawled obscenities and curses. And a few crude drawings. Olgi took no notice. He had been inside twenty years.

9

The pain in his chest was still there; under the breast-bone and through to his back. Olgi knew what that pain, that symptom, meant: it was his heart shouting stop it, I'm sick of beating, I've been working forty-six years for you, what's the use?

I'm not delaying you, Olgi told his heart, I'm just as tired as you are, but . . . today, today of all days, just when I'm moving, are you going to stop?

And he stretched out on the bench, shutting his eyes, avoiding thought, breathing evenly, so as not to give any help to the agonizing pain that was trying to snuff out his life. His expression was no longer defensive or insolent; he just looked like a poor man.

Half an hour went by. An hour. The pain eased, and the man lying on the bench smiled. It'll be all right, he said, childishly happy, I'll be off . . .

The carabinieri came – three of them, a fat old NCO and two strong lads. The NCO was holding a paper. He read it, and as a mere formality asked:

"Are you Valnisi, Olgi, son of Pietro?" scarcely looking at the prisoner.

"Yes," answered Olgi.

The NCO looked at the sheet again, and said:

"You've got 870 lire, right?"

"Yes."

"Then we can go."

And they moved off: first one of the young men holding the end of the chain; then the sick man, firmly handcuffed; then the other lad, watching him carefully; and beside him the fat NCO with a leather bag under his arm.

They went through a gate, then another gate, into a court-yard larger than the inner one, and much cleaner – with flower beds and small trees, for the offices of the chief warder and the prison warden were there. And even that heavy gate had a gay and civilized air to it – newly painted and with ornamental plants at the sides.

Grey in the sunshine, the prison van waited.

The van – a prison on wheels, completely closed – left and drove through noisy streets. Olgi heard women's voices and children's shouts; life was there all round him, and within him as well, in insistent echoes.

The van turned, stopped. The NCO opened the door from the outside and Olgi saw a narrow street, shops and windows, people passing and watching curiously: a boy flashed by on a bicycle, a dog barked. Life was going on, just as it had done before: his fate was of no importance, and knowing this, he felt melancholy but at peace.

The courthouse, less ugly than the prison, was also in that street, and nine men, handcuffed and chained in threes, came out of it. Nearly all of them were young and still wearing their own clothes except for two who were dressed, like Olgi, as convicts; they were carrying bulging haversacks and boxes tied up with string, and some had suitcases.

They were cursing and protesting, because the chain hindered their movements and when, in the confusion, a man pulled or moved a bit abruptly it hurt the wrists of the man chained next to him. The van was too small to hold all of them as well as the carabinieri on guard; it was hard to breathe . . .

"Close up, close up together," the man in charge of the guard kept saying. "Christ, it's not far!"

A man with a great grinning mouth and a Roman accent trod on Olgi's foot and prodded him with his elbow, without apologizing. There was not much light in the van, and in the half-light faces looked uglier than ever.

In ten minutes they reached the station. They were taken into a room where there was a table, a fat young man wearing a white uniform with white gloves and a revolver, a poster advertising the beauty of the Alpine lakes, and three benches.

Olgi sat down; so did the two dressed as convicts and those chained to them. The rest remained standing, three on one side and three over by the door. The Roman twisted his great mouth. His long hair gleamed with brilliantine, and he wore shoes made of plaited rope. A squat fellow with a moustache and sun-glasses, and a tall, thin, hungry-looking man with a crooked nose, were chained to him.

Olgi watched attentively, love and compassion in his eyes. He always watched everything with interest. Especially people. Forced to live enclosed in a few square yards – and this for more than seven thousand days – he had made up for the smallness and narrowness of his physical life by developing his mind and imagination.

A tall, young fellow with a hard, aggressive gangster's face, was on the other chain with an elegant but insolent-looking man and a dark, silent one. The others had no personality; they were insignificant, the sort that one can meet in the street and forget at once. And yet among them there was one who had cut off a woman's head.

One thing aroused Olgi's curiosity: who was the showy youth in the white coat and gloves? He couldn't be a waiter with that great revolver dangling. Nor was he a carabiniere, because no carabiniere in history has ever worn white. White isn't severe. Maybe he was a city policeman. But what on earth could city policemen have to do with trains?

He could have asked, and appeased his curiosity, but he was ashamed of showing such ignorance of the world. He had been standing still so many years, but the world was moving ahead, and changing.

Trains went by, full of people, some without stopping, others stopping for a few minutes; and there was always a pretty girl or elegant young lady at one of the windows. A glance, a smile, and away, each to his own destiny.

They were waiting for their train, a slow one called the poor man's train – not because it was really the poor man's train, but because it had a prison coach and on its way picked up hand-cuffed men.

The genial and obviously happy young man, who was dressed like a waiter or an ice-cream man and was made to feel safe and important by that big revolver, announced that the train was running an hour late; none of the carabinieri looked disap-pointed, maybe they were quite used to set-backs like that. Standing there four-square and solid, armed, as their repressive, watchful job demanded, what on earth could they be chewing over, Olgi wondered? Small concrete, reassuring thoughts, about their safe pay-packets, their virtuous wives at home, their nice children at school, or elevated thoughts about Duty, Re-sponsibility, Command . . .

In the stink and sweat a raucous voice yelled 'ice-cream', offering a cool heaven in the hell of that heat. A child awoke in Olgi's heart – oh the joy of having an ice, even a single one, a tiny one, and enjoying it in peace, like a reason for living.

A train rumbled past and carried away the voice of the ice-cream man.

II

THE AUGUST HEAT HUNG HEAVILY IN THE ROOM, and his thoughts were trapped in it, like flies.

'Visit our wonderful Alpine lakes,' said the poster; and there were mountains, clearly outlined, beautiful trees reaching up into the sky, and the blue, cool-looking water. Everything there must be harmonious, happy and pure.

Olgi's neighbour nudged him with his knee.

"Excuse me," he said, in a strong southern accent, "have you come from the prison here?"

He wore an old-fashioned jacket and a funny striped cap. The eyes in his olive face were sad.

"Yes," said Olgi. "I've come from the prison here."

"And what's it like? Is the food good?"

"It's prison food," said Olgi.

The man gaped, thinking or feeling or suffering something he could not translate into ordinary, acceptable words. So he said:

"Hot, isn't it? But it's August. See all those people going to the sea? I'm from Lecce. Lucky we're not kept locked up here. You should see how it is at Bari, or at Naples! And it's no joke in Rome, either."

"If they had a place to put us here," said Olgi, "they'd lock us up in it. You get no advantages."

The words meant just that, but in his thoughts Olgi meant something else. The fact was he no longer cared about any privileges that might or might not be given him. That was no longer the problem. What counted was finding advantages within an unpleasant reality. At one time he too had loathed being shut up in the station cell because it was sad, nearly always dirty – a dead place in which even time died. He was forgetting for a moment that the cell also had a bed, where an old convict could lie down and rest his bones as he waited patiently for the train to take him away.

The man from Rome, chatting and joking the whole time, continually twisted his nimble thief's hands in the cell of his handcuffs, shifted his feet, shook his head – full of youth and life, untroubled by conscience. And the short man, with the moustache and impenetrable black eyes, laughed, fierce teeth showing through hair as hard as a boar's bristles. The tall thin man with the crooked nose didn't laugh; nor did the man from Lecce. The fair Sicilian laughed. And the tall young man smiled a little ironically.

The chief guard was now reading a newspaper, a serious

official newspaper, holding it unfolded in front of him. Olgi, who was opposite could read the headlines.

'Cold war continues.' 'Noble speech by our Foreign Minister: safeguard peace in freedom and justice.' 'Thieves caught breaking and entering.' 'Kills wife with axe and jumps under train.' 'Inherits eighty million from an uncle he thought dead.' 'Rousing words from the Minister of Information,' etc.

The NCO folded the newspaper in four and fanned himself with it. His face expressed no special feeling or thought. As he fanned the newspaper to cool himself a little, sometimes on the right and sometimes on the left of his face, he threw those facts, those events, about in handfuls, one here, one there, like confetti.

The fat young man dressed like an ice-cream seller was talking. Turning to a keen-looking young carabiniere, but obviously wanting a wider audience, he told how he had been with his girl-friend the previous evening – and he said 'girl-friend' as one might say my Alfa Romeo – to see a film where monsters, as tall as skyscrapers, were awakened or resurrected – and here his explanations became a little confused – by atomic radiations.

"A science fiction film," smiled the keen young carabiniere.

"It may have been science fiction, but my girl was scared out of her wits."

"Excuse me," the man from Lecce said, nudging Olgi's knee again. "Are you going to Gorgona, by any chance?"

"No," said Olgi.

"I just don't see. We're all together, they make us travel together, and I'm the only one going to Gorgona. What bloody luck . . ."

"But look," Olgi said, persuasively, "it's you who's lucky to be going to Gorgona. You may be the only lucky one among us. Gorgona's a farming prison. D'you think it's nothing to work out of doors, in the sunshine? To look at the sea? The sea's glorious round those islands in the Tuscan archipelago; you can even bathe if you want to, and can swim."

"But they told me," said the man from Lecce, sticking firmly to his convictions, stubborn in his dislike, "that the food there's no good. And if the food's no good what's the use of sun? What's the use of sea?"

"Well supposing," said Olgi, his eyes full of ironic amusement but anxious to enlighten the poor devil all the same, "supposing the food's nothing special. You can always stoke up with the fruits of the earth, pull up a nice onion and eat it with salt; or some beans; or greens."

"But I can't do farm work. And if I can't, why send me to a farm camp? I had a small business in oil. But where they're sending me I won't be selling oil. If I've got to stay there for my whole four years I'll die. I've got a wife and four kids. Who's going to feed my kids?"

So said the man from Lecce in the funny striped cap, and as there was nothing to answer, Olgi turned to look at the square shoulders, big feet, big hands and revolver of the ice-cream man – who fascinated him – and then stared dreamily at those incredible trees by the Alpine lakes. He felt as if thought and feeling were suspended, as if he had to draw apart and shut himself away, because he was steeped in suffering and couldn't take any more.

Olgi was shaken out of his trance by the Roman and the tall young man talking excitedly. Again he was filled with curiosity, full of love for life. The two weren't quarrelling, although such men could easily exchange insults and even blows (but chained and handcuffed, that wasn't so easy); they were expressing male excitement, as if with ruffled feathers and reddening cockscombs, about a female of the species passing by with nothing on.

"Why, she's naked," the Roman exclaimed. "She's naked, she's naked," echoed the tall young man.

There was a rush, heads almost knocked together to see this portent. Even Olgi stretched out his neck but could see nothing

16

because she was already on the other side of the pavement. But he 'saw' her just the same, walking naked among the people (and of course young and beautiful) showing with immodest pride what women usually keep hidden.

Olgi soon realized his mistake and laughed inwardly at his lively imagination, pleased and even proud that it was so youthful and alive. It was only a bather who was showing sunburnt thighs through a slit in her dress – the beach was only about three hundred yards from the train. Olgi 'saw' the beach, with all its usual peculiarities and characteristics. And above all he saw and heard the sea.

Far away, but not so very far, they heard a train puffing. It drew nearer and nearer, and slowed down as it entered the station. It was coming from the south and might be any train going north, but it might also be the slow train they were waiting for, with the prison coach on the end or behind the engine. A train that was in no hurry, and that for better or worse would always reach its destination.

III

IT WAS THE SLOW TRAIN. IT STOPPED ON THE NEAREST line, with the prison van by chance outside the first-class waiting-room. It was a long gay train, full of people.

The people at the windows, on the platform, and coming out of the waiting room turned and looked curiously at the group or human herd, which, though handcuffed and chained, was taking along its own luggage, or fodder. They either could not or would not leave their things behind, even though they were chained and obviously uncomfortable; so clearly they were also going on a journey, were also passengers.

"What have they done, I wonder?" the onlookers thought

curiously, not "Who are they, I wonder?", since they could see perfectly well, or thought they could see, what they were. And those who were travelling with visibly light luggage and without any visible chains, were glad not to be travelling so wearily, so uncomfortably, without freedom and with shame.

But the man from Rome was not looking with shame at those who were 'free but daft', on the contrary he glared at them scornfully. Nor was it shame or contrition that the tall one showed on his gangster's face, or the squat fellow with the moustache. Or the fair Sicilian, or the tall man with the crooked nose. But the dark silent man, the man from Lecce and the others may have felt shame.

Olgi did not; he was unashamed but not barefaced, unhumbled yet not arrogant. He had paid the long price of suffering, and had settled his account; he could look anyone calmly in the eye. Now that he was near his goal his luggage was light, although at first it had been heavy, terribly heavy, and at every station he had left something behind.

Olgi was the first on. They had unchained him but not removed the handcuffs; the running board was high, and to avoid falling he had to grab the handrail. A vigorous hand helped him from below. It was the tall gangster who, though handcuffed and carrying his own luggage, had enough strength for two.

"Thanks," said Olgi and looked at him, not surprised to find he had a kind expression.

"This way," said a gigantic carabiniere, and Olgi trotted after him, the haversack, which had slipped off his shoulders, thumping against his belly, the too-wide striped cotton trousers hanging down on his hips so that he was nearly tripping over them, and on his face an expression that was half ironic and half desperate.

They went down the left-hand corridor and half-way down the right-hand one. The cell doors were bolted, and faces appeared at cracks to get a breath of air or out of curiosity; the whole prison coach, which seemed sad and dead from the outside, was in fact full of bustle, voices and human noise.

The gigantic carabiniere shot back a bolt and said:

"In here."

He loosened the handcuffs and bolted the door again.

"Thanks," said Olgi.

There were three men already in there, but room for four. A glance was enough to classify the three: they were long-term convicts. They sat there quietly, uncaringly.

Better to travel with clods like these, thought Olgi, than with crazy fellows like that Roman. And, being wise now, he was glad the door wasn't quite closed, glad to have the handcuffs loosened so that he'd be able to slip them off (and in fact he did slip them off and put them on the rack beside his haversack, like the others). He sat down.

And almost gaily, without really meaning to start up a conversation, but just for the sake of talking and to get his own back on that snail-like train, he said:

"Let's hope the driver of this hearse hasn't dropped off and won't keep us boiling here for too long."

"It's off at one," said the man sitting opposite him, who had a thin pale face. His accent showed he came from the Marche.

"An hour and a half to wait!" exclaimed Olgi, speaking and gesticulating like a travelling business man who has no time to waste.

He realized this and laughed. But the pale man didn't laugh. He looked at Olgi, his eyes alarmingly alive and penetrating in that dead face.

I've seen that face, thought Olgi. But where?

"I believe I know you," he said.

"Me too," said the other. "But I don't remember where."

"I think I know you, too," said Olgi's neighbour. He had a big face with a tiny pink nose, like a baby's.

19

"I've seen you too," Olgi said. "But where?"

"That's right," said the tough man with the baby's nose. "Where? Inside, of course. I've been inside fifteen years. I'm from Calabria. Name's Enrico."

"I've been in sixteen," Olgi said. "On my present sentence. But counting my previous sentence I've done twenty."

The man with the small nose whistled, as if it was a record to admire.

"I've been inside seventeen years," said the pale man from the Marche.

Olgi glanced at this man's neighbour, who looked like some sort of middleman. But the middleman shook his head.

"We've never met," he said peremptorily.

"I think you're right," said Olgi.

"I've been inside four years," the man explained, as if apologizing for having done so little, "and I've done them all at Sulmona. You've never been at Sulmona. If you had I'd have seen you because I was quartermaster and knew everyone."

"I haven't been at Sulmona," said Olgi, "but I've been at Porto Azzurro, at Perugia, Lucca, San Gimignano, Procida."

He said this to prod the memory of the man from the Marche, who shook his head however.

"At Civitavecchia?"

"No."

"At Fossombrone?"

"No."

"At Montelupo?"

"Yes, five years at Montelupo: from 1945 to 1950. And under strong guard the whole time, in a *letto di forza*,"* said the man.

Then Olgi remembered him clearly – he was the man who didn't speak, didn't eat (they examined him every six days), and

*A board to which the prisoner is strapped by his wrists and ankles. It used to be applied to prisoners affected by – or suspected of being affected by – epilepsy.

lay stoically in the stink of his own filth. A trickster with the heroic toughness of a saint.

"And how did it end?" asked Olgi, feeling a little appalled again.

"For five years I stuck it. Five years are about eighteen hundred days. I defy anyone to do it under those conditions. I thought I'd win, I thought they'd admit my mind was completely sick and so I'd get off penal servitude. But they were more pig-headed and more patient than me and could have waited not just five years but a lifetime, because they weren't suffering, but just watching me suffer. That's why they won," said the lifer without bitterness, but with indifference, as if he was now beyond struggling and hoping.

"Got it – it was at Porto Azzurro," exclaimed the man from Calabria. "It was at Porto Azzurro we met."

"Yes, I think it was," said Olgi.

"I was the fellow who saw to the straw. Don't you remember? I used to bring it round."

"Yes, now I remember."

"You've got an eagle on your chest," said the man from Calabria delightedly, "haven't you?"

"More like a chicken than an eagle."

"Doesn't matter, so long as it's there and I could recognize you. But . . . how you've changed! You're like someone else."

"I look like someone else," said Olgi. And he thought: but I am someone else.

But he couldn't say it, it had no meaning. There was no point in saying it, only in feeling it within him, like yet another punishment that later became a reward. He couldn't change his skin, but what was a little tattooed skin?

And he had to say where he'd gone after leaving Porto Azzurro, and listen to the other man's talk of prison things, and prison thoughts. Outside were marvellous trees, girls with flower-like faces, romping children, sparrows in the sun, and the song of the sea.

The train suddenly jerked and started to move, as if it wanted to be off. And, in fact, it gathered speed – but quickly tired. The train had simply moved on to an unused piece of track.

IV

INSIDE THE PRISON COACH THE UPROAR AND shouting had increased but the noise wasn't made by all the men – just by a few. Always the same five, six or seven who shouted defiantly or mockingly from cell to cell, from corridor to corridor, region against region; Neapolitan against Milanese, Sicilian against Piedmontese, and the man from Rome against everyone.

Olgi and the other three were now silent, no longer able to communicate, strangers who happened to be travelling together. Only Enrico, the man from Calabria, burst out with acid, ugly remarks. He spared nothing and no one, everyone was his enemy, but he was specially riled by those four or five 'idiots' making a noise.

"Bicycle thieves," he said, "suitcase pinchers; they may snatch the odd bag now and then but they're really pimps to their own mothers and sisters. They come in for a year or two, they've got a bit to spend so they behave as if they owned the place. Listen to them blowing their tops; but just you wait, you, and one fine day you may find you've got me to deal with and then you won't squeal through your mouths, oh no, you won't even squeal through your . . ."

If a carabiniere passed he spat into the corridor; and he bared his arms to show he too was tattooed.

Something was happening in the meantime, something that

had begun in the first cell of the left-hand corridor and was coming towards them as bolts were drawn on the doors and something was said. It was about buying food. No wine. But nearly all of them wanted wine.

"No wine," the sergeant said each time, "all the food you want, travelling packs and so on, but no wine. Wine's forbidden."

He reached Olgi's cell and began again.

"No wine, but food if you want it, travelling packs but no wine."

"How much is a travelling pack?" Olgi asked.

"It is 850 lire."

"No, thanks."

The lifer said nothing, nor did the man from Calabria. The middleman sat wondering for a moment, but he, too, remained silent, preferring not to buy anything, in case he had to share it.

"I bought a travelling pack in 1951 on this very line," said the man from Calabria. "I paid 750 lire, and afterwards I was hungrier than ever."

"What was in it?" asked the lifer, interested.

"Two rolls as big as this." He joined his finger and thumb to show the size of the rolls – "Some processed cheese, an orange, and a chicken's wing."

"Chicken?" the lifer said. "Chicken, wow!"

"And since then," said the man from Calabria in a melancholy way, "I haven't tasted chicken. Since 1951."

"I haven't since 1944," the lifer said. "But with that distinguished face of his," and he indicated Olgi, joking amiably, "imagine the chickens he must have eaten! One a day."

Olgi smiled, flattered. It wasn't the first time he'd been told he had a distinguished face. The sort of face you might find in the Cabinet!

And for another fifteen or twenty minutes they said no more. How hard it was to find pleasant subjects of conversation! And then it was so hot: the walls, gleaming with varnish, threw back a furnace-like heat.

A long sharp whistle, not from the engine but from a factory somewhere in the town, announced midday; and Olgi 'saw' workmen in overalls or summer sweat-shirts coming out from the factories, clerks in respectable collars leaving their offices, pretty typists and dressmakers gaily, although they had a living to make, hurrying to lunch and glancing sidelong at the handsomest men.

"How about eating ourselves?" Olgi said then, almost gaily too.

He took down his haversack, and opened the bag of olives. The man from the Marche and the Calabrian opened theirs as well.

"Green olives," said the man from the Marche, "what fine green olives!"

"They are," said the Calabrian.

"Help yourselves," Olgi said.

They took one each. Olgi gave the man from the Marche as many as he could hold in the hollow of his hand, and an equal number to the Calabrian, which left him with about the same. In exchange the Calabrian gave him some slices of salami and the man from the Marche a piece of cheese.

"No, no," Olgi protested, his distinguished face rather red.

He did not have any ulterior motive. But the others were already munching, with the sad concentration of animals, as was the middleman who had turned away from the others and was eating his roll; Olgi began eating too.

Afterwards they smoked, except for Olgi, a thick dark tobacco that filled the cell with stinking smoke. Each of them blissfully wrapped in his own foul breath.

There was a shudder as a train rushed by, then another train that arrived, and stopped and went on again noisily.

It was a train full of soldiers singing; that they were soldiers was clear from the sort of songs they sang. The middleman, who was sitting by the crack in the door (how Olgi envied him that place!) like a traveller at the window, also said they were soldiers.

"They're soldiers," said the Calabrian, who had also gone to peep through the crack. "They're braying like donkeys in the sun."

He scratched his shaven head, as if to extract an idea from it.

"They must be happy," he said, surprised and envious.

"Balls," said the lifer, "we've been soldiers ourselves."

And Olgi, who had shut his eyes, saw himself again walking gaily in warm sunshine (it was March, 1936) in line with other gay young men, called up to serve their country at sea.

His mother, already old at forty, her frail head full of foolish fears, dragged along behind him in her slippers; Olgi kept his neck stiff as a bantam's. What a lot of pretty girls around! – that was what mainly interested him.

When the train whistled his mother hugged him with clumsy tenderness and held out a small greasy package.

"They're two veal chops," she said softly.

Her lower lip trembled, Olgi kissed her on the cheek and got on quickly because he was afraid of bursting into tears among all those strangers.

The rapid clatter of the wheels carrying him away, far from the rathole house, from unemployment, from humiliating days that were always the same, made him feel gay and exalted, as if he had drunk some wine.

Olgi opened his eyes again, the noisy train had gone, and he ached with longing for his own train to leave as well.

V

THE TRAIN STARTED WITH A JERK, FEEBLY, LIKE AN
animal reluctant to move, but then loosened up and gained
strength, and all its wheels sang powerfully.

"See how it runs," said the Calabrian and laughed.

Olgi laughed too, given over to the movement of the train,
as he had been that far-off day. Could things miraculously repeat
themselves? He lived on hope, knowing that there was none,
and clung obstinately to the promise of a future of which he had
already been deprived.

The train now had to run through a stretch of barren country,
where at one time only buffaloes grazed and malaria spread
from the swamps. Then the land was drained and that proud,
desolate, Old Testament landscape became more habitable and
more modern (Olgi knew this from his reading, not because he
had stayed or travelled there. As he knew about Mauretania or
the steppes of Central Asia.)

But there was no smell of earth in the air, only the foul stink
of the heat inside the car.

The train, as though exhausted, slowed down and stopped.

"It was doing fine," Olgi said, disappointed.

"It's a slow train," said the man from the Marche, as if
defending a lost cause, "and it stops because it's got to. At
every station, even the small ones, someone gets on or off and
that's what it's for. It's not the Rome-to-Paris line, you know,"
and he shook his head pessimistically, because things were so
obvious but no one would understand them.

"At this rate it'll be night when we get there," said the
Calabrian peevishly.

"And what's that to you? If you get there in daylight the
night'll come just the same," said the man from the Marche.

"What's the time?" asked Olgi.

The middleman shrugged.

"Can't see a thing," he said.

Ignorant beast, Olgi thought of him, with your great lumpish soul. You've got the world before you and can't see a thing.

"Excuse me," he said and settled himself between the legs of the middleman, who shifted to make room for him.

Olgi looked. The world was an oblique strip the width of his hand – that was the width of the crack at the door – and in that strip the station wasn't included, only an extension of it, an ugly enclosure, a horseshoe-shaped hedge with two huts inside it, one for men and one for women.

A half bald, bandy-legged man with a bag on his back went by, looked at the train as a horse might look at a house, and disappeared. Olgi went back to his place, feeling immensely lonely and sad. It's never-ending, he thought, this agony. Everything now, squalid or cruel or pointless jarred him unbearably. He closed his eyes.

The train started up again.

And Olgi, since he was alive and still kept on living, opened his eyes again. For the first time he noticed the gleam in the eyes of the man from the Marche. It was a consoling feeling of comradeship. And he realized, though in fact he had realized it before, long before (only sometimes he forgot it), that it was shutting one's eyes that was agony, not wanting to know that other people were living and suffering too.

All the wheels of the train sang their song, and hearts might be gay or sad, but the wheels kept turning; come life or death the wheels kept turning. Only Olgi was no longer listening to the song of time. He had already arrived.

But what was the other trying to tell him? He smiled as he looked at him. But he didn't speak, it was Olgi who spoke.

"So after ten years we meet again."

"Yes, we do."

"On a train."

27

"On a train."

Was this what they wanted to tell each other? Or did the words really mean something else? Olgi noticed, meantime, that the man's hair was grey. He must be about the same age as himself. He had 'come inside' at twenty-six or seven, maybe twenty-eight, and would never get out. Never. He too was travelling with a haversack, where, among a little old linen, there might be some photographs.

"And where are you going now?" Olgi asked.

"To Porto Azzurro, of course. From S. Stefano to Porto Azzurro, and then from Porto Azzurro to S. Stefano, if I want a change. Till . . ." the lifer said meaningly.

And it was as if everything had been said. But Olgi wanted to know more, more . . . but how could he ask it? They looked into each other's eyes. But it isn't true that eyes speak.

"And where are you going?" asked the man from the Marche.

"To Saluzzo."

"Saluzzo?" said the man, as if Olgi had said Biarritz or Copacabana. "Saluzzo in Piedmont? Whew, what a bit of luck! You'll be able to see the mountains, Monterosa."

"No, Monviso," Olgi corrected him, "Monviso where the Po rises."

"The Po, the biggest river in Italy. I've learnt a bit of geography myself. How many trees there must be along the banks of the Po!"

"D'you like trees?" asked Olgi, surprised.

"Yes, maybe because I was born in a town, and I like mountains, and rivers. If I had the choice, I'd like to be buried without a coffin by a river, between two big trees."

Whereas, thought Olgi, they'll bury you at S. Gerbone, inside an ugly deal coffin, and they'll carry you out on the gardener's cart.

The train had stopped, briefly, and was now on its way again, moving freely and rhythmically.

The Calabrian kicked at the door.

"I want to go to the toilet," he shouted.

The very tall carabiniere opened the door, and didn't bolt it again, but stood there stiffly, solemn as a monument. Olgi took advantage of this to look farther out, into the sun caressing the earth. But he saw little: fields flying past, houses scattered here and there, and the tangled thorn hedge beside the railway line.

The Calabrian came back, having relieved himself. He was humming through his teeth, in a kind of happy grumble, but he soon stopped, rolled himself another cigarette, and sent stinking smoke blowing through his nostrils, an ugly look in his eyes once again.

The train slowed down again, whistled, and stopped.

"Who's for Orbetello?" asked the sergeant's voice in the corridor.

"Here," shouted the middleman getting up and hastily taking down his own luggage. He had a big brown leather suitcase, a bulky mountaineer's bag, and a haversack twice as big as a normal one. He put his own handcuffs back on his wrists and shouted again, "Here, here, I'm getting off at Orbetello," as if he was afraid of being forgotten.

"Hey, what's the hurry," said the sergeant, a jolly fat old fellow soon to be pensioned off. "The train's not leaving yet. It'll stop for half an hour. Is all this stuff yours? Why don't you bring your bed along with you?" he said, teasing cheerfully.

"Oh, not his bed," said the Calabrian with heavy sarcasm, "his wife can use that."

And when the middleman had gone he called him a dirty pig, a cuckold, a filthy skinflint and a notorious moneylender.

"He's got 800,000 lire in the bank and smokes tobacco from stubs. He's got houses and land and eats prison food. At Poggioreale he bought himself a herring, at Regina Coeli a few figs. He said he killed by mistake, ha ha, and they believed him. They always believe people with money. And now he's going to do his last months in a nut house. Whereas I'm going to Volterra. Is that justice?" he asked and spat on the floor with disgust, and then rubbed the spit out with the sole of his shoe.

The lifer smiled cynically and stared fixedly ahead of him, fidgeting his hands as they lay on his lean thighs – dry yellow hands like those of a dead man.

Olgi thought: We've left Lazio, we're at Orbetello, we're already in Tuscany. Orbetello, what a beautiful harmonious name! How many people live there? And he felt distressed, regretful, that he hadn't visited that town, Orbetello, when he might have. Like so much else he had thought unimportant he had left it irreparably behind him, without ever having known it.

But why didn't the other two take the middleman's place? It was the best seat, it was like the window seat in a first- or second-class compartment. You could look out and get the wind on your face. They had a right to it, one or other of them, and Olgi hadn't, he'd come last and couldn't take it.

But the pair of them clearly didn't want the privileged position. They were quite happy where they were, it seemed. Some people might be annoyed, rather than pleased, at having the wind in their face. And why look out, if everything looked the same?

Then Olgi yielded to temptation and said:

"Well, let's have a look at this Orbetello."

VI

HE SAW A RUSTY ROOF, AND A BIT OF YELLOW WALL, an old but not beautiful fountain, the usual fenced-in place – why were people so keen to put fences up everywhere? –

and then olive-trees and more olives, as far as the eye could see.

"This wretched driver," Olgi exclaimed, half serious and half joking, "keeps stopping the train on purpose outside the station, out at one end or the other; he never stops where the train ought to stop."

"It's because we're on the end of the train," explained the man from the Marche, with the resigned, afflicted air of a man talking to a mental deficient, "that's why we never get the station in front of us when the train stops. I've never seen a prison coach put on so that we get the station in front of us, the way the other carriages are."

"It depends," said the Calabrian, "what the station's like. If it's big the train can fit in completely, but if it's small part of the train's outside. It's like giving a tall fellow like you a small bed. What happens? If you stretch out at least your feet are outside. But if the bed's big enough you can fit in it completely. It's like that with a train in the station."

"But this is quite different," said the other. "What's that got to do with it? I was talking about the tail-end of the train."

"If the station's big enough," insisted the Calabrian, "being at the head or the tail just doesn't come into it."

But the man from the Marche went on maintaining that however large and well arranged the station, a train always had a head and a tail.

"It's elementary. Can't you see it's true?"

These words impressed the Calabrian, but he still insisted:

"The prison coach isn't always on the end of the train. Sometimes it's right behind the engine."

"And what difference does that make?" said the other man, modestly triumphant. "It doesn't alter a thing. There's still a head and a tail."

Olgi was distracted, and wasn't listening to this odd conversation, which was as pointless as life itself. He continued looking out at the thick green of the olive-trees, and brooding over some thoughts of his own, which the olive-trees had nothing to do with. They might be any other sort of tree, or thing, without affecting the way he was reasoning and thinking at that moment.

In fact his were independent thoughts, divorced from objects, self-sufficient; but this wasn't his favourite way of thinking. His favourite way of thinking was a thought that presupposed a feeling.

All the same, even as he meditated, he heard the sound of water at the fountain, and looked at it at once. A woman was drawing water in a bucket. She wasn't beautiful like Liz Taylor, nor was she even very young, yet it was pleasant to look at her, and see what was typically feminine about her. Her breasts, for instance. They swayed gently as she pumped the water. And her buttocks, too, which were round and broad, as only a woman's can be. It was doubtful if she had anything on under her dress. Her eyes were laughing at him.

Olgi began to warm up. He wasn't selfish, so he said:

"There's a woman at the fountain."

The lifer said:

"There are about one thousand three hundred million women in the world."

But the Calabrian, less of a philosopher and more of a man, asked, "What's she like?"

"About thirty-five, plumpish."

Then the Calabrian got up and went to look. He twisted his mouth and said, "She's had at least six kids. She's a cow."

The 'cow' moved off with her bucket full, and out of Olgi's line of vision. He sat down. That seat was now his, which made him feel almost gay; and this gaiety was mixed with the desire which the sight of that fine fat woman had aroused in him, and made him chatty and amusing.

"Well," he said, his voice tinged with amusement, "fancy

calling a fine plump wife like that a cow. I'd be touching heaven with my finger if I could just touch the hem of her knickers."

"She's no Sophia Loren," said the Calabrian, "she's no Gina Lollobrigida, she's no Soraya."

"But she's a fine healthy wife," exclaimed Olgi, "a warm live creature. She must smell like a field of corn."

The Calabrian insisted she must stink of the washing. When he wanted to think of one he wasn't going to think up one with tits hanging down to her navel, like the Africans, but of Gina, Sophia, Soraya, Marilyn, etc.

"So you make your imagination work too," Olgi said, laughing.

"Imagination? I don't imagine anything. I look. I've got them all here," and he indicated his haversack. "At least a hundred of them. Film stars, dancers, singers, princesses, models, beauties from all over the world."

"And have you got Liz?" asked Olgi, narrowing his eyes like a jealous lover.

"Liz? Who's Liz?"

"Why Elizabeth Taylor, of course! The most beautiful woman in the world."

"The most beautiful woman in the world is Gina Lollobrigida," said the Calabrian. "Even nursery school kids know that. Even he knows it."

"Me?" said the old lifer, surprised and disgusted. "I spit on the lot of them." And he spat. "When I want it I get myself a boy."

And a smile lit up his sad face, half affectionate and half obscene.

"You're wrong, you know," said Olgi. "The most beautiful woman in the world is Elizabeth Taylor."

"The most beautiful woman in the world is Gina Lllobrigida."

"No, it's Elizabeth Taylor."

"No, it's me," grinned the man from the Marche.

The fountain gurgled again. Olgi looked. It wasn't the gay, exciting wife from earlier on, but a sad wrinkled woman.

"Big arse again?" asked the Calabrian.

"It's an old woman," said Olgi. "Very old."

"An old woman?" said the lifer. "Oh, it's a long time since I saw a really old woman."

He moved over to look at her.

"Yes," he murmured, "she really is old."

What was his face now showing? Was he moved? Was it tenderness?

"She must be over seventy," he said.

And he stayed there, his arms resting on the door, his forehead on his arm, looking at her, till the old woman had filled her bucket and, bent and unsteady with the effort of carrying it, moved off with her slow, old-animal's walk, a decrepit old woman still fond of the pain of living.

The lifer sat down, without speaking. Suddenly the Calabrian said:

"I lost mine a couple of years ago, she was sixty-two. If she hadn't had cancer she'd have seen me free. She always said so, poor soul: 'I don't want to die before my Enrico comes out.' She was a bright old thing, my mother was, she still did all the housework, and the washing, and at night she pinched hours from her sleep to earn a bit making stockings and sent it to me. If it hadn't been for that cursed cancer that devoured her in six months she'd have seen me out."

So the Calabrian spoke of his mother, and looked at Olgi, and at the man from the Marche.

"My mother died last year, in winter," said Olgi. "Old women nearly always die in winter, when they're poor. She was seventy-two. She too used to say she didn't want to die before she'd seen me free. But she didn't make it, in spite of her longing and her love she didn't make it."

34

"My mother's still alive," said the lifer. "She's sixty-six and waiting for me. It's crazy, but she's waiting for me. She prays and weeps, for me and for the woman in the cemetery. Because mothers are like that: they weep for us and for those we've killed as well."

Again water gushed in the fountain: and Olgi looked again, glad that this time it was a boy. He had run, he had played, and now he was drinking avidly, his face under the violent jet, his mouth wide open, and a spotted dog jumped round him, whining.

The train whistled, and the wheels started up again, with jerks and tugs between one coach and the next, before it became a smooth continuous speed. There appeared and disappeared, in quick succession, a church's pointed bell tower, some rough anonymous buildings, a piazza; Orbetello, that no longer fascinating town, was already far behind them, and Olgi sat down, suddenly tired, bored with looking at a monotonous fleeing landscape, envying the Calabrian who had stretched out on the seat and could sleep, and no longer think, no longer remember, no longer suffer, only sleep.

VII

THE CALABRIAN LAY CURLED UP ON THE BENCH. HE was snoring lightly, and his face looked harsh and stubborn, though this was partly belied by the quaint attractiveness of that childish nose.

Olgi looked at the lifer whose position and expression hadn't altered for three hours. Had five years in a *letto di forza* turned him to stone? And yet he was living, he too loved his mother. Perhaps he had other attachments, other supports, but to Olgi the human problem to be solved wasn't that. He already knew that 'even a murderer's a man', what he wanted to know was something further. But what words could he use to ask it? He didn't even feel he had the right to.

And yet the need to know kept seizing him, irresistibly. Wasn't the Calabrian asleep? Weren't they alone? Facing one another? He could risk asking his question.

Suddenly he remembered the man was called Galloni. It was like an inner voice telling him so. He said:

"Galloni."

The man turned and looked sharply at him, a hint of cautious surprise in his impassive eyes. He said:

"After ten years you remember my name. Odd."

"I'd forgotten it, I suddenly remembered it, without trying, like visions suddenly flash inside you sometimes."

"Odd," the man repeated.

Olgi smiled in a friendly, familiar way.

"Galloni," he said.

"Well, what d'you want?" said the man, in a hard suspicious voice.

"Tell me truly, are you sorry?"

"Sorry for what?" said the lifer, genuinely surprised.

"For having killed, are you sorry you killed? Not just sorry because you've got into such a filthy mess, with results that'll last out your lifetime."

"What business is it of yours? What are you, a priest, a confessor?"

"I'm a man, like you, who has spent many years in prison."

"Did you kill as well? And now, when things have gone badly, prate of repentance?"

"I never killed anyone, but I might well have done so."

"I see, you're innocent, we're all innocent, or all unlucky in here, what baloney."

"I'm not innocent, I've done things too, but the problem's no longer this, at least for me. I need to know if . . ."

36

The lifer laughed.

"All you want to know is if a man's repented, well, it's a mania like any other. You ask everyone, or maybe you don't, seeing there's no point in asking a bull if he repents having gored someone." (Obviously by this he meant the sleeping Calabrian, for he winked in his direction.) "I understand – I understand practically everything – why a man may have this curiosity, or need as you put it. I knew a man who asked everyone he met: 'Are you happy?' He was a wise man and people laughed at him as if he were crazy. Another man used to ask even old men in their seventies: 'Do you masturbate?' And they all said he was a queer, but he wasn't, he was just curious about it."

He sucked in his lips and teeth, as if trying to swallow his own laughter.

"No, I haven't regretted it and why should I? That woman deserved to die not once but a hundred times. But I've regretted being fool enough to get caught. I was inexperienced in those days, though."

Olgi got up and looked out at the fleeing landscape. Everything had been said, yet it was as if nothing had been said, they were back at the beginning again, words fled away like the landscape which, though motionless, seemed to be fleeing. Only man remained.

But thoughts fled as well, and it was tiresome, perhaps vain, to chase them, to ask them the why and wherefore. And Olgi looked at the world fleeing past, an oblique strip of the world fleeing past, with scared surprise.

He felt tired and sat down. The Calabrian grunted, woke up, and yawned.

"This bloody train'll never get there."

The lifer was now reading, he had put on a pair of old spectacles and was reading a copy of *Science and Life*. Olgi thought, oddly, if he'd worn glasses for reading in those days, would he have committed that ugly crime just the same?

37

He was pleased to find intellectual interests in his companion. "So you read *Science and Life*," Olgi said.

"I read *Science and Life*," said the lifer, "but not only *Science and Life*, I read the classics and the great nineteenth-century writers too, Russian and French, Balzac and Stendhal, Tolstoy and Dostoievsky, and books of history and philosophy as well. You've got to do something in prison. Some people make sailing ships, some breed canaries, some turn queer, some become pimps, some cultivate one mania and some another. And some people read and study. I started learning chess but then stopped because I realized I'd never become a great champion like Capablanca or Botvinnik. And I started studying languages: English, French, Spanish, German. Knowing these languages is of no practical use to me, but what does that matter? I've passed the time, I've done something, I've made my brain work. For five years I lived like a hog. I started writing too, but then stopped, it's too difficult."

"Yes," said Olgi, "writing's hard work. Horribly hard."

He said it in the tone of a professional.

"D'you write?" asked the man. "You've got a writer's face."

Olgi laughed, amused. "I didn't know you could tell a writer by his face."

"By face I mean eyes. Thief's eyes, copper's eyes, greedy eyes, always on the alert. If you can't gobble up life, the whole of life, you can't even describe it."

Olgi confessed that he wrote. He'd been writing for twelve years.

"But it's hard," he repeated, "terribly hard."

Olgi looked into the man's eyes.

"Why did you stop writing? Because of what you might call technical difficulties, or for inner reasons of your own?"

"I stopped writing for the same reason that I gave up chess. I realized I'd never become a great writer like Stendhal or Tolstoy, so why go on?"

"One doesn't write just to become a great writer."

"What for, then? Ambition, protest, to make money?"

Olgi shrugged.

"Then why d'you write?" the lifer asked him, relentlessly.

"Because I suffer and love life," Olgi replied, "and because I must express myself. I need to express myself."

"That's a fine phrase, a writer's phrase," said the lifer.

They laughed together. Then they had a short conversation in English, because Olgi had studied English as well. Then they spoke French, because Olgi had studied French, too. And finally in Spanish, because Olgi had also studied Spanish. Whereas in German Olgi knew only the ugly words *arbeit*, *scheisse*, *kaputt* . . .

The lifer smiled, but not in his usual cold manner, which might have been his way, less cruel but no less wicked, of continuing to kill his neighbour; he smiled the friendly, happy smile of a man who, with liking and trust, tells another man his thoughts and interests, intimate and true and good.

Olgi smiled too, his distinguished face pink with pleasure, delighted to have found not just a reason for chat, though chatting was pleasant, but a way of escaping his filthy, squalid life, that was no life at all, by expanding and revealing oneself in real talk about human things.

And he would have liked – perhaps as much as having a girl to enjoy: the two wishes were quite disparate, but equally intense – to go for a walk with this man, this murderer who had suddenly become brotherly, on the sea-shore or along a river, between rows of graceful trees, free at last, free within and without, and to walk along talking, or better still silent, in the cool clean air, in the calm silence of the night until dawn.

The train had whistled insistently, and stopped, and the pair of them hadn't even noticed. Perhaps they didn't even notice that the train was now moving again, except the Calabrian who couldn't see how anyone could talk so long and so excitedly

39

about things that were no earthly use to anyone or were just lazy people's pastimes, books especially, which weren't life, and so weren't even truth. The few he'd skimmed through had had as characters rich people who were modest and charitable, priests who were all saints, reformed criminals, chaste girls, timid lovers, and other pretty lies, which was why he'd stopped reading.

He also felt a little humiliated to be cut out of the conversation; and so, taking advantage of a pause in their talk, he said:

"At Porto Azzurro you'd a fine pair of whiskers. Why did you cut them off? Without whiskers on that great mug of yours, you look like a priest."

"They were too thick," said Olgi, "stopped me breathing."

He hesitated, and then added:

"What's the use of whiskers? They're no use at all."

The Calabrian, who had no moustache, said whiskers must be some use for so many people to wear them.

"Or are they to hide behind?" he said, making an obvious mental effort, "so as not to show other people what we're really like?"

"I think that's why myself," said Olgi.

The Calabrian tried other topics of conversation.

"Now I'll tell you why I'm going to Volterra as a punishment. I am going to Volterra as a punishment because I told the warden there were worms in the food. 'Worms?' he said, astonished. 'Sergeant, d'you find there are worms in the food?' 'No, sir, absolutely no worms in the food,' he said. But I insisted: 'There are worms in the food,' I said, 'as big as earthworms. You could go fishing with them.' 'No wisecracks from you,' said the warden, 'and don't contradict the sergeant. The sergeant's here to keep order and discipline.' 'Order and discipline are one thing,' I said, 'and worms in the soup's another.' 'You can go,' he said. 'See the food improves,' I said, 'or I'll go to higher authority.' 'We know what you're like, a regular bad one, undisciplined, violent, sulky. You've been punished twelve times,' he said. 'What's that got to do with worms in the soup?' I said. 'Of course it's got something to do with it, because you're a liar, a backbiter, a mixer, that's what you are,' he said. 'Don't abuse our patience and our goodness,' he said, 'Next man in.'

"And that's why I'm off to Volterra as a punishment," the Calabrian concluded. "Is that justice? Ha ha! Is that democracy? Ha ha! Is that civilized? Ha!"

The train whistled sharply several times, and sounded as if it too was blaming civilization, democracy and justice, whereas in fact it was whistling because it had reached Grosseto.

VIII

THE TRAIN HAD MOVED ON TO ANOTHER LINE AND was now waiting motionless, like a snake in the sun, for a train from the north and another from the south to go by, before it could carry on.

"Another hour's wait, shut up in this oven" said the Calabrian desperately.

Olgi said nothing but he too was appalled. His chest and head were hurting again. This journey's never-ending, he thought to himself. Or rather it would end abruptly and dramatically for him, with irritation or even horror, or perhaps pity, for the others. He was resigned to going, but not in that way, on a violently sunny afternoon in a train full of people even though they would notice none of it. At the first stop they would send for the ambulance and take him to the mortuary.

It's ridiculous, it's ugly to end up this way. I won't.

He must lie down.

"Please, Enrico, would you give me your place? I've got to lie down."

The Calabrian noticed his pallor and the breathless bewildered air that cardiac patients have when an attack is imminent.

"D'you feel ill? Shall I send for someone?"

"What for? It is just my lumbago giving a twinge. What can you expect at my time of life . . ."

"I thought it was heart," said Enrico.

He spat into the corridor through the crack.

"Swine!" he said.

He had to vent himself. And did.

"Twenty years for a couple of thefts! And not a day commuted. Bastards," etc., etc.

He went and sat down beside the lifer, who was reading imperturbably. He was reading an article on a new method of cultivating mushrooms artificially . . . Suddenly the Calabrian's irritation vented itself on him.

"Oh, you . . ." he said, "you dry old stick, you."

The lifer never moved an eyelash.

"What's in your veins instead of blood? What's in your soul?"

"Soul?" said the man haughtily. "What nonsense is this? No one knows what the soul is."

"Well anyway," shouted the Calabrian, "are you a lifer or aren't you? Yes you are. And don't you care? And do you know or don't you that you'll die inside, because people like you are never let out? You know that. And I never hear you ranting against the man who sentenced you. You never curse anyone . . . if you'd repented it I could see why. But you haven't repented. So?"

The lifer raised his comical old glasses. He had his same ghastly smile.

"Listen," he said. "We're here, alive, and for better or worse are behaving like living men, while those who sentenced us are

42

now underground. The judge who sentenced me was seventy and in poor health, and so was yours. So by now they're rotten. Doesn't this thought comfort you?"

"Comfort my eye," said the Calabrian.

"Well it comforts me a good deal," said the lifer, and began reading again.

Olgi was getting away from the slime of pain, loosening the noose that was trying to strangle his life. That one day wouldn't see him dead, either. And he was strung between regret, considered regret, at once more not being dead, and joy that was wholly instinctive at finding himself alive again.

Olgi knew it took luck to die, in the same way as it took luck to live. A sister of his, the one he had loved most, had lived for twenty years – as long as he had spent in prison – with death breathing on her continually. And she was innocent. From childhood Alba had suffered from valvular disease of the heart, and yet she had grown up, had developed and gained experience like every human being, had known love and pleasure, had borne a child; then the illness grew worse, and after three years in hospital she died.

Olgi knew it took luck to die. He had seen a man die suddenly, who was young and strong and irascible, and had kicked his pregnant wife to death. The whole town thought ill of him, he had previous convictions, and was certain to get a life sentence. But the wretch was lucky. He died suddenly, of cerebral or coronary thrombosis, while walking in the yard. He fell down and died at once. The infirmary guard rushed across to him and injected a corpse.

Olgi knew it wasn't easy to die, either; and he opened his eyes, saw the impassive, and perhaps still cruel, lifer reading, the Calabrian glumly picking his nose, heard the oaths and laughter of the Roman, the Sicilian, the Neapolitan; and in his mind he quoted, he who hadn't much faith in literature, the poem of a poet he loved: the living discount death.

43

"You really have aged," said the Calabrian with satisfaction, "you're not the man you were. I've lasted better. At Asinara I worked out of doors. Inside, a man who doesn't work's done for in a few years. I've always worked. At Porto Azzurro I was storekeeper, at Spoleto cook, at Fossano smith. At . . ."

"But you've never had a book in your hand," said the lifer, who had finished the article on mushrooms.

"Books? Hell! All gossip and lies."

He went back to where he had been interrupted.

"But five years ago you were still a strapping fellow."

"I could lift three hundredweight," said Olgi proudly.

"Three hundredweight?"

"No exaggeration. At seventeen I worked on the docks, till I was twenty. We were all of us strong in my family. My father was nicknamed the Crane."

"And at twenty you went into the navy."

"I didn't go, I was called up!"

"And there you got five years inside."

"Yes, but I did only three. Till June '44, when the Allies turned up. Barely three months' freedom, then inside again. And no knowing if I'll ever get out this time . . ."

"Whew, this heat," said the Calabrian, "and this thirst of mine. What wouldn't I give for a bottle of cool beer. I'd even settle for a slice of water-melon."

Again Olgi saw the hot boy slaking his thirst at the jet of the fountain. Once – when? – he too had played and drunk like that.

Melancholy, he looked outside, and in the calm blazing sun saw only torn-up, twisted, rusty sheets of metal, wrenched-off carriage doors, broken seats, as if some time ago there had been a crash, a disaster, and these were left as witnesses, but they were now quite without horror, and had become useless old things, suggestive if anything as remains, left-overs of a dead civilization, where boys might squat. But there were no boys about; besides, there was a high dirty wall to keep them away. Still lazy, prudent lizards must come out of cracks to enjoy the fierce sun.

"Tell me," said the lifer, "have you ever written poetry?"

"A bit, some years ago," said Olgi. "When I started stammering and wanting to express myself. I wrote poems of eight, six, even three lines apiece. But when I discovered poets like Ungaretti and Lorca, I immediately stopped writing poetry."

"And turned over to prose," said the lifer shrewdly. "The opposite to what happened with me. I started by writing great big novels, then got discouraged and started writing very short poems. I still do. Would you like to hear the last one I wrote at S. Stefano?"

"With pleasure," said Olgi.

The man recited:

> *This morning*
> *as soon as I was up*
> *I went to the window*
> *Laid my forehead on the bars*
> *and looked at the sky and the sea.*
> *When shall I too be*
> *like the sky and the sea?*"

"What d'you think of it?" he asked anxiously.

"Not bad at all," Olgi answered. "Essentially it expresses a state of mind, and then there's a pantheistic intuition in it that's really interesting."

"Really? Is there really all this in it?"

"Of course there is. You put it there yourself. Making all due allowance, you write like Ungaretti. You've read Ungaretti, I'm sure."

"No, I haven't. How does he write?"

"Here's one of his poems: 'Between one flower picked and another given – the inexpressible nothing'."

"Why, he writes like me," the lifer exclaimed. "Is he . . . is he a great poet?"

"Perhaps the greatest contemporary poet."

"Thank you," said the lifer.

The Calabrian snorted. Now that they'd started yammering away again about all that stuff, they might go on till kingdom come. And he'd thought of someone, someone Olgi had known as well, a man who'd hung himself, and even if it didn't hurt him to keep it in, he felt he must communicate the thought, fling out the memory, because the only time he felt really comfortable was when his head was perfectly empty.

"Remember Pinzi?"

"Pinzi?" said Olgi, frowning.

"Yes, Pinzi, you must have known him, tall thin chap from Milan, with a scar on his temple."

"I don't really, there've been so many."

"All of them scarred at the temples? Why, you're bound to remember him. He was at Porto Azzurro when you were, he killed a guard in '44 trying to get out, and another prisoner walloped him on the head with a mattock."

"Of course, I remember now. Pinzi, that tall thin chap with crazy eyes."

"The bugger!" said the Calabrian.

"Who? Pinzi?"

"Of course not! I mean the Tuscan who knocked him on the head with a mattock, when he'd done in the guard and was just going to open the ammunition store and set everyone free. He was a lifer himself, the swine. And d'you know, for what he did they pardoned him?"

"The way they look at things is different from the way we do," said Olgi. "You've got to bear that in mind."

"But his crime was a hundred times worse than Pinzi's," the Calabrian exclaimed disgustedly. "He killed three people while they were asleep and then burnt the house down. And a little

46

girl of seven among them. This monster got his freedom back·
Is that justice? Ha ha! Whereas poor Pinzi hung himself. After
twenty-three years inside he hung himself."

The engine whistled.

"We're off, praise be," said Olgi.

He would have liked to talk of poetry again, but he could feel
the effects of his last attack and lay down, forcing himself not
to think of what had happened to Pinzi.

The train left at last and Grosseto vanished quickly as well,
and stayed in his memory as a scrap-iron yard between grass
and sun, and a high dirty wall to keep out children's happiness.

IX

THE TRAIN HAD STOPPED AGAIN, AND THEN AGAIN,
and was now on its way to Livorno, half the journey over, and
the other half to be done, mile after mile, station after station,
till they reached their destination.

The Calabrian got off at Campeglia, where a bus was taking
him on to Volterra, the lifer at Piombino, where a steamer was
taking him to Elba.

"All in all," Olgi said to himself, "I'm luckier than those
poor wretches. I'm going to Saluzzo." And he thought Saluzzo
as he might have thought Biarritz or Copacabana.

He was almost rejoicing at the feeling of being alone, no
longer hemmed in and suffocated by other lives, free in his
melancholy solitude. But not always alone, and not necessarily
unhappy. Sometimes the clinging, living happiness in his blood
even made him lively and gay.

He now recognized the landscape, finding something that
belonged to his own home in it: those endless pinewoods, those
sudden glimpses of the sea. The cool sea smell was in the warm

47

wind made by the train's movement, the smell of pine was strong and alive in the sunshine. And that should help to make his journey pleasanter.

"Now I'll lie down," he said to himself, "and have a snooze." But the seat was narrow, and short, and hard, and besides, the train was jerking, and then how could he possibly sleep by day if he couldn't even sleep at night; yet he remained lying down, as it was more restful.

And he began thinking again of Saluzzo, conjuring not obvious images of prison, barred door, gate, etc., but gay, unexpected things – the bonus of cool fresh drinking water, water from the mythical Monviso, and air, such heavenly air that they would feel like eagles, for the penitentiary was set up high, and from up there he could even use his spy-glass, the forbidden observatory, as he had called it, cunningly hidden during hundreds of searches.

The bolt was drawn, the door opened and someone else came in.

"Hullo," said the man, "I'm Armando."

"How d'you do," said Olgi, looking squarely at him.

He had the jolly red face of a heavy drinker, and he stank of wine too. With a broad gesture of greeting, and his red face oozing roguish gaiety, he flung his haversack on the seat, and his striped cloak on top of it, sat down, ran a large, not over-clean hand over his face, rummaged in his pockets for a long time, pulled out a twist of greaseproof paper with tobacco in it, laid a pinch of tobacco inside a strip of toilet paper and with a drunkard's clumsy stubbornness rolled it over and over again. The twist of paper he had laid on his knee fell off, the tobacco scattered on the spit-stained wooden floor, and the drunkard ran his shoe over it, raging and cursing, but his red face still remained cheerful. He looked at his attempt at a cigarette and said volubly:

"What an ugly old bitch you are. You're uglier than my wife,

but I'm going to smoke you, just the same. No I won't. I'll
smoke it, I won't . . ."

He threw it into the corridor through the crack.

And a good thing too, thought Olgi, who loathed the stink
of strong tobacco.

"What did you say?" said Armando.

"Me? Nothing," answered Olgi, and thought, slightly worried: Can he be a mind reader? Primitives like this sometimes
have remarkable intuition.

Mind reader or not, he was the sort of man who was immediately, cheerfully likeable.

"Where have you come from?" asked Olgi.

"From Volterra."

"Then you got on at Campiglia."

"Yes, but I should have got on yesterday. The train wasn't
there, though – at least there was a train, but it wasn't the right
one, it hadn't got a prison coach. They took me to the local
gaol, but the crew there didn't want me. 'It's not too secure
there,' he said, and 'he's got a heavy sentence.' 'But this is a
good chap,' says the sarge, 'I know Armando well, he won't get
out even if you leave the door open. All you need do is give
him a drink.' 'Ah, but have you got what it takes?' says the
screw. 'Nothing doing if you ain't.' 'Course I have,' I said, 'I
got two thousand lire.' 'And what d'you want? Lemonade?'
'Bottle of wine.' And I put away three bottles in a row. Then
the screw starts yelling: 'Paolina, Paolina, come and see a
marvel.' So his wife comes along to see the marvel. 'Never seen
such a marvel in all my born days,' says the screw. 'This
Armando's got through three bottles of wine.' 'Mind your
step, Ernesto,' says his wife, 'convicts are the very devil. Maybe
he's got a bottle hidden in his belly.' And she patted my belly
with her dear plump hands. Gorgeous, it was! Now there was a
good fellow, that screw! And his wife as well. And her dear
plump pretty hands!" Armando sighed.

Olgi liked this Armando.

"So you've drunk all your money. What now?"

"What now? I'll carry on, same as ever. Don't they feed me? Right. Don't they give me a place to sleep? Right. So I've got everything, or practically everything. If only they gave out a bottle of wine a day it wouldn't be too bad inside."

"I suppose you say that because you haven't been inside long."

"Not long? I've been in since 1943," said Armando.

"Christ," said Olgi. "You've beaten me by a couple of years, if you don't count my previous sentence. And where have you been all this time?"

"All over the place, in prison," said Armando.

"Porto Azzurro?"

"Certainly, Porto Azzurro among them. From '49 to '53."

"I was there too, in those years. What were you doing?"

"I used to sweep out for the old lifer."

He was sitting opposite Olgi, sadly shaking his head, but the gay red face refused to grow sad. Yet it was with a strange melancholy that he said:

"You don't know who you've got before you."

"Why, you're Armando, aren't you? That's all I need to know, I'm not nosy," said Olgi.

"Yes, I'm Armando, but I'm a jackal as well."

Olgi showed no surprise, no disgust or fear.

"D'you know what a jackal is?" asked Armando anxiously.

"It's an animal," Olgi said, shyly.

"Yes, but what sort? Tell me that."

"Well, let's say not a very pretty animal, a native of North Africa or a bit farther down, who goes for left-over titbits and isn't exactly a lion in the matter of courage."

"But that's a harmless creature," said Armando, "whereas I'm a real jackal, an ugly beast born of the war."

"Well, don't take it so hard, there are plenty of others like you," said Olgi consolingly. "Have a snooze instead."

But Armando insisted on telling his story, and explaining why he had become a jackal.

"I took some bits of wood from a factory that was no longer a factory but a heap of rubble," he said, "to cook up a pot of beans. They gave me thirty years. And I've got to do the lot because I'm a jackal, and jackals deserve no pity."

From the gloomy way he now spoke it seemed as if his drunkenness had gone, but his expression was still just as it had been, a drunkard's face or a clown's.

"And where are you going now?" Olgi asked.

"To Pisa, to the hospital at Pisa, to have an operation for an ulcer, but it may be cancer," said Armando with that bravely, absurdly cheerful face.

Olgi began to look at the landcape: small undulating hills as soft as a woman's breasts. And plots of ground as quiet as graveyards. The distant sky was a blue so pure there was no point in watching it.

He turned to look at Armando's red face. It was now smiling, quite naturally.

"Well, brother," he said. "You've been inside long enough yourself!"

"We're all condemned to death," said Olgi.

"Luckily," said Armando. "Luckily, brother."

X

ARMANDO WAS ASLEEP. IN SPITE OF THE JERKING and noise of the train, in spite of the short wooden seat, he was the sort who would sleep lying on the coal in the tender. Olgi admired him, envied him a little for his capacity to adjust himself to the brutality of things, a capacity he'd also had as a youngster and later lost.

As he slept he whistled hoarsely, and Olgi thought: If he's really got cancer he'll be dead in a few months. Olgi's father had died of cancer too.

Olgi now knew the country-side better, and could sniff the briny air, though they were still inland. Houses appeared in the greenness, mostly small and prettily painted, but farmhouses too that looked modest and solid, with tidy haystacks, well-stocked chicken-runs, good cattle too, and washing, lots of washing hung out to dry on the barn.

He also caught sudden glimpses of groups of small ugly houses, almost huts, or else large new buildings, geometrically alike. A sign the town was drawing nearer and nearer.

And that town on the sea was the town where Olgi was born and had spent the first twenty years of his life. There his father and mother were buried, and one of his sisters, there lived people to whom he was attached by family bonds. Face glued to the crack, he looked out greedily.

Yet he couldn't put names to those familiar places, which distressed him, almost shamed him, as if it were a betrayal of love, and he justified this by thinking the train was going too fast to allow him to identify the various things they were passing and that anyway he wasn't looking straight out of a window but through a door that was ajar, opposite a window in the corridor, and always facing the same direction.

But when the train turned – it was running down along the side of a hill full of chestnut-trees – Olgi suddenly saw the gulf, a sinuous curve stretching from Castiglioncello to the light-house at Meloria, with a promontory that plunged into the sea and was, in fact, Castiglioncello, a great arm held out as if in defiance of the raging Tyrrhenian sea, which meant the wild reefs of Calafuria; there, in the country, must be Antignano, there Ardenza, set sweetly among orange-trees and oleanders, there the sea-front with bathing huts packed close all along it, sea-bathing for rich, and poor, and everyone; and then the

Naval Academy, and what had once been Ciano Terrace but was anyway still a terrace, and the Naval dockyards; and then the port, the old port and the new, the Medici fortress, the Lanciotto canal, the Mandraccio, the Draga.

He recognized everything, remembered everything.

Suddenly the train vanished into the ground, ran through the bowels of the earth, and then came out on to a concrete embankment, but Olgi now had the sea within him, and those creeks and beetling cliffs and reefs, and dives and shouts and adventures.

"How fast my youth went, before I even realized it."

Now the train was running more slowly between rows of low white houses, as pretty as small country houses, each in its own little plot or garden. In a quick row of pictures Olgi saw a man shaving, a woman bent over a bowl washing clothes, a blonde girl combing her hair at the window, a man in a paper hat sawing a table, children running, children munching slices of bread, a black cat on a balcony, an old man with glasses reading a newspaper, two sunburnt girls arm in arm, exchanging excited confidences, a pregnant woman sitting with legs apart, fanning herself with one hand.

Olgi's eyes were hooks out to grab all the life they could, stealing life from life. How many people, how much life! he thought. And yet all this was here before, all this beauty existed before, all this life was life before and I never noticed any of it. I was like a blind man, I rushed blindly about among people, walled up in my prison, carrying my prison within me. Or are we all, or nearly all of us, so blind? Are we so deceived that we live without realizing we're alive? I don't know. I only know that it took me twenty years of life, twenty years of filthy, careless life, to learn to appreciate life, to love life. To want it cleaner, juster, and happier for everyone.

The train ran a little farther and then entered the station, dropped its passengers and goods, and ran a short way out of the station, where, among old grass-grown, coal-strewn tracks,

53

a man on point duty unhooked the prison coach, and the engine went on with the other carriages.

The sun was setting over the houses.

In one of those houses lived Olgi's sisters. A widow with three daughters to support, and an unmarried mother who also had two daughters. When his sisters wrote to him they expressed themselves more or less thus:

"You're in prison and you suffer, but our life's a prison as well. You at least have bread and soup every day, even if you're in bed you eat just the same, the government looks after you prisoners, whereas from morning till night we've no respite from this dreadful problem of food. And if it were only a matter of food! We've got rent to pay, and light, and gas (because cooking on coal these days isn't as cheap as cooking on gas) and then there's shoes, clothes, all sorts of things we need, things we've just got to have, which are all terribly expensive. You just don't know what it is to support two daughters, three daughters. If it weren't for these innocent souls we'd have killed ourselves, by now."

Or else they wrote:

"The children often ask about you. They say: Mother, why doesn't Uncle Olgi ever come and see us? You say he loves us so much, but he never comes and sees us. Why is he always travelling? Why doesn't he ever send presents?"

Olgi avoided thinking of those children who waited in vain for presents from their mysterious Uncle Olgi. He had photographs of the little girls, who were plump and smiling in spite of their mothers' poverty and sacrifices; he kept them inside a book. Olgi often opened the book and read a few pages to recharge himself spiritually (it was a book that seemed to have been written especially for him, or by him), but he nearly always avoided looking at his nieces' photographs.

And so now as well he kept away from the thought of them, and looked at things, distracted himself by thinking of things that might even take him back in time, ashes of things enjoyed, melancholy of things lost, but with a soft, sweet, almost pleasurable sadness; whereas the thought of those little girls waiting for presents from him and saying to their mothers, 'But why doesn't Uncle ever come and see us if he loves us so much?' was an ugly pain, was torture.

Just beyond the station wall was the street, where there were houses, shops, and a small factory (all this had been there for years, as Olgi well remembered), but those large prison-like buildings had been built recently, had one after another eaten up the patches of grass and rubbish heaps where boys had once played glorious games. (Come to think of it, where had their glorious games gone to, since their eviction? Did boys still play?)

The day was over but it was not yet evening, a few windows opened, a few young women looked out. And this was enough to change the stony grey of those ugly blocks of flats into vitality and joy. There were even geraniums on the window-sills.

A few windows lit up, a few stars shone in the distant house of the sky. Even the prison coach lit up.

The engine came along, and took the prison coach into the station, a train was made up again and set off, jerking hard as it moved breathlessly along; and as it jerked Olgi's head bumped against the door, but only lightly, hurting just enough to distract him from a greater pain.

The pain grew fast, and overflowed.

"No, no," Olgi suddenly cried, strangely desperate and muted, and "Why, why?" he cried as well.

His head banged hard on the door, and so did his fists.

"What's up?" said the tall carabiniere, bending down to peer through the crack. Under a military cap, and an honest, stubborn brow, a single eye appeared, vast and suspicious. "Want to go to the toilet?" he asked pleasantly.

"No," said Olgi, "no thanks."

"You knocked, I thought you wanted to go."

"I just knocked absent-mindedly, I'm sorry."

Armando the drunkard slept, snoring open-mouthed. Lucky man, in three months he'd be dead.

XI

FROM LIVORNO TO PISA IS ONLY TWENTY KILOMETRES, all of it built up; it was the stretch of railway line Olgi knew best. That large quiet enclosure, shaded by cypresses, was the cemetery; in front of it ran the street with its noisy traffic; behind it, between tall grasses and thick reeds, ran a river where couples went to make love. Olgi himself had enjoyed his first girls among those reeds, indifferent to the dead near by.

In the darkness flecked with lights, he steered clear of pain and distracted himself by thinking, there's the Anic works, there's the small airport for tourist flights, and villas and chalets on the edge of the great pinewood; American military stores; Triero's restaurant must be here, between the level-crossing and Torelli's factory; Mombelli's farm must be there; and here are the goods sheds and towers of Sangobè. They've rebuilt it all, after the war damage, newer, bigger, more progressive, more efficient.

This last scrap of his mental conversation he not only thought but said, speaking cynically. He said it to Armando, who was asleep.

"They've rebuilt everything bigger, newer, more progressive, more efficient."

Even asleep Armando's red face was gay.

"Start getting ready," said the tall carabiniere, "we're at Pisa."

In his voice there was gladness, gladness at the thought of rest and refreshment in the barracks, and perhaps at the thought of other pleasant things that awaited him at Pisa.

Olgi slung on his prisoner's striped cloth bag and woke Armando.

"Friend, we're there," he said.

"Where?" muttered Armando, between yawns.

"At Pisa, aren't you going to Pisa?"

"It's true, I am. And where are you going, brother?"

"I'm going to Saluzzo, but changing at Pisa."

"I was at Saluzzo," said Armando, "in 1956."

"Ah," said Olgi and was tempted to ask him what it was like, but didn't, since Armando was sure to answer: "What d'you think? It's inside."

Armando was rubbing his big grubby hands.

"I had a dream," he said. "Oh, what a dream it was!"

"That you had wings and were flying in heaven?"

"You can stuff your wings and heaven! If I didn't know I was the drunk, of the two of us, I'd say you'd had a bit much yourself. I dreamt of Paolina."

And he told in detail how he had dreamt of Paolina, in a dream as exact as physical reality. More than what he said, his red face showed his glowing happiness at having dreamt of Paolina.

"You still react like a boy," Olgi complimented him. "The engine's still working."

"Oh, it works, it works all right," said Armando, who, drunkenness notwithstanding, had always reasoned clearly. "It's just that a key without a lock's no use."

"Are you married?"

"She's dead. For ten years she was ill and then she died."

"Have you any children?"

"I had three. The eldest poisoned himself, the second was killed by the carabinieri during a demonstration, the third works in the Argentine but never writes to me or sends me anything."

"And now you're going to hospital in Pisa to have an operation for your ulcer," said Olgi, as if adding an amen to his litany of misfortune.

"It may be cancer," Armando said.

The train drew into the station, under a long reverberating roof. The escort began carefully putting on chains and handcuffs again, and the jolly sergeant with a bulging brief-case under his arm kept saying:

"Now be sure and get off the minute the train stops, otherwise we'll get hauled off to the engine-shed and have over an hour's wait."

Everything went smoothly, the prison van was already there, a large new one which took them to Don Bosco in a few minutes. There they were taken into a bare room, from which, after a short passage and three doors, one came to the prison office.

Behind the bars was the usual thick grille, but the bench to sit and rest on, which had been there in 1945, was no longer, Olgi observed, there in 1961. To balance this they had put up a large crucifix. The walls smelt of fresh whitewash.

There were ten of them, but not all those who had been at Civitavecchia, for some had got off during the journey, and others had got on. There was the tall man with the crooked nose, the blond Sicilian, the tall boy with a gangster's face, the little man with the moustache and sunglasses. The others were wearing the official striped cloth cloaks, two with dull faces, one dark hairy man with a scar on his cheek, and a fair slender man who, even dressed as a convict, looked like a gentleman.

Three of them sat on the floor, smoking strong tobacco, talking wearily, and the man with the dark scarred face was actually lying down, head on the bare floor, eyes shut, hands on his chest, as though dead.

The blond Sicilian and the tall boy with the gangster's face walked quickly up and down, smoking good cigarettes and laughing. The Sicilian was very smart, a fashion model. The gangster was more sporty, with wide comfortable trousers, and a coloured shirt hanging outside his belt.

"If you just take my tip and come to Rome," said the smart Sicilian, "we'll be stinking rich in no time. There's no place like Rome for getting stinking rich in. Now just you take my tip, Claudio, and come along to Rome. Change your trade, lad, growing turnips'll take too long to bring in the lolly."

Claudio laughed, and seemed undecided whether to accept the new job.

"Well, I'll do these last six months and then we'll see," he said.

An elderly guard, fat and bald and with red stripes on his sleeves, opened the end door of the three.

"Who's come for an operation at the hospital?"

"Me," said Armando cheerfully, "me."

"Here again? Why, it's your third operation in eight months. What's it this time, an enema? You just enjoy being cut up and sewn together again, you do."

"I've got an ulcer," said Armando, "but it might be cancer."

"Get moving and collect your things, you ape," growled the fat guard, who disliked jokes.

"Everything's here," said Armando, slapping his half-empty haversack.

"Then go along in there."

Armando waved his hand in Olgi's direction.

"We'll meet again, brother," he said, and trotted off as sly as a dog, or as the jackal he was.

"You take my word for it," the Sicilian was still saying fervently, "come to Rome, there's no place like Rome to make fools of people."

The thin fair man who even dressed as a convict looked like

59

a gentleman stood leaning his back against the wall, his stiff pale face gazing at the lozenge-shaped tiles of the floor.

The guard with the red stripes came back, and called out three names. After these three names came three others. There was an interval of about a quarter of an hour between calls. Each man called picked up his things and went into the office. Olgi, the dark man with the scarred face and the thin fair man were called last.

The fat clerk bent over his register was sweating, as if instead of writing he was digging.

"Valnisi Olgi," he said, enunciating carefully, "are you called Valnisi or Varnisi?"

"Valnisi, with an 'l', as in Livorno."

The clerk then looked closely at him, recognized him, and exclaimed:

"So you're really Valnisi, Valnisi from Livorno, you old scoundrel – but how you've changed! Don't you remember me? I'm Dolce."

"Signor Dolce," said Olgi. "Why of course I remember you. Haven't you always been in this office?"

"Yes, always, I've been here for twenty years. Ah, you wretch, the trouble you gave us, but no one breaks out from here nowadays."

"I've no need to break out any more," Olgi said calmly.

"You were a terror," said the clerk, with a hint of admiration in his voice. "You and Nanni L'Urbani. Bbbrrr! I'd sooner lose you than find you."

"Nanni's been dead fifteen years," said Olgi.

"Well, we must all come to that," bumbled Signor Dolce, and shouted gaily:

"These three settled as well."

PART II

XII

THE DARK HAIRY FELLOW WITH THE SCARRED FACE
named Careddu, went to sleep at once. Olgi didn't, nor did the
thin fair man who looked like a gentleman. Now that he had
taken off his prison clothes and had put on his own clean
pyjamas he looked more a gentleman than ever. He was one,
too. Before settling down to sleep, Scarface had called him
'engineer'. He had said:

"Engineer. Let me have a cigarette."

The engineer had glanced at Olgi two or three times. He
looked as if he had a rather embarrassing question to ask, and
out of delicacy, or shyness, couldn't decide to do so. Then, just
when he appeared to have given up the idea, he asked it.

"Excuse me, but when are you leaving?"

"In four days," answered Olgi.

The engineer went back to gazing at the black crucifix nailed
above the door, whereas Olgi looked at the red knob that made
the toilet flow if you pressed it. But the flush didn't work. It
hadn't worked in 1945 either, Olgi remembered.

Several minutes went by. From outside, from the street
beyond the prison wall, came the sound of cars; from farther
away, from Piazza Grande or Corso Matteotti, the blaring of
music on the radio; from still farther, but only at long intervals,
the fleeting rattle of a train.

There must be a great moon in the sky, because it illumined
even the top of the cell window.

The engineer leant his pale face over towards Olgi and said
wearily:

"I'm leaving on Friday."

"After me," said Olgi, almost happily.

The engineer began looking at something moving slowly between the black wooden crucifix and the ceiling. He was rather short-sighted, and put on his spectacles – a fine, expensive pair – to see what it was. "It's a bed-bug," he said, as if he thought the man in the next bed was short-sighted as well.

"It's a bed-bug."

"Yes, it's a bed-bug," said Olgi. "Nothing odd about that."

The engineer gave a short stifled laugh. "That's true, nothing odd about that."

He was staring at Olgi. His short-sighted eyes, now armed with spectacles and seeing quite clearly, were seeking an exact view of reality. Then (without really needing to say it, perhaps to justify his insistent stare) he said:

"If there was just that one, we'd be justified in killing it," obviously alluding to the bed-bug on the wall.

"But it's not the only one," Olgi objected, "there are any number, and you couldn't dig them out and destroy them all if you spent the whole night at it. They have the foulest smell when they're squashed. Better let them live."

"And also because we're forbidden to kill," said the engineer. "It's written in the Bible: thou shalt not kill. It's not specified whom, but I suppose the ancient law-giver meant to imply: thou shalt not kill any living creature, not even a bed-bug."

These apparently light-hearted words were spoken with an extremely serious expression. The engineer was no longer looking at Olgi, but at his own feet. They were neither handsome nor ugly, but just a man's feet, made for walking on, the big toe rather fat and tufts of reddish hair between the toe-joints. He must have found them unpleasant to look at because he covered them suddenly with his bedclothes. A church clock somewhere near by struck twelve.

"Midnight," said the engineer.

"Checking time," said Olgi.

And in fact the sound of doors and gates being opened and

64

shut came up floor by floor from below, now louder, now softer, as the rounds were made on each floor. The men who were checking came to their cell too: a sergeant, a corporal, and three guards. They looked, they counted, they went out, they shut the door again.

The engineer smoked his twelfth or thirteenth cigarette, and again turned his stiff face to Olgi, with a smile that was conventionally friendly.

"Where are you going?" he asked.

"To Saluzzo," Olgi answered, "to Saluzzo," and his face laughed, inexplicably.

The engineer spoke to the smoke that hung round him, saying shortly and neutrally that he was going to San Gimignano.

"I've been there," said Olgi.

The engineer seemed incurious about the way things were at San Gimignano. He cared nothing for San Gimignano, he cared nothing for Saluzzo.

For an hour or more they were silent, each in his own prison.

The clock struck one, half past one, two. The whole city was silent, idly shipwrecked in the night.

The engineer raised his face from his hard pillow, and looked at Olgi with hatred.

"Why don't you sleep?" he burst out.

"And why don't you?" retorted Olgi calmly.

"Because I'm a fool who thinks," said the engineer with comical anger. "You must be a fool who thinks too. Look at Careddu. He's asleep, as happy as a sandboy. And he's killed three people."

"Actually," said Olgi, "I haven't killed anyone. I've only stolen. And they gave me twenty two years. A trifle."

"Whereas I . . ." said the engineer in an altered voice, but didn't finish the sentence. Then he turned to the wall and said:

"Good night."

"Good night."

The engineer didn't move again. Was he sleeping, or was he pretending to sleep? Olgi looked at the door, at the grille, at the lavatory that hadn't worked since 1945, looked at Careddu's feet and shoulders and hard impenetrable animality, looked at the back of the engineer's head, and his no less impenetrable humanity, looked at the black wooden crucifix nailed to the whitewashed wall, and a fly squashed on the wall; he shut his eyes, calling on the mysterious powers of sleep, the merciful gift of unconsciousness, but his eyes kept cruelly opening again, and there was still the gate, the door, the squashed fly against the wall; they would always be there, till the end of his days.

"Why don't you stop now?" he said to his heart, with quiet despair.

XIII

HE GOT UP AS USUAL AN HOUR BEFORE THEY WERE called, without making a noise, with the sober movements of an old convict used to moving in a small space, folded his bed-clothes, covered the mattress with its cover, washed his face and hands, using soap only to wash his hands, cleaned his teeth with a brush but without toothpaste, defecated, and found himself facing a day he didn't know how to fill, an endless desert of boredom.

Lucky I'm here for only four days, he thought. And to think I did a year here, the whole of 1945.

He hated that prison more than he had hated Portolongone or Volterra. Whereas Fossombrone or Civitavecchia he hadn't hated. Nor had he hated San Gimignano. For certain small advantages and compensations even a prison can offer: a better library, pleasant work, a loving friendship, the chance of playing chess, etc. Procida he had actually loved.

He had gone to Procida in 1954, after five years at Portolongone and three at Volterra. The window of the cell where they put him was uncovered, and through it he could see the sea, a bit of sea, a bit of countryside, and some houses. The first time he put his face to the bars he rediscovered the world, life, and the right perspective and dimension of things human: that slow steamship below, those fishermen throwing out their nets and drawing them in again, that fast motorboat, those small houses among prickly pears and vines, that peasant working in his garden. He saw all this again, after seeing nothing for years but tomb-like whitewashed walls, and his feelings were so tender and so violent that he burst into tears.

He now lay down on the mattress because there was nothing else to do, and started thinking of Saluzzo again. Everything would surely be better there.

The engineer got up with a deep furrow between his eyebrows, yet he said 'good morning' politely, washed, looked at Olgi, seemed embarrassed. Olgi understood, and went over to the window, where he leant his elbows against it while the engineer quickly relieved himself.

Outside the bars there was a kind of stone ridge, and trickles of rain had worn away the paint and showed up the hard stone in all its nudity. Well, it was only stone.

The morning alarm-bell rang imperiously, the prison sprang to life and became a lodging-house.

Careddu awoke, with the bestial dullness of his long sleep still on him; then, with a look of vaguely human intelligence, he said:

"Engineer, will you give me a cigarette?"

The door opened and white coffee was distributed, a cross-eyed orderly carrying the pot of it against his belly while a warder dipped the ladle in and served it.

67

They came round for the check-up: sergeant, corporal, two guards. The sergeant carried a notebook, one of the guards beat on the bars with a piece of iron, the corporal looked under the beds, and they went out in order of seniority: first the sergeant, then the corporal, thirdly the guard who banged on the bars, and lastly the guard in charge of shutting gate and door.

The door was shut again.

"Engineer, let me have a cigarette," said Scarface.

He didn't thank him; in his way of looking at the engineer there was a willing submissiveness that seemed to demand something in return. He was glum and silent, but not sad.

They went out for exercise: this was in small courtyards that were parallel but divided, with bits of broken bottle on top of the dividing walls; in each courtyard thirty or forty men walked up and down with a kind of crazy tidiness, up and down, one behind the other, monstrous ants in the prison's guts.

There were men who had been sentenced and men awaiting judgement, northerners and southerners, old and young, most of them poorly dressed, and ragged. They looked wretched. But they were unhumbled, and felt no shame or sorrow at what had happened to them, which might not in any way have altered, or worsened, their wretched existence. Most of them laughed coarsely, and exchanged obscenities and insults. Two of them came to blows, biting one another like dogs.

Olgi avoided looking at the mouths, noses, and foreheads that seemed to cut him like knives. As he walked he tried to feel isolated and different among those swarming criminal cockroaches, persuading himself that he was taking a healthy morning walk, in order to avoid the horror of feeling forcibly swept up among those feet, and mouths, and noses, and guts, sucked inescapably into that absurd shuffle up and down between two dirty walls.

The engineer walked without looking at anyone, either, protected by his pride perhaps, invulnerable or less vulnerable than the others, yet still a man, with things about himself to reveal and other things to hide. He too walked fast, just to keep on the move, for prison makes a man rusty (or was he fleeing as fast as he could from something which, alas, existed but he wished did not?).

Above, far above, where the air was no longer stuffy or foul, an aeroplane must have been flying. Its motor was silent and invisible, but it had drawn a white line in the blue sky, like a chalk-mark on a slate.

Exercise ended, and the men (for they were still men, as Olgi knew, and had long known, though he sometimes forgot it) went back to their cells, their holes, on the first, second, third or fourth floor.

After an hour the door opened and bread was handed round; after another hour it opened again and soup was served.

"Engineer," said Scarface, "give me a cigarette, will you?"

And calmly, belly stuffed, he settled down to sleep again.

The engineer, sitting on his straw mattress, smoked and smiled, and stared crazily at his hands. Or else he peeped at Olgi with a spiteful, repressed amusement. Till he burst out:

"Don't you think he's perfectly splendid?"

Olgi, who had understood perfectly, asked nevertheless:

"Who's perfectly splendid?"

"Why Man, of course," said the engineer, openly mocking, "Man. Don't you find him splendid?"

"He is what he is," said Olgi, but this answer meant he put himself outside or above the question; so more humbly, he added: "We are what we are."

The engineer grimaced, in a way that might have meant agreement or disagreement, and continued to pull hard on his cigarette, and take refuge in its smoke.

Outside the door they heard a hoarse laugh and saw an eye flash behind the spyhole. Eye and laugh belonged to the cross-eyed orderly.

"Christ, what a place to put you in!" he grinned. "This is the cell Vito Morandini hanged himself in. Last month. He was on his way to Portolongone and for fear of going there he hanged himself."

"Who is this fellow?" said the engineer, with immediate, remarkable interest.

"The cross-eyed orderly," said Olgi.

"Not him, the one who hanged himself."

"He told us: Vito Morandini."

"But who is Vito Morandini?"

"He was, he no longer is. He was the 'monster of Pontoglio'. Don't you read the papers?"

"Very rarely. And besides, news like that's generally cut by the censor."

"But we manage to hear of it just the same. All you need do is listen. Come out of your shell a bit," said Olgi, half annoyed at him for having, by the look of it, made his misfortune the centre of the universe.

The engineer wasn't listening. He was staring at the bars, from which a man seemed to be hanging. Without ceasing to stare at him he asked:

"What had he done?"

"Eight or nine murders. Old couples, peasants who weren't even well off. He'd come to a house, kill his victims as they slept, burn down the house and carry off their few possessions. He was arrested on suspicion of stealing, and suddenly confessed all his crimes."

"And last month he killed himself," the engineer said thoughtfully. "Why?"

"He was scared of going to Porto Azzurro," said Olgi.

The engineer shrugged.

"That's Squint-eye's version. Piquant, but hardly logical. A man who kills so càsually can't be afraid of going to Porto Azzurro. He can't even be afraid of going to hell."

70

"Maybe he disliked being called the monster of Pontoglio," said Olgi. "Maybe he felt remorse. Or he may have preferred a quick violent death to this long insipid agony. Vito Morandini had already been in prison, so he knew well what lay in store."

"Five minutes," said the engineer, still staring at the bars, "That's all it takes to be free."

He was now speaking with strange calm. He looked at Olgi and Olgi looked at him. The engineer shook his head.

"Don't think I mean to commit suicide. I have meant to but I'm now resigned to living. How many years have you done so far inside? A lot, I should think."

"Sixteen, nearly seventeen, not counting my previous service imprisonment."

"That's a fair amount," said the engineer. "I've done seven."

"Seven's a fair amount too."

"How many have you still got? Forgive me, I don't take much notice of others as a rule but . . . I like you."

"Five, which'll make twenty-two."

"No hope of getting out sooner?"

"Maybe," Olgi smiled.

"A pardon?"

"Let's call it that," said Olgi.

"I shall be leaving soon," said the engineer. "There's an article, number 105 I think it is, that allows conditional freedom to be given when there's not more than five years still to run. There must be other favourable circumstances, of course." His tone was ironic. "Have you ever heard of anybody getting out through this article?"

"Four or five, in sixteen years. Their families were rich and well connected."

"My family's rich too," said the engineer with a grimace. "My father's an architect, his second wife has a smart boutique, my step-sister's a graduate in chemistry, but works as production secretary to a film company. Not to mention my other relations, who are all well-placed socially, and suitably married, with important friends and relations. They'll just have to give me this reprieve: it's what I've got a right to and deserve, as my distinguished, pettifogging lawyer puts it."

Paradoxically for some unknown reason of his own, the engineer's face oozed sarcasm and loathing. He continued:

"Deliberate, premeditated murder: I deserved a life sentence. Whereas I got away with twelve years, without even the tiresome extra of a psychiatric hospital. You stole and they gave you twenty two years. But you're a poor man, which means a dangerous criminal. Oh, my lawyer's touching trumpetings! 'A fine, basically good young man, swept away by his crazy love. Your Honour, Gentlemen of the jury, you must judge him calmly and fairly. This tragedy would have moved, nay, would have inspired Shakespeare . . .'

"Don't you feel moved?" he asked Olgi aggressively.

"I don't see why you're telling me all this," said Olgi.

"Forgive this childish outburst," the engineer stammered apologetically. "I forgot that our troubles never interest others."

"I can understand the troubles of others," said Olgi, wanting to have it out. "But you're not sincere."

The engineer started as if he had been slapped, and for the rest of the day they didn't exchange a word.

XIV

IT WAS AFTER THE MIDNIGHT CHECKING THAT THE engineer unexpectedly resumed the talk he had broken off nine or ten hours before, as if there had been no long, embarrassed silence in between.

"Look," he said, and his voice had no resentment in it, or if there was he was controlling it. "The feelings I expressed were quite sincere."

"I may have been wrong in my judgement," Olgi said, soothingly. "Everyone makes mistakes and I often do."

"Look out," said the engineer, with unexpected good humour, "now it's you who's not being sincere."

"I am, I am," protested Olgi.

"Then let's say sincere but incoherent," retorted the engineer, "I'm often sincere but incoherent myself."

The talk got going again, and all they need do was continue it. The night was long, and talking was a diversion, a way of passing the time, even if it contributed little to their knowledge of one another.

"Of course," said the engineer, "you must read a lot."

"Why of course?"

"Anyone who doesn't sleep reads."

"I read a bit, and write a bit."

This took them on to talk of books, of those a man might read if he chose from the prison library, and those he might manage to get from outside. The engineer said he had twenty books in his suitcase, his small personal library, and he always took them with him and always read them.

"Of course," said Olgi, though with a touch of involuntary irony, "they're twenty masterpieces, the great classics of world literature: Dante, Cervantes, Shakespeare, Manzoni, Goethe, and so on."

"Not at all," replied the engineer, aroused, "why d'you attribute such old-fashioned tastes to me? In literature, as in other things, I'm against tradition and authority. My twenty authors are modern: Ungaretti, Thomas Mann, García Lorca, Kafka, Joyce, Lee Masters . . . Give me a poem like *The Rivers* or the *Lament for Ignacio*, and you can burn all the other poems in the world. Don't you agree?"

"I agree that *The Rivers* and the *Lament for Ignacio* are two

73

very beautiful, very human poems. But why would you destroy all others? There'll never be too much beauty in the world for everyone's enjoyment."

The engineer paid little attention to what Olgi was saying. Like anyone obsessed he thought his own opinions absolutely right. He sighed.

"Think of writing a poem like *The Rivers*," he said. "If I could, I'd be a happy man."

"Even in your present state?"

"Or course. In fact, especially in my present state. I'd be happy the way you're happy."

"I'm happy?" exclaimed Olgi with wonder. "Do I seem happy to you?"

"You don't seem happy, you are happy," said the engineer. "And like all happy people you don't realize your own happiness."

"I've stopped tormenting myself over so many silly trifles. And so if I'm not happy I'm a little less unhappy than I used to be. You could do as much yourself."

"It takes time to be wise," said the engineer. He took off his spectacles and put them on again. "And then, d'you know what? I'm not really tempted by this wise happiness. Unhappiness has its advantages, you know, suffering makes you feel more alive."

"Why, you were praising death before," Olgi observed. "Death conceived as the paradise of non-being. What a muddled pessimist you are!"

"Leopardi, and even Schopenhauer were no less puzzled than I am."

"Why, Engineer . . ." laughed Olgi. "To think of putting yourself in such illustrious company!"

"Laugh away but don't call me Engineer, I loathe it. My name's Silvio and I'd rather you called me that."

They talked until four in the morning.

74

The church clock struck the hours: one, two, three, four . . .

"Thank you," said the engineer sincerely. "It's years since I spoke with so much pleasure about things that seemed dead to me, or anyway quite outside me, even if they were still alive. Whereas just talking about them has made me feel them alive inside me. Part of me. Prison is terrible because it makes you unable to use the old words, or too reserved to do so, and to feel and admit that they aren't just words."

"You're telling me . . ." said Olgi. "I can count on my fingers the chances I've had in as many years to talk over things that have become a reason for living to me."

"A real reason for living?" exclaimed the engineer.

"Yes," answered Olgi, "a reason for living. How could I carry on living, otherwise?"

"He's alive as well though," said the engineer, indicating the dark bristly Careddu who, as he slept, made a strange dull noise that was not exactly snoring but seemed more like the purring of a cat or some animal of the kind. "What does having a reason for living mean? Millions of men live thinking they have a reason for living, all sorts of reasons for living, solid, unshakeable, but nothing lasts, man dies."

"And if he didn't die, mightn't he be more unhappy?"

Olgi smiled as he said this, but the engineer's face was desperate.

"It's after four," he said, "shall we try and sleep a bit?"

"Let's try."

The following day was like the previous one, with one variation, which had been foreseen, like everything else, by the invisible adjuster of the clockwork: Careddu's departure. It took place soon after the soup had been brought round. He slung his haversack over his left shoulder.

"Engineer, will you let me have a cigarette?"

He lit it, and calmly, belly full, went towards his fate.

At once the cell seemed larger to them. It had in fact become

75

so, since everyone takes up space, and there was precious little of it; but above all it was within themselves that they no longer felt stifled.

They talked. Not to pass the time, or to stretch their brains, or to show off their culture, and so forth, but to reveal themselves, and because they needed to be understood.

"In the seven years I've been in this crazy, disciplined hole," said the engineer, in the polished yet crude way he spoke, "I've met all sorts of oddities but no one as extraordinary as you."

"But why do I seem extraordinary to you?" asked Olgi. "Is it because I know Kafka and Edgar Lee Masters, as you do?"

"That's one reason. You don't often find a porter, or a docker, who reads Kafka or Edgar Lee Masters."

"But I'm no longer a docker," Olgi protested humorously. "I've taken my convict's degree."

"And you can say quite indifferently: I have stolen, because, in your peaceful vision of things, you've quite got over any shame or pride in these actions. Whereas I can't say that."

"But you haven't stolen."

"Worse, I've killed."

"There's no crime," said Olgi, quoting an author, "that can prevent the birth of pure goodness."

"Words," said the engineer, annoyed. "I can't cure my pain with fine words, I'm still on earth, my bones smashed, and no word-medicine's going to give back my health and balance again."

"But life can," said Olgi.

"Life," said the engineer enviously, "this life without meaning, this absurd adventure we're involved in without asking to be."

"I've heard this sort of outburst somewhere before," said Olgi.

"Well," said the engineer shyly, "it's . . . it's a thought of Heinsenberg's."

76

"A sentence of Heinsenberg's," said Olgi. "Phrase for phrase, I prefer my author's one. At least it helps one to live."

And he laughed. And the engineer laughed as well, though rather forcedly.

XV

NEXT DAY – IT WAS THE THIRD OF THEIR FORTUITOUS yet ever more profound and pleasurable time together – the engineer did something that contradicted Olgi's notion of him as parsimonious (this not through meanness but through continence, whether natural or acquired he didn't know: a spartan way of living in prison). When the creaking trolley of things for sale turned up – a cornucopia, a veritable sack of Befana*, yet the torture of Tantalus to the many poor wretches without money – the engineer not only failed to say "No, nothing," as before, but stopped the trolley.

"What's good?" he said.

"What would you like, sir?" said the guard, with the instinctive respect of such people for the man whose fat cheque book shows his social importance. "There's excellent salami, soft cheese spread, gorgonzola, stracchino, ham, bacon (but I don't honestly advise it, not in this heat . . .), bananas, figs and almonds, black or green olives, Cirio jam, tinned tunny fish, nuts, Pavesini biscuits, eggs, pears and apples, red wine and white. But for you, as a special treat, there's even Marsala." (Very softly, very secretly.) "I really oughtn't to give Marsala, but considering who you are . . ."

*The 'good fairy' in whose name sacks or stockings are filled with toys, as are Christmas stockings in other countries, on the eve of Epiphany (January 6).

The engineer bought 4,000 lire worth, and his bed was piled high, like a sumptuous table.

"Celebrating your grandma's golden wedding?" said Olgi. He joked about it, but touchy in his poverty felt oppressed and hurt by this show of wealth.

"My grandmother's been buried half a century," said the engineer, glum and desolate as ever in speaking of death and perishable things. "My mother's been buried thirty-five years, too. I never knew her, I was a few months old when she died."

He was wandering bewilderedly among ghosts and gloomy memories again, but with an effort took hold of himself.

"Let's lay it out on the bed."

"What for?" said Olgi.

"To eat it, of course. We'll eat and toast our acquaintance. It will be a symposium of friendship."

They ate. The food, which, even if not delicious, was varied, and in comparison with their everyday soup seemed exquisite, the Marsala especially, made the two friends even more expansive.

"Yes," said the engineer, dipping a biscuit into the Marsala, "life would be acceptable if we didn't see so many faces around like dogs, like monkeys, like parrots. That's what scares me: the lack of nobility in the human race. From time to time one authentic man emerges from the filth and flatness, and then meeting him and recognizing him is joy indeed. My dear Olgi, you're one of those rare true men who ennoble the race. A man, from head to foot. If I were a woman I'd adore you on my knees."

Olgi felt pleasure and shame, as if a shameless declaration of love had been made to him. The engineer's grey eyes, usually without tenderness or pity, glowed softly. Slightly embarrassed, Olgi began to shell a nut. He had already realized what the engineer was getting at . . .

The engineer then changed the subject, and began talking about himself.

"My life's gone wrong from the very beginning. Teachers hired to guard me, then the school dung-hill, with its filth and small utilitarian lies, and its wretched sneers and cruelty. And then my father's second marriage, and my inability to become part of the new family's plans and atmosphere. Like a sick animal I mistrusted everything and everyone: without friendships or love, I would listen to the gremlins whirling round in my brain. Even my university days were cold and dark. They'd made me pick engineering because an uncle on my mother's side, who was getting on and a bachelor, had a factory, and I'd been chosen to succeed him. But I'd sooner have got a degree in literature. I thought I'd inherited my mother's artistic nature, wrote poems in the current fashion, and a little prose poetry as well. Flimsy rubbish, I now see quite clearly: the cavortings of a dilettante. But in those days I was as pleased with myself as a dog with two tails. I scorned the idea of getting others to judge these early efforts of mine. When I decided to get an opinion I chose the most authoritative and important critic available, certain that at the first lines he'd exclaim: 'Why, this boy's a genius!' Whereas what he said was: 'Dear boy, these are just exercises, and you're really not very deeply involved. It's a long hard trail in any of the arts. Work, practise, persevere, and in five or ten years come and see me again.' I was foaming at the mouth with rage and scorn. The old bastard! I'd show him what his opinion was worth! So I went to another distinguished critic: you'd think they'd sadistically got together and agreed to blast me. Another critic, who was also right at the top, confirmed what the other two had said. So then I burnt those despised fruits of my misunderstood genius (fewer than thirty exercise book pages! And to think that in ten years you've written about ten thousand pages just to get your hand in, just to learn the job!), and flung myself headlong into living. Yes

Olgi, smile away. Does it remind you of Rolla, of D'Annunzio's heroes? D'you know what 'living greedily and intensely' meant at university to us youngsters from nice bourgeois families, in those cheerfully chaotic pre-war days when the chap who was always right kept urging us to asceticism, renunciation and manly expectancy? Well, apart from going to brothels and dashing around in one of the gang's car, it meant getting together on Sundays at the home of someone – boy or girl – with accommodating parents, to dance in bathing dress as we imagined our contemporaries did in New York or Paris. It was after one of those aphrodisiac dances that I rashly deflowered my first virgin, a dear, good, decent girl who let me do it just because she loved me and felt it was so important to me that it seemed cruel to deprive me of it. A girl who gave me her virginity for love, and never asked me to make it up by marrying her! This marvellous girl, so sincere and so utterly unlike the scheming little hot-pants I'd met so far – all of them either frigid or frivolous – had simply got to be my wife. I took my degree and got an executive post in my uncle's factory. We'd bought the furniture, our new house was nearly ready, the love-nest waiting to welcome us . . . I was bloated with gorgeous platitudes, and quite without doubts or worries. At last I was living, like everyone else on earth, longing to be united with an adorable girl, and to hand on the flame of life myself. But clearly I was to be denied normality and happiness. One day, like a fool, I bragged that I'd enjoyed the favours of a cousin of hers. She said nothing, but the following day her brother came and gave me back the ring. I managed to see her, but there was no shaking her. I wrote her long imploring letters, and at last she replied:

"'I was wrong about you. Forgive me. I can't be your wife.' Then I turned ugly. All the devils of my odd, rebellious youth returned, and in my rage I plotted death and destruction with the pleasure of a man possessed. I compared myself with Pavese, with Weininger. Through an act of cold will, I too would escape this wretched slavery of life and leap into the ineffable void . . . Actually I was like an angry child, spoilt by having too much without any sacrifice to deserve it and, denied a toy, deciding to smash it. I'd destroy myself at the same time as the toy. I thought I could, I didn't yet know what a cowardly wretch I was. And now I'm alive, grieving for ever because I killed the only person who really loved me, and loathing my filthy self."

Olgi was glad the door suddenly opened, and the guard said:

"You're lucky to be passing through just now – there's a film on today and you can see it. You going?"

The engineer stared ahead, wrapped round in the hard cocoon of his lonely sorrow.

"Of course we're going," said Olgi, "this cage at the zoo hasn't so many distractions that we can afford to refuse one."

And he took the engineer's arm and dragged him off.

"It'll be the usual idiotic stuff," protested the engineer. "Some clown fooling around with a lot of girls, or a weepy about a little orphan girl."

"You sometimes get something decent," said Olgi. "A while ago I saw *Friendly Persuasion*, with the great Gary Cooper."

In the din and laughter two men went by. One was thickset, like a boxer, the other thin and lanky.

"What's the film, Aurelio?" said the lanky one.

"*Room for One More*, with Cary Grant."

"There's room for one more in the graveyard," said another man, who looked like a chicken thief, roaring with laughter.

"Belt up, you queer," said the lanky man.

Chicken thief retorted with a rude noise.

"Hear that?" said Olgi, childishly pleased. "Cary Grant's in it."

The engineer shrugged.

"Well, he's a good actor," said Olgi.

"Oh, he can act, but he's too smooth. I don't like him."

The hall was oblong and low ceilinged, with benches on either side. With only a single small window at the end, its air was already foul with the smoke of cigarette stubs, and the stink of sweating, flatulent humanity. All their faces seemed hideous, stamped out in coarse clay from a single mould. There was noisy, rough, undemanding gaiety.

From the start Olgi followed the story of the film with interest. In an orphanage a group of very respectable old ladies was listening, smug and absent-minded, to the heart-rending speech of an elderly spinster, the principal or vice-principal of that gloomy institution. She complained of their ever-growing numbers, new children daily dropping down on them from heaven, and needing to be cared for with the small funds available; she blamed people's selfishness, the materialism of the age, the dearth of love and charity. The respectable old hens looked round at one another, virtuously certain they'd no cause for reproach, took out scented handkerchiefs, aristocratically lifted their beaky noses, and fluttered the feathers of their ridiculous hats; then at last they left.

Left behind was a woman who was still young, not strikingly beautiful but pretty, simply and cleanly dressed, with large, lively tender eyes, and a profile that was at once sweet and resolute. The principal, who knew that gentle woman and her passionate nature, said she was keeping something very suitable for her, a girl of about twelve who had had an unusually sad childhood, was morbidly sensitive and had even tried to kill herself.

"To kill herself at twelve?" exclaimed Signora Anna.

She recoiled in fear, seemingly eager to flee, yet stayed there fascinated, subdued by the force of motherly love that seeks to spend itself on others – the most deprived, the most unfortunate.

Then came the inside of a typical American house, with all the necessities but none of the luxuries. Signora Anna's husband, the nice Cary Grant, was an engineer not exactly over-worked in a firm where he wasn't exactly overpaid, and where the usual puritanical old bore, nicknamed Codfish, kept ranting; now, shirt-sleeves rolled up and wearing his wife's apron, he was getting lunch ready competently but a bit absent-mindedly, while three healthy, chatty brats peered nosily under the side-board where the cat was about to have kittens.

Olgi enjoyed the film, in sympathy with its simple, eternally human themes, and sympathized with its heartfelt, ingenuous emotions.

"D'you like it?" he whispered to the engineer.

"Superficial optimism, typically American pseudo-evangelical slush," muttered the engineer.

More than once Olgi furtively wiped away a tear, afraid his diabolical neighbour would mock him. Afterwards in the cell they argued hotly. Olgi accused the engineer of not under-standing the poetry of little things, of being a gloomy cold fish; the engineer said that in spite of his endless trials and tribulations, Olgi was still a splendid example of blind vital force.

"Say I'm an incurable idiot without beating about the bush," exclaimed Olgi, annoyed.

The engineer looked affectionately at him.

"When you're angry your neck swells, and that's another fine example of vital force."

"It's just how the blood vessels swell."

"So it may be. It's a question of terminology. Our whole futile life's a play on words. Anything else to eat?"

"I've had enough for a week."

"Then let's have all these titbits wrapped up and taken away."

"Why?"

"Because I want them taken away."

"I can understand how you feel like being philanthropic, but hasn't it struck you that people may not want your philanthropy?"

"Then let's halve it. We'll divide it up fraternally. Fra-ter-nal-ly. There's another fine word for you."

He looked into Olgi's eyes. Sharp and peevish though they were, the engineer's eyes, Olgi realized, sometimes had a defenceless sweetness about them, like a girl's.

XVI

THE NIGHT WENT BY, AND ANOTHER DAY BEGAN. Another few hours, and each of them would go his own way. Would they meet again?

The engineer went on with his desperate, crazy? monologue.

"I loved her and I killed her. She was my reason for living and I destroyed her. I'd decided to kill myself too, but that pistol shot had taken all my strength, and I watched her dully, as she died so quickly. When I wanted to kill myself again it was too late to do it, at least it wasn't so easy. A gun simplifies the effort, and bolsters cowardice. Without one, what could I do? I was shut up in a cell, watched continually, my life no longer belonged to me. On the one hand was the power of the law, with everything in black and white, severely put into practice; on the other were my relations, with their money, their know-how, their influential friends. Between them there was me, with my weariness, my disgust, my longing to get it all over.

"Among several possible forms of suicide I chose one that was particularly foul and possibly not even certain. It was achieved through steeping four or five packets of strong tobacco in a bowl of water, and then gulping down the filthy mixture. I knew death wouldn't be immediate, but that I'd die of septicaemia, through a blockage of the renal passage after hours of terrible pain. I'd bear it without a groan, strong as Socrates. Arrogant, wasn't I?"

"It's hard to be a hero," Olgi said indulgently.

"I wasn't alone in my cell. With me was a carefree young thief and a middle-aged con-man nicknamed the Marchese. I had to buy their silence, so I let them have the run of my bank account. Why of course, Engineer, why certainly, sir – they'd have licked my boots. They never disputed my plan to kill myself, and I gave them everything I had in the cell. The Marchese had an eye on my suit, and wanted to swap it for his. He wanted my spectacles as well.

"'In any case,' he said seriously, 'once you're buried, a corpse needs no spectacles.'

"I told him the spectacles had been a present from her, and that I wanted to take them to the grave with me, so he must forgive my silly romanticism . . . I was waiting till they had done the checking at five o'clock to end the whole absurd squalid business.

"At three I had a talk with my lawyer, a man in his sixties who had the manner of a young ladykiller. He roared with laughter, triumphantly, and told me, with a wink, that it was all in the bag, the girl's family (with suitable compensation, of course) had dropped legal proceedings against me and the judge was a 'very good chum' of his.

"'Don't look so glum,' he said, with good-natured cynicism. 'What are you worrying about? None of my clients ever gets a life sentence or thirty years. All it takes is cash. Oh, what a little hard cash can do . . .'

"While this sly scoundrel was chattering so dishonestly, I was thinking of my darling dead girl and saying to her: 'I'll soon be like you. With you, in the realms of bare truth and pure silence .. Outside the visitor's room a sergeant was waiting for me.

85

"'For organizational reasons,' he told me unctuously, 'I've got to put you in another cell.'

"I realized then that somebody had 'squealed'. (I later learnt that it was the Marchese.) I tried again and ended absurdly, and was convinced that I was a coward, irrevocably a coward. Seven years have gone by. Are seven years of this filthy life enough to expiate what I did, or not? Are twenty years, thirty years, a life sentence, enough? They are idiotic sums. Repentance is something spiritual, it's born from within and is a punishment quite unlike the sufferings others may inflict on us. That's why, though I accept repentance, which belongs to *me*, I reject all the rest. Is this what's called solipsism, anarchical individualism, Tolstoyism? Let it be. Labels and definitions make me quietly laugh. There's something, though, under the gloss of words. Every man is what he is. I'm attached to my own way of facing life. But the trouble is my repentance is sterile suffering; if only I could turn it into active feeling I'd have a reason for living again."

"Knowing what you need," said Olgi, "is half-way to getting it. All you need is a bit more sincerity, a bit more humility, and above all fewer big words. You hate these words, yet you whirl about in them till it makes one's head spin."

This time the engineer didn't flare up.

"Have you never thought of killing yourself?"

"No, never. Why do the hangman's job for him? Nature sees to killing off its creatures in her own good time. But I thought of escaping. I thought of it for five years on end. Twenty-two years inside seemed too great a punishment. Twice I managed to escape, and twice they caught me. There's prison and prison, as you know, and mine became specially hard, it was prison at its blackest. Always under the strictest conditions, ceaselessly, obsessively watched. Not knowing what else to do, unable to do anything else, I began reading, first of all whatever came to hand, just to pass the time, then choosing more carefully and knowledgeably. Having read so much, I felt the need to write and tell people something myself. At first I was encouraged by a good deal of presumptuousness, and even by an eye to the main chance. Then luckily, after I'd had two rejections from publishers, I imposed a strict discipline on myself and aimed at the very highest artistic result I could manage. I've made progress, but I'm hardly ever satisfied with what I write."

"And has no one helped you?"

"Can a man be helped to become a writer? I doubt it. But I've had approval and encouragement."

"From whom?"

"From E. V., from V. P., and from C. M. two years before he died."

"These are highly distinguished writers and critics," said the engineer. "They wouldn't easily give praise. If they've encouraged you it must mean you've really got qualities. But apart from this encouragement and approval, what have they done for you?"

"Nothing, and I'm glad of it. To become a real writer you've got to suffer above all, you've got to suffer a great deal."

"Too much suffering can dry you up as well," said the engineer. "You may lose the taste for human things. What definite hope have you of getting out? I think I understood you to say you were hoping for a pardon from the President. Forgive me for saying so but in your position I think that's rather foolish."

"I wasn't talking about a pardon," said Olgi. "What I meant was, I'll very likely not finish my sentence because I'll die first. In '57 I had a stroke. I may have another, and next time it may carry me off."

"You say it so calmly. You've overcome the fear of death," said the engineer, with admiration and envy.

"I've overcome the fear of death, but not the love of life, even 'this life'. Life is sweet. This intimate talk we're having now;

studying Socrates or Kafka, the ancient Greeks or the modern Chinese; finding a spatial problem as exciting as a woman's beauty, even if it's only on a magazine cover; a football match, a lyric of Lorca's; and everything, everything there is in life and in the world, including today, which is quite different from the infinite number of other days that have gone before it and will come after it: thinking that I'll have to leave all these things makes me feel melancholy."

Thus they talked, man to man; and the time came for Olgi to leave.

"Listen," said the engineer hastily, "this is my home address. I'll write to my father and he'll be happy to do something for you. And so will Dina and Sandra. There's so much you need, you've got to have conditions in which you can work calmly. And I want to help you. I'm not doing it out of philanthropy, and Christian charity and so on and so forth, but because among all these monkeys, parrots and dogs I've found a man at last. You are a man."

But Olgi, though smiling, was shaking his head.

"I'm nothing special, I'm not worth much, believe me," he said. "And besides, I don't need anything. You must believe me, I don't need anything."

"Do please accept, I want to help you, I don't say I should but I feel the need to help you," the engineer insisted, as if he were asking, begging to be helped.

The guard had already opened the door and the gate.

"Hey, what are you waiting for, you're leaving aren't you?"

"Goodbye, my friend," said Olgi.

"I'm sorry," murmured the engineer, "I'm sorry . . ."

Olgi was still smiling as he went downstairs and as they put on the handcuffs, but he stopped smiling when he was inside the dark van, a fast-moving prison where he could hear, in waves of sound, the city's tremulous life.

PART III

XVII

THE SNAKE-TRAIN DROWSING IN THE SUN WAS awakened by piercing whistles, and began swallowing people. It became gay and bustling with their gaiety all along its meandering length, until, puffing and whistling even harder, it uncoiled itself and ate up the never-ending railway line.

"We're off," said the handsome Sicilian with white teeth exultantly, and remarked that with two in a cell they were fairly comfortable. And, he went on to explain, the fact that there were two of them travelling comfortably, instead of four, crammed together and stinking foully, was all due to him.

"You've got to get them to listen, and see your point of view," he said, handsome, virile and hairy as he was. "Did you see how they gave way straight off?"

"There aren't many of us and there are plenty of empty seats," said Olgi. "In a case like that, being kind costs them nothing."

"Kind?" said the Sicilian, supremely disdainful. "Kind, d'you call them?" And crudely he told Olgi what they were. "You can say the chief of the escort's from my part of the country – that's more like it: he's from Agrigento."

He was standing, legs wide apart, at the crack in the door, swaying gently in time with the vibration of the train.

"One day when I was on a trip," he said excitedly, "I saw a peasant girl . . ."

"You mean she was doing it in public, in full view of the train?" Olgi said cheerfully.

"Right out in the fields. The train wasn't there, it turned up suddenly, and at a hundred kilometres an hour you can't see much," said the Sicilian regretfully. "I did see her arse, though. Just like a hill in the moonlight."

This had happened in Campania, he went on, on a memorable day in the year 1955, while he was going from the prison at Ucciardone to the one at Poggioreale.

He looked out again.

"Hell," he burst out, annoyed and disappointed, "you can't see a thing. I might go the whole length of Tuscany, and Liguria, and Piedmont, and Lombardy, and never see what I saw in Campania."

He sat down and quickly changed the subject.

"So you're going to Alessandria too."

"I'm really going to Saluzzo," said Olgi, "but I'm stopping off at Alessandria."

The Sicilian said Saluzzo wasn't bad, but Alessandria was much better. He said Alessandria and Padua were the two best prisons in the whole of the Italian republic, and that he'd got the choice of going to Alessandria or to Padua, or any other prison he liked. And he added, to clear up the mystery, that he had a cousin at the Ministry.

"I've an uncle who's a priest as well," he confided and turned his velvet black eyes on Olgi, who said seriously:

"An uncle who's a priest can get you into Heaven."

The handsome Sicilian, now launched on his boasting, began overdoing it.

"Now I'll get them to open the door."

He was wearing prison clothes like Olgi, but much more smartly. His shirt was new, and had a collar, his trousers were new as well and had been altered, and the regulation shoes, originally tan-coloured, had been polished a fine shiny black.

He called the chief of the escort in dialect, drawling softly and hoarsely, sweetly, almost lovingly complaining. The chief came over idly. He wasn't a sergeant, only a lance-corporal, but important all the same. A crooked nose was stuck sadistically in his yellow face.

"What's up? What d'you want?"

The Sicilian prisoner continued to speak in dialect, trying to soften and persuade him. He said it was hot, horribly hot, that he suffered from asthma, and so on, and that, in fact, he'd like the door open and kept open, for pity's sake.

"Can't be done."

More persuasive reasoning follows.

"Can't be done," repeated the lance-corporal; and, to prevent further useless argument, added:

"The rules won't allow it. What's humanly possible I do, but I won't disobey the rules. I've put just the pair of you in here, I've left the door ajar, I've left off your handcuffs, what more d'you want?"

He returned to the end of the corridor and sat down, vexed and tired, and the handsome Sicilian got his own back by saying that with a face like that he couldn't fail to be a miserable old bugger.

"And now I'll make coffee," he declared gaily. "D'you like it?"

"I never drink it," said Olgi.

"If I don't drink it I'm done for. I've just got to have at least two cups of coffee and ten cigarettes a day. Else what's the point of living? You been inside for long?"

Olgi told him how long. The handsome Sicilian said he'd been in eight years, was now thirty, and would be out when he was thirty-four. He said prison was hard mainly because a fellow couldn't have a bird there. He was going to Alessandria to study accountancy. Three years of it, then a diploma, and he'd go home a qualified accountant. When he left to go to prison he was a groom, and he'd go back an accountant.

"What a laugh – me an accountant."

He gestured with his thick hand, palm upwards, meaning

that he'd have everyone in his stupid town in the palm of his hand when he was an accountant.

He frowned, and his lecherous velvet eyes gleamed proudly.

"Of course," he said, "even if I went home without a diploma, they'd welcome and respect me. I've done nothing to be ashamed of, and nothing my family can be ashamed of. I haven't stolen, I've killed. I avenged the honour of a cousin of mine. I'm Sicilian. We Sicilians aren't like you polenta-eaters, who don't give a damn for your horns and settle it all among yourselves. Nothing personal of course, because you might say you've always been inside, but isn't that so?"

"L'homme heureux est celui qui est cocu," said Olgi.

"What sort of lingo's that?"

"It's what a man called Rabelais thought," Olgi explained.

Proud paladin of outraged womanhood, the Sicilian was gay and busy, meantime, making coffee. He had a minute coffee-pot, as pretty as a toy, and all sorts of gleaming pots and pans.

"You're well organized," said Olgi.

"I've got everything I need," the Sicilian boasted. "I get 5,000 lire a month from an aunt, the mother of the cousin I avenged, and with that I get along."

"And how about your uncle the priest?" said Olgi slyly.

"He's stingy," said the liar from Agrigento, "but he's a saint."

On a spirit-lamp with a cotton wick soaked in alcohol he boiled up the coffee, drank it and clicked his tongue. He smoked, his handsome face glowing with bliss, which came, not from the coffee and tobacco, even if these occasioned and aroused it, but from the depths of his animal life. Olgi knew that perfect, unthinking happiness – he had enjoyed it himself in the days when he was like a vessel filled with life, without a hint of illness or of death within him.

The train slowed down and stopped, and the Sicilian leapt over to the crack to peep out with his beautiful greedy eyes.

"Nothing but the sea."

He went and sat down again, obviously thinking it pointless to look at the sea. Then Olgi went over to look. As far as the eye could reach there was sea. Just sea. A strip of sandy land, and then sea to the horizon. Not still and blue and man-sized as it is in paintings, but immense and irridescent, strangely and fearfully alive, incomprehensible. Fascinating, in fact, for what he couldn't understand about it; like the stars, and, in general, like everything on earth.

Then the train moved, the strip of sand widened and became solid ground, with houses, a few factories, and trees, more and more trees, that hid the sea.

"Any arses in sight?" asked the handsome Sicilian, laughing.

"Trees," said Olgi. "Just trees."

They had tall, delicate trunks, and thick foliage at the top that spread richly. What's the name of those trees, Olgi thought longingly. I don't know what they're called. Just trees, as we call ourselves men?

The trees came to an end, and he saw houses, trees again, and then again houses, and the white walls of green gardens, fountains in squares, glimpses of the sea. Until the carriage jerked to a halt with the rest of the train.

"We're at Viareggio," said Olgi, and the Sicilian looked out and said Viareggio wasn't anything.

"You can't see a thing."

The prison coach had stopped spitefully by an ugly wall built there for some unknown reason. All the sunny happiness and beauty of that seaside town died, stifled by that ugly wall.

"But it's only a wall," exclaimed Olgi, "and Viareggio isn't this wall." (He said Viareggio but he meant the world.) "I've been to Viareggio. Twice. Once as a sailor. You're quite wrong to despise Viareggio, the pearl of the Italian California. Its sea, its sky . . ."

The Sicilian yawned.

"All I know about is horses. When I'm an accountant . . ."

"Its women . . ." Olgi went on fervently. "Ah, the wonderful women of Viareggio!"

The Sicilian pricked up his ears.

"What are the women like at Viareggio?"

"Soft and passionate."

"What are their tits like?"

"Superb."

But the Sicilian wasn't satisfied with poetic adjectives. He wanted Olgi to describe them with prosaic exactness. The air of the cell was filled with exciting curves and protuberances. The Sicilian clicked his tongue.

"Ah, the wonderful women of Viareggio," he said as well.

He got up and went to gaze passionately at the wall.

"Ah, the wonderful women of Viareggio," he repeated.

He looked at Olgi with admiration and envy.

"Had many?"

"Many what?" said Olgi, surprised.

"Why, the wonderful women of Viareggio."

"I was never a Don Giovanni," laughed Olgi. "I'd a good appetite but not much to feed it. One of them, though, I did manage to get. The loveliest girl in Viareggio and, I think, in the whole world."

"What was she like? What was she like?" said the Sicilian.

"I was twenty," said Olgi. "And handsome, at least so I thought. In my smart sailor's uniform, with my cap at a rakish angle. I sauntered about and the world seemed mine. Then I saw her. She had a white dress, a red mouth. And then I was certain, without having to think it out, that I'd lived and waited twenty years to meet her. In short: we agreed to go for a walk. It was summer, the sea was before us, the acacia woods behind. And of course there was moonlight too."

"What's moonlight got to do with it?" muttered the Sicilian, shocked.

"I didn't invent it. Anyway, we didn't stop and gaze at the moon. We kissed."

"Uhu," said the Sicilian. "And then?"

"Then we said goodbye."

"But before saying goodbye, what happened?"

"I told you we kissed."

"Nothing else?"

"It's quite something to kiss a beautiful girl in a white dress," said Olgi thoughtfully. "Sometimes it can be enough to fill a whole life."

"Mmmm," said the Sicilian.

The train started up again.

XVIII

AND VIAREGGIO VANISHED, THE WHITE DRESS AND the red mouth he had remembered vanished, his pleasant, light memories flew away, and all that was left was the heavy grinding of the wheels in his heart.

The train often made short stops, and other longer ones between them, to unload goods or to load up with them, or simply because the timetable said there was no hurry. And each time the Sicilian went hopefully to look out, and invariably complained:

"No good, you can't see a thing."

Or rather he could see something, but not what he wanted to see. And he was so irritated at not seeing what he wanted, that he refused any merit to what he could in fact see.

"Why, what ugly houses," he said, "what ugly streets and piazzas, what ugly people. Look at that one, he's like Pinocchio. And that woman with three humps."

Then he began telling a long, muddled tale, of doubtful

authenticity, in which the main parts were played by himself, the groom, and a young blonde countess who had 'lost her honour' to a dazzling officer, her mother's lover. Horses came into this story of love and intrigue, and with them our Sicilian, who though socially modest enough, was man enough to interest even a young countess. This noble girl had a horse, but since it was old she was ashamed of riding it. So, with begging and praying she got a new horse at last, a fine bay three-year-old, but with such a wicked nature no one dared ride him. But our man undertook to break him. And he beat him so hard and broke him so well that when his pretty mistress made ready to mount the horse used to bow to her.

Of course, such cleverness and devotion deserved a prize: and in the traditions of chivalry, there was a kiss.

"A kiss?" said Olgi, puzzled.

"Certainly, a gorgeous kiss," said the handsome groom, mawkishly, "a kiss in the wood."

"And then?" asked Olgi. "You're not telling me that there was just a kiss."

"And what else should there be?" exclaimed the groom.

"Why, she wasn't an innocent girl," said Olgi. "And then a wood's a powerful aphrodisiac."

"But she was a countess," yelled the Sicilian, "and aren't there some things you can't do to a countess?"

Olgi allowed himself a small laugh and went to look out through the crack. The landscape was all strewn with stones, from the ripped up Apuans to small towns of two or three thousand people who lived on the marble industry, and larger towns, almost cities, whose names referred to the stone, as to their tutelary god: Pietrasanta, Forte dei Marmi, Massa Carrara ...

At Massa a fellow from La Spezia got on, who was going to Genoa to appeal, and was shut up in the cell with Olgi and the Sicilian. The Sicilian made no protest. The newcomer had no luggage, and was raggedly dressed in all sorts of colours;

besides, he was thin, extremely thin in fact, and so not much of a nuisance. And then he was new, a distraction, rather like a magazine to look through. He said that, one fine day when he'd drunk a bit too much, he'd lifted his elbow and insulted a policeman, which got him eighteen months straight off. He'd done twelve, and was now going to Marassi to appeal.

"But I'm not very hopeful of getting any off," he said, reasonable and pessimistic. "I haven't even got a lawyer."

When he heard how long the other two had been inside he rubbed his hands.

"Six months won't be long," he said cheerfully.

"I'd do them squatting," said the Sicilian. "What did you do outside?"

"I did a number of jobs, till I realized the best job was doing nothing. You manage just the same and save yourself lots of bother. But in the summer I was a guide."

"A guide?" said Olgi.

"A guide, what d'you call it? An interpreter, something like that. I speak French, je parle français, parbleu, I used to go round with tourists, or rather lady tourists, ah Frenchwomen, mes amis, faut-il avoir du bon machin avec elles."

The Sicilian's greedy eyes narrowed. Though he knew neither French nor France he thought he knew plenty about Frenchwomen's ways and temperaments.

"Ah, Frenchwomen," he sighed.

Olgi asked the newcomer, in French, if he had been to France.

"Mais oui," he said. "A Marseille, et puis à Paris. Trois ans à Paris, mieux clochard à Paris que prince à Rome."

Olgi was interested to hear he had been a tramp in Paris, but the Sicilian thought nothing of it, Paris meant practically nothing to him, just as Tokyo or New York meant practically nothing to him, but he was deeply impressed with the story of the guide kept busy satisfying Frenchwomen.

"I'll learn French and when I get out I'll be a guide myself,"

99

said the handsome, hairy Sicilian. "And we'll see who tires first, them or me."

"But they come in groups," laughed the ex-tramp. "And how can one man alone satisfy a whole tribe of women, and French-women at that?"

The Sicilian smiled very smugly.

A Sicilian . . . he seemed to imply. "You married?"

"She's left me."

"Left you? Ha ha. Why?"

"Not that I cared," said the man. "I just wish she'd done it twenty years ago. I'd sooner have scarlet fever than her."

"Have you got any children?" asked Olgi.

"Two, but they're grown up and on their own. I haven't even got a home. I've nothing, now. And although I've got nothing, my friends, I'm better off now, believe me, than I was when I thought I had something."

"Then you can't mind prison much," the Sicilian remarked sarcastically. "Work you're not too keen on, women are too much like hard work, if it rains open an umbrella, if you haven't got an umbrella get in a doorway, and if the sun's too hot lie down in the shade."

He carried on mockingly; then paused to listen to a high, twittering laugh, not a man's but a woman's, that came from somewhere in the prison coach, not from outside.

"Why, that's a woman's voice!" the Sicilian burst out. "There's no doubt about it: it's a woman. Only women laugh like that."

He looked questioningly at Olgi.

"It's a woman," Olgi agreed.

The newcomer said it was Marcella, night-club dancer from Versilia. She did other things as well, and had got two years for infringing the Merlin law. She'd been inside a year, and was on her way to Genoa to make an appeal.

"She was with me at Massa. A fine gay tease she was."

"Young?" the Sicilian asked ardently. "Pretty?"

The newcomer said she was thirty, maybe more, maybe less (guessing a woman's age, he said, was a pretty hard thing to do); her flesh was in all the right places, and she smoked forty cigarettes a day. Her man sent her a money order every week and she blew the lot in a day.

"She's so mad keen on it," grinned the newcomer. "And she admits it, the hussy."

Again they heard the whore's shrill laugh. The Sicilian began calling her, comically, lustfully, and with suggestive movements. Then he banged on the door, saying he wanted to go to the toilet, but it was an excuse to see her. But Sourpuss was inflexible, incorruptible. He sent him to the lavatory but stood outside it, an implacable sleuth.

A lively lot of insults followed, after which the Sicilian returned to his favourite subject.

"Big tits, has she?"

"Huge," said the newcomer.

"Bigger than Silvana's?"

"How do I know Silvana's?" said the newcomer.

"Long legs or short?"

"Long."

"And her thighs?"

"I haven't seen them."

"Well, you can see what they're like through her dress. Are they thin as sticks or thick as pillars?"

"Thick as pillars."

"Ahahaha!"

Fast and excitedly, the Sicilian told them what he'd do with her. And as he did so the train reached La Spezia. It was the newcomer who told them they had arrived.

"We're at La Spezia," he said, and his thin, worn face had a glimmer of feeling or fond memory in it. Even when he had spoken of Paris it had never lit up like this.

"I did my military service here."

"At the depot or at sea?" asked Olgi.

"A few months at the depot, then aboard the *Grecale*."

"I was in the *Maestrale*," said Olgi. "What a coincidence!"

"What year was it?"

"In '35."

"I was in '36."

"I heard," said Olgi, "that both the *Grecale* and the *Maestrale* were sunk during the war."

"That's true," said the newcomer, "but by the time it happened I'd been posted to Sardinia. Then they sent me to Lero."

"Whereas I was already in a military gaol," said Olgi. He laughed, not bitterly, but as if oddly amused. "I was born to spend my whole life inside."

The newcomer looked at him, as if searching for something in the face of this man who had spent so many years in prison; then he shook his head and said:

"Pooh, the whole world's a gaol."

XIX

BUT OLGI WASN'T THINKING OF PRISON, HE WAS brooding on his lost happiness at twenty, a happiness he hadn't even noticed. But that it had been real was proved by its un-self-consciousness and spontaneity, which depended not on natural things but came from the very centre of life itself.

The newcomer scratched his back, with his air of a whipped cur happy to be whipped just a little less than usual.

The Sicilian whistled.

And then the wonderful thing happened. The half-whore, whom Sourpuss had condescended to let sit beside him so as to lighten his boredom with indelicate chat, was shut up in the cell next door to that of the three travellers, awaiting an inspection later on. Just above the luggage rack there was a strip of holes in the wall, through which, by standing on the seat, one could look into the next compartment.

The Sicilian commanded silence by eye and gesture, took off his shoes, and as cautiously as an Indian on the warpath climbed up on to the seat. There he stretched on tiptoe, his heart thudding.

Before him he saw a pair of mocking eyes and a bit of tongue coming out of a red mouth. It was Marcella, who had had a similar inspiration. Finding herself unexpectedly before that dark face, burning with excitement, her craziness burst out.

Filled with shame and confusion, the Sicilian pretended he was looking for something in a box, and then climbed down, crestfallen, and put on his shoes.

"Hi, Attilio," said the gay sinner, "so they shoved you in here?"

"Yes," said the newcomer "they shoved me in here."

"And who are these others?"

"King Farouk travelling incognito," said Olgi, indicating himself. "And this fine dark youngster with virile whiskers is the best groom in the whole of Trinacria."

"I'm Sicilian," said the man from Agrigento, who had started burning with excitement again, "from Catania."

"You make my head spin, the way you talk," said the woman. "But d'you know you're really like King Farouk? If you'd got his moustache you'd be the very image."

"Well, at Reggio Emilia they used to call me King Farouk," said Olgi.

"At Reggio Emilia where the looneys are?"

"Yes at Reggio Emilia where the looneys are."

"I like looneys," said Marcella, "at least they're sincere. I was shut up at Maggiano for three months. I'm a bit looney myself."

And she laughed.

"Let's talk softly. Sourpuss doesn't like me talking to the

prisoners. As if they weren't as good as him. As if I was Lady Muck and not a prisoner myself. I'm inside myself, you bloody old phonies, you! They make the laws! And fine laws they are! Putting poor girls in prison who just do what they can with what they've got! They say they want to moralize Italy. Moralize yourselves first, you swine!"

Having vented herself, she lit a cigarette.

"Have you got any smokes? You got smokes, Attilio?"

"I've got a few stubs," said Attilio.

"I've got ten," said Marcella, "but I'll give you five. Then I'll see what I can get. Maybe some off old Sourpuss."

She laughed shrilly again.

"Let's talk softly."

The Sicilian wanted his chance.

"D'you know you're very pretty, signora?"

"Thanks for the compliment, handsome. They wanted me on the films in Rome. But it was Hollywood or nothing for me. Anyway I'm not signora. I'm still signorina."

She burst out laughing uncontrollably again, then took four or five quick puffs and became thoughtful.

"What d'you think, Attilio, will this appeal do me any good?"

"Well," said Attilio. He shook his head sadly, like an old featherless bird. "I no longer believe in people's consciences. But I do wish you well with all my heart, and hope you'll get out soon. You're a fine girl, Marcella."

"Thanks," said Marcella. She seemed moved and her eyes glittered.

"Poor Attilio! When I think of all the crooked things there are in this filthy world I want to kill myself. But sometimes I want to laugh at everything. Yes, let's laugh at everything instead."

But instead of laughing she remained silent for a while, as if brooding, then she sighed:

"But if I have to spend another year inside . . ."

"Cheer up, Marcella," said the newcomer. "You see this fellow, who looks so gay? He's done twenty years inside."

"Twenty years inside?" exclaimed Marcella, shuddering. "And he's still alive? He still hasn't hung himself? He still hasn't slashed a vein?"

Her eyes peered through the holes of the grating to see this human phenomenon better.

"You poor thing. How d'you do it? . . ."

"Man gets used to everything," said Olgi.

The Sicilian broke in, annoyed not to be the centre of attention: "I've done eight years. I'm young, so my eight are more than his twenty. I was twenty-two when I came in and now I'm thirty."

"Poor darkie," said Marcella. "What did you do, pinching?"

"Pinching? Me? No, I killed. I avenged my cousin's honour."

"What's that? You avenged your cousin's honour? Well, well, just think of that!"

Her voice was suddenly mocking and malicious.

"Have you ever wondered whether women really want you poking your nose into their honour? Whether they want you defending their honour so fiercely and hypocritically? Stinking honour, too! Oh, you punks from Calabria! You southern blockheads! Hasn't it ever even entered your great fat clumsy southern head that your cousin mayn't have given a damn for the loss of her honour?"

"But, signorina . . ." said the Sicilian.

"Signorina . . ." she answered, her language worse than a docker's yet her face still fresh and pretty, with a pair of lovely brown eyes. "I just can't stand you, your stupid jealousy, your disgusting, treacherous killing."

"But signorina," protested the Sicilian, "you talk like that because you're a woman. If you were a man . . ."

Hearing him call her signorina instead of whore appeased her. Basically he was a nice fellow, and handsome too. Marcella softened towards him.

"Get up and give me a kiss. Why should we quarrel? We're all in the same boat."

The Sicilian glowed, like sunshine. He pressed his face to the grating. It wasn't the kind of kiss that two youths make when they come together completely, and seem to want to enter one another. There was more iron than mouth about it. Yet to the Sicilian it meant heavenly joy.

"Eight years," he moaned childishly, "eight years since I kissed a woman."

Marcella felt a vital warmth and melting tenderness all over her, a longing to give herself that she had not felt as intensely since she was a girl climbing out of the window to meet her lover in the moonlight. Unable to give him the most living part of herself she put out her tongue and then, without shame, they enjoyed one another through the hole in the grating.

The newcomer watched as cheerfully as an indulgent father watching his children's nonsense, but Olgi felt his legs tremble.

"Now let's give him a bit of fun too," said the altruistic Marcella, "we mustn't be selfish."

But the Sicilian's eyes glittered murderously.

"Come, **my** big Farouk," said Marcella. "come and kiss me. It's twenty years since you kissed a woman, you poor wretch."

But Olgi, though burning with desire like a youngster at his first discovery of sex, said without irony:

"Thank you, with all my heart, Signorina Marcella." And he shrugged, meaning: now, at my age . . . "You two carry on."

They carried on. But all happiness is brief. Sourpuss came to take Marcella away. He saw or guessed what had happened and glanced severely at her, but she waggled her hips and brushed past him.

XX

THE TRAIN, OR AT LEAST THE END PART OF IT WHERE the prison coach was, had stopped in a tunnel, like something shameful that must be hidden. The tunnel was as dark and cool as a crypt, but not as sepulchrally silent, for even there they could hear the sound of the busy port.

"Or is it the arsenal?" said Olgi. "I can't remember whether it's the port or the arsenal. Are we near the station here? I didn't know there was a tunnel near the station."

"Filthy tunnel," the Sicilian burst out. "Filthy world."

"Why, the whole district's full of tunnels," said the newcomer peaceably. "There are more than a hundred between here and Genoa."

This might arouse edifying thoughts: for instance all the work and human effort needed to cut through so much land to pierce mountains and so on, so that civilization could run faster than the seven-league boots.

All it took was a ticket and everyone could run: clerk, soldier, tart, businessman, priest, married or single, intellectual or blockhead, stout or arthritic. And they were running too, shut up in their prison coach, enjoying the benefits of civilization.

The Sicilian lay on his back on the seat, and said tragically that the world was bloody, but that if he could have Marcella beside him just then he'd feel a god.

Outside the endless work of the port continued, hammers rang, sirens moaned, cranes creaked.

The newcomer was standing silent. He was a weary man rather than a wise one, who took up little room, and was humble in a way that aroused no pity.

Olgi had copied the Sicilian and was taking up the whole of the left-hand seat, not because he was a strong, arrogant man asserting himself but simply because he needed to rest. In half an hour the train set off again. Although Olgi had shut his eyes while they were in darkness, he hadn't managed to sleep or lighten the intense working of his mind, the hard abstract thought he mistrusted, whereas imagining, making images of memories . . .

Until the train moved, and came triumphantly out of the tunnel's shade and into the sunshine again.

"We're off," said the Sicilian, leaping up, "we're off."

And he cried:

"Marcella, oh Marcella," with the tuneless urgency of a rooster.

Olgi got up, stretched himself, and looked at the newcomer, feeling vaguely guilty at having kept him off the seat – so thin and threadbare he seemed pitiful. How hard life had hit him!

"Ça va?" asked Olgi.

"Ça va," he answered. "Of course, it must."

Olgi shook off the faint pity, or solidarity, or whatever it was, and began looking through the crack at the landscape, crouched up like the Sicilian, who was looking out as well. The train was running along the sea-shore: and the sea was slightly rough under a west wind. Yet how many people were there all the same!

"Stop, train, stop you foul train," said the Sicilian. "You never stop where it'd be nice to stop. God, God, look at all those birds – just look . . . They don't come to the sea to bathe, they come to show off all a man gets with marriage, and they want everyone to share, whores that they are . . . I wish . . ." and so on.

He joked obscenely with the same desperate face the engineer had shown when he spoke of his painful search for an inner balance and for a new reason for living, or of his inability to create poetry.

But Olgi was no longer thinking of the engineer, no longer thinking of anything, horror, vain misery and torment were all wiped out, he was simply living, as he had lived when he was happy and ignorant and twenty, with a living, happy warmth and a lustful vitality in his eye that was like an extension of sex.

"Oh, stop, just stop a minute, you bloody blind horse," panted the Sicilian. "Oh, this is terrible."

Then Olgi laughed, because it was a comic, typically human despair, and the newcomer laughed as well. And so, with outbursts and linguistic oddities from the Sicilian, and mild chat from the other two, they reached Sestri Levante.

"What comes after Sestri?" asked Olgi.

"Chiavari, and then Rapallo," said the newcomer.

"And Portofino?"

"We don't touch it, but it's near by, you go on another line, a branch line."

"Have you been there?"

"Yes, it's nothing much."

Paradise, Eden, accessible only to millionaires: it was nothing much.

Olgi sat down again. The train was running through another dark painful tunnel. Olgi would now have liked to talk, to dig and get to know those other two. Not see them, but hear them.

A glow announced the end of the tunnel and it was daylight, ordinary, exact, and without secrets; and as everything seemed flatly what it was, Olgi again gave up the idea of talking.

But the Sicilian, inexhaustible on the subject of sex, went on chattering; and sometimes he became ironical.

"But you who were a guide," he said poking his crooked finger into the newcomer's skin, which was pretty hard, "what sort of a guide were you when you can hardly stand on your feet!"

"A man does what he can," the newcomer said modestly.

"And then with that old codfish face of yours, those Frenchy girls must have been pretty keen on it."

"Everyone's got the face God amused himself to give him."

"But what did you live on when you were outside? Crickets, lizards?"

"Whatever I could, young man. But I can tell you that if you'd been where I've been, crickets and lizards would have seemed like lobsters and pheasants, if you'd got them."

"What, were you dying of hunger in Paris?"

"Belsen, Dachau," said the newcomer gloomily.

But these terrible names meant nothing to the Sicilian, who whistled at a seductive bikini in the distance. And with that image of erotic joy in his heart, he was carried into another dark tunnel.

"So you were at Dachau as well," said Olgi.

"Yes, I was at Dachau as well," said the newcomer.

They sat side by side, brothers in misery, and the newcomer smoked. He coughed and said:

"I was at Lero at the time of the armistice. Our detachment didn't surrender to the Germans, so most of them were killed and the rest sent to Germany in sealed trucks. That's how it started: starvation, hard work, blows. It was hard, but worse was still to come. At Dachau they died like flies. Those who could keep on their feet had to carry the dead to the crematorium ovens. And the dead weren't always completely dead."

The train left the tunnel, and ran along in the sunshine, and Olgi looked at the weary face of the newcomer, who, slightly bewildered, said:

"It's incredible what a man can bear, the evil he can do, and then, in spite of everything, how he can start living calmly again."

Was it a reflection, or a hint of confession?

The Sicilian had begun to sing.

XXI

WHILE THE NEWCOMER WAS TALKING TERSELY ABOUT
events and misfortunes, both collective and personal, mostly
personal, Olgi was grateful to the young Sicilian whose oaths
and chitchat made his thoughts less gloomy.

It was a silly song, and so ideal to chase melancholy away.
Olgi suddenly began to sing it too, in his deep voice.

The contrast was funny in itself, but only the Sicilian was
amused. Gravely Olgi told the newcomer not to boycott gaiety.

"I can't sing," the newcomer apologized humbly.

"You don't have to, to join in this."

"I don't even know the words."

"They're easy. It's not like learning bits of the *Divine
Comedy*, you know. Come on, say it: there's a zebra."

"There's a zebra."

"Daddy's present."

"Daddy's present."

"Ha ha ha."

"Ha ha ha."

"Très bien, mon vieux. Now let's all three start again together: "There's a zebra, there's a zebra, there's a zebraaaaaa
..."

In spite of the efforts of Olgi and the newcomer to be gay,
their faces, marked by a thousand sufferings, remained irrevocably sad.

"Will you shut up?" yelled Sourpuss.

"We're having a bit of fun," said Olgi. "Are citizens of the
republic forbidden to have a bit of fun? You've got to pass the
time. We've been in this cage eight hours. Eight hours to do a
hundred and fifty kilometres."

"And what about me?" said Sourpuss angrily. "Where am
I? In Taormina?"

"Well, go there," said the newcomer. "Get along there, seeing you can. Or are you a prisoner too?"

Not knowing what to reply to this sally, which cut rather too near the bone, Sourpuss said:

"Elderly people making such a racket! You ought to be ashamed."

"Now you're really insulting us," said Olgi facetiously. "I feel as if I were twenty."

The man went off, swallowing his bile, and Olgi said:

"What a pill!"

They heard him quarrelling at the other end of the passage with someone who had got on at Chiavari or Rapallo.

"If he hadn't gone," said the Sicilian, "I'd have got myself another trial."

They had entered still another tunnel and Olgi sat down, suddenly feeling what he was; old, tired, ill, even radically changed, in his nature and ways. He longed for this absurd journey to be over soon, and to leave these temporary companions.

After another three tunnels the train stopped.

"Where are we?"

"At Santa Margherita. No, at Nervi."

Olgi looked. He could see the outside of a low building and, through leaves like lace, something white which was a flight of steps.

"Well, that's something," said Olgi.

But the Sicilian said with irritation that it was nothing, in fact worse than nothing. Then Olgi, looking at the indifferent newcomer, murmured:

"Le néant, la philosophie du néant."

And rather crazily he laughed.

The sun had already set. They began to see the outskirts of a large town: huge, dark boxes, in painful rows. Olgi always felt bewildered and depressed when he saw these cold cubes for living in. Nearly all the windows were shut. Were they voluntary prisons?

"Get ready, put on your irons, collect your luggage."

It was Sourpuss's truer voice. And he was running up and down to check that his orders were being obeyed, ceaselessly barking: "Hurry, hurry."

They were all now in the corridor: the four from Pisa, the newcomer, and another five picked up on the way. (Marcella was segregated in the other part of the coach.) Three were very young, almost beardless, and the other two were between thirty and forty. One of the boys was tall and healthy and fair, with a transparent raincoat, and looked Nordic.

"Bolzano," said the fair boy, with an attractive smile, "will you give me a cigarette?"

"I haven't any," answered the man from Bolzano roughly. He was tall, and thickset, and wore a cap with a visor, like those the Nazis wore. His face was pitiless. He spoke in angry outbursts, bitter and proud.

The train seemed to have arrived, but that obsessional row of houses never ended. The air had grown livid. Lights glimmered here and there. Half an hour passed, and the train continued manœuvring, running up and down, sometimes pausing to puff away like an asthmatic old man, then suddenly doing a bit more, running fifty or a hundred yards and then stopping again.

It was the fault of Sourpuss, for not getting out with the other travellers, but requiring separate room for the prisoners and, a particular rite, adequate security measures.

The man from Bolzano was trembling with hatred. They all felt it, and even Olgi caught it. But he was too tired or too wise to give way to such a pointlessly violent feeling, and took refuge in watching the fair youngster's face. It was as beautiful as a girl's, but without a girl's affectedness and delicacy.

At last they were taken out on to a patch of grass which was dying from suffocation by coal dust, between a tumbledown fence and black heaps of clinkers. The prison vans were waiting for them, engines running. And they jerked off along unseen streets.

The man from Bolzano had settled himself at the end, on a seat in the dim light of a lamp in a kind of cage; with his solid chest, his animal jaws, and his SS cap, he looked like a sleepless, hungry and therefore evil warrior on the way to a massacre.

At last he spoke excitedly, as if to avoid bursting, and absurdly threatened to write to the Minister.

"It's a scandal," he raged, in his harsh half-German voice, "a scandal you'd only see in Italy. Making prisoners travel without a proper head of escort."

The two young carabinieri exchanged looks, sitting solemn and dignified and watchful by the barred door of the prison van.

"But there is a head of escort," said the elder of the two, "the lance-corporal."

The man from Bolzano croaked with scorn.

"A lance-corporal! It ought to be a sergeant, and where there are more than six prisoners being moved it ought to be a *maresciallo*. The Rules are perfectly clear about it. I know the Rules, why aren't they applied?"

The two young soldiers were silent, either prudently or disdainfully. But the man from Bolzano, determined to add something important to complete his triumph, was not.

"It's an ex-warrant officer you're talking to, my friends," he told them ironically, and it was implicit, in fact explicit, that this warrant officer wasn't just any warrant officer but a warrant officer of the Third Reich.

Olgi was embarrassed. He looked at the fair boy, as if hoping to get some support from him; but his face was on his knees, laughing.

PART IV

XXII

THEY GOT THROUGH THE REGISTRATION IN A FEW minutes, being nearly all in transit: rather like parcels in the post. Parcels without value.

"All done, all checked?" said a fat sergeant jovially.

"Hey, calm down over there. The storekeeper'll be along now and he'll fix you all up in five minutes."

He touched the fair boy's belly, indecent but innocent. The boy laughed, a child. The fat, fatherly sergeant gave him a cigarette.

"I want the priest," said the fair boy. "The reverend."

"At this hour?"

"I came at this hour."

"But the priest isn't here.'

"He is here. Don't tell lies. Don't you know that people who tell lies go to hell?"

"He's out, he was sent for. Why d'you want to see the priest? D'you want to go to confession?"

"I want him to give me a thousand lire," said the fair boy.

The sergeant laughed. His belly shivered. He opened a door.

"Be patient, boys."

And professionally careful, he locked the door.

It was a bare room, with a bench fixed to the wall. There were obscenities and curses written on the wall. And some crude drawings. Olgi looked at them. He had a feeling that nothing had happened, that he hadn't travelled, that since the distant day of his arrest he had always lived in a bare room with a bench fixed to the wall and curses and obscenities on the walls.

But time had passed, something had happened, something had matured, something had changed; and he heard the youngster's shrill living laughter, the harsh voice of the man from Bolzano, and that too was life. He came out of that silence of agony where his own selfhood was sometimes shipwrecked, and recognized others, felt himself alive in relation to others.

Noticing his own tiredness, he convinced himself that he had in fact travelled, and went to sit down on the bench, leaning his back against a real, solid wall. The room had a toilet and that too was a comforting sign of life.

One by one the men all went to make water, not bothering to hide, with the immodesty that becomes second nature in soldiers or convicts, and is due to the lack of privacy. Some who still had cigarettes smoked. Some walked up and down, some searched in their luggage or put something away that they could leave in the store.

Two had been travelling with Olgi from Civitavecchia, the tall thin hungry-looking man with a crooked nose and the sturdy fellow with a moustache and sun-glasses. One was going to Asti, the other to Turin.

Olgi wasn't curious, at least not with the superficial, gossipy curiosity that feeds on outward facts, and he avoided making judgements, too. As a rule he relied on impressions, inner movements of liking or dislike. When someone interested him he approached him, trying to extract as much of the essence of him as he could; otherwise he would ignore him.

Olgi was now feeling really ill again. Not only his heart but his whole body was like a seed-bed of pain. He hated this big body that had betrayed him, and he lay down on the bench, using his haversack as a pillow.

What a worm I've become, he thought of himself, and that fierce and almost humorous knowledge of his own state, which excluded pity, turned into strength, and prolonged his vitality and resistance.

He looked at the fair boy, who had taken off the raincoat that made him look wretched. He wore a short-sleeved shirt open on the chest. His skin, through sunburn and the warm flow of his blood, gleamed golden.

Olgi couldn't take his eyes off him. Through that handsome youth, all his unquenchable love of life rose again and stood triumphantly on the ashes of his misery. Nothing really died on earth: youth was immortal, beauty indestructible.

This certainty – of the perennial flow and renewal of life – made him suddenly forget his own ills, his own troubles. But there was still a part of reality that was bitter and intractable, that no gleam of beauty or love could warm or light up, that cut man off from nature, and from real life, although it did not extinguish it. And he was seized with what seemed an anxious motherly love, that made him long to speak words of life to the boy, to illumine and strengthen him with the terrible truth of his own experience, to put him on guard, to save him. Save him? The impossible beauty of that word made him tremble. He couldn't save anyone. No one could save anyone.

The storekeeper turned up.

"Five of you come along," he said, "and then the other five," and the fair boy went out and vanished, unaware that he had illumined anyone.

Olgi lay there still, with his eyes shut. No illusion or miracle now could change the reality of this locked room. It was a cork-cell; in less esoteric language a transit room. A dirty transit room. But what did it matter now? Innumerable horrible days had levelled even horror, suffering had become tedium, repentance dust.

The guard came back.

"Let's get a move on," he said. He looked at his wrist-watch. "I ought to have finished and been home by now."

On his left hand he wore a gold wedding ring, obviously he hadn't been married long, a young fellow like that. Tired though he was, Olgi saw the inside of a modest house filled with the blessed family cosiness that has now become hackneyed: a vase of flowers on the table, a young woman sewing, a child toddling and lisping, perhaps an old man as well, his father or hers, an old prison guard now pensioned off and reading a government newspaper . . .

But the vision gave Olgi no happiness.

"And where's your stuff?" said the guard, longing to be off.

"My stuff's all here," Olgi answered, indicating his haversack.

"Right, take what you want. We'll leave the haversack in the store."

"Done," said Olgi and showed his hand, which held a toothbrush, a piece of soap and some lavatory paper. In the middle of these he had hidden his ball-point pen. It'll get through, it won't, he had thought with the fatalism of a man playing a game of chance. He got through.

"Everyone take his bundle," said the guard, "come along now, please get a move on."

Silly idiot, thought Olgi of himself. I keep imagining things like a visionary and forget what's practical and useful. I might have taken my exercise book into the cell. What shall I do for these three days? Lucky I brought some toilet paper. What fun for the bibliographers: a book worth something written on lavatory paper! Oh, laugh away, you cynic. The fact is, you old clown, you don't want to write any more. It's an effort to write, I know, and it brings no return. Far more fun to look through your spy-glass at pretty girls undressing isn't it, you old satyr?

If confusion and racket meant gaiety, it was a gay prison. But jammed full of people like a rush-hour tram. A large port, with its trade and its social anomalies, usually turns out a great many gaol-birds.

"Go upstairs," said a guard who was eating.

The effort of going up with a bundle on his back. At one time he boasted of carrying three hundredweight. Could this bundle really have grown so heavy? A blanket, two sheets, a pillow case, a towel, a mug, a mess-tin, a spoon. A pretty poor outfit. Yet it was heavy.

"Where are these to go?" said the guard on the first floor.

"Three in No. 29 and one in 14," answered a dressed-up prisoner, the section clerk. With a clinical eye he examined the new arrivals, concluded there was nothing to be got from them, and went with dignity into a tiny hideout, which was his office.

When the Sicilian saw that he would have to share the cell not only with Olgi but with the tall man with the crooked nose he seized his own bundle and went out. He talked to the guard and at last came to an agreement with the all-powerful clerk.

"Right, that leaves the pair of you," said the guard, and added with friendly roguishness: "That fellow says he's got to be on his own because he's got colitis. All the better for you, you'll have more room. There are your straw mattresses. D'you need anything?"

The tall man looked stolidly at the ceiling.

"No, nothing," said Olgi, "thanks."

"Good night."

"Good night."

The tap didn't turn off properly, the light was feeble and indirect, the water-closet stank disgustingly, the bedsteads wobbled, the straw mattresses were all holes and lumps. Despair for so little? These were trifles in prison; and Olgi undressed and lay down, glad that another day was over.

XXIII

HE WAS SITTING ON THE WATER-CLOSET, SINGING softly a kind of loving comic lullaby, with words made as he went along to the tune of an old Sicilian song.

Olgi, who slept lightly, awoke. He looked with loathing at the dawn light coming in through the prison window. Another wretched day to live through! The squalor and filth of that cell entered into him like the drip from a sewer, sinking him in disgust. He gritted his teeth.

"The cowardice of the cliché: the force of habit. You get used to everything, you resign yourself to everything. No! I'm not used to it, I'm not resigned. I'm a man, and I want to keep intact all my faculties, all my rights as a man. Even this poetic extravagance of loving things that are beautiful and clean. I won't degrade myself, I won't annul myself till I become like that latrine."

The outburst calmed him. He had grown wise enough, and had enough sense of humour besides, to avoid stiffening into extreme attitudes. He opened his eyes and accepted reality for what it was. That madman singing on the toilet was amusing.

He sang like a troubadour or a minstrel:

"I'm the man who seeks the love of all women – I'm the great man who loves all women – I'm the handsome man all women love – Oh pretty, pretty, pretty girls – how pretty women are – Yes, yes, how pretty women are."

"Fine," said Olgi. "So you're the handsome man all women love. Actually I hadn't noticed."

The other was straining over something that refused to come out. He made a constipated grimace that gradually turned into a smile of relief. The relief became triumph.

"Yes," he said exultantly, "I'm the handsome man all women love. I'm the great man who seeks the love of all women."

"So you're fine and handsome," said Olgi, "but you stink as well. Press the flushing knob."

But the knob – foreseeably – didn't work.

"No good," said the man.

"It's lost its voice," said Olgi. "Turn on the tap and swill it out with the bucket until it goes down."

The day seemed as long, dry and monotonous as the Sahara desert; but cheer up, traveller, don't lose heart.

And Olgi turned back his shirt-sleeves and tidied up the cell a bit. After all, for three days this was his home. When he climbed up on the bed he made a discovery that filled him with jubilation. An oasis in the Sahara? More or less.

Between the top of the grating and the top part of the window there was a space of about twenty centimetres, and in that space was framed a delightful slice of the world: a new building flaunting its newly-painted window-frames and balconies, on the right old houses that looked grey and resigned, on the left a builder's yard half hidden by grass, and even a piece of hillside. All this was too far away for him to make out images and details. But Olgi could get over that. He would set up his spyglass, his forbidden observatory, and the hours would pass pleasantly.

"We'll enjoy outselves," he said to the tall man who was lying down again and smoking a cigarette butt. But the man didn't even look at him. Having stopped singing and filled his belly, he let the world go to hell.

This thick-headed indifference irritated Olgi.

"Where are you from?"

The man went on smoking and gazing at the ceiling.

"I'm talking to you," said Olgi, nudging his arm roughly. He was behaving in his old crude, quarrelsome way.

"I'm from Asti," the man muttered. "But what d'you want, let me alone, get out, you murderer you."

Should he hit him in the face, straighten that crooked nose of his? But the new man won, and the old man trotted crestfallen away, and went and crouched up near the ceiling.

The door opened and white coffee was handed out.

"So little?" the tall man complained.

"It's the ration," said the guard.

Olgi gave the tall man his share and even a roll he had left over. So they made peace. Olgi now no longer felt the pointless weariness of life: he had small, agreeable, practical problems to solve. He must get hold of cardboard and a little glue. In place of glue he could use sticking plaster. He must talk to the nurse or the sweeper.

"Exercise," said the guard.

"Don't they shut the doors?" Olgi asked a rough, bandy-legged man, wearing patched trousers and a white cap with a nautical-looking anchor on it, who was smoking a pipe.

"Why should they?" said the cop. "Not during exercise."

And he went on sucking away at the stem of his pipe, with his hands in his pockets, as if he were on the deck of a ship.

Olgi politely called the sweeper, an ugly, slovenly youth, who laughed stupidly and glowered.

"Please, could you give me a little cardboard?"

"Cardboard!"

The youth quickly considered the chances of getting paid for such a service, and concluded there was nothing doing.

"Cardboard?" he said sarcastically, spitting saliva about. "What for?"

"I'd like . . . I'd like to make a little gondola," Olgi lied.

"A little gondola," mocked the fellow. "No, I haven't any cardboard. And where'd I find it?"

"Forgive me, Your Excellency," said Olgi.

He had mistaken his tactics, but even if he had turned up with his sleeves turned back and his shirt open on his chest to show the tattoos, probably the result would have been no different. You cannot trade with men with empty hands.

"I've got to go to the surgery," Olgi said to the guard.

"Go along then," said the guard.

"Where is it?"

"There, at the end of the passage."

"Can I go alone?"

"What are you waiting for, a guard of honour?"

Olgi went to the end of the passage and there found several doors with notices nailed on to them: Accounts, Surgery, Library, Chaplain's Office.

"Shall I get some books? Old rubbish, very likely."

But sometimes he managed to find something that interested him. Hadn't he, at Civitavecchia, found among a hundred volumes of hagiography and biblical exegesis a book by Anna Maria Ortese, another by Truman Capote, and Pratolini's *Cronaca familiare*? He grinned:

"Who knows, I might find Joyce's *Ulysses* here!"

He knocked discreetly.

"May I come in?"

"Come in," said a voice.

Sitting at a table, on which worm-eaten books were piled up anyhow, the prisoner librarian, flaunting donnish pince-nez and a dignified bald head, was cataloguing.

"Could I have some good book to read?" Olgi asked with a friendly smile.

"There are authorized days for giving out books," said pince-nez drily.

"But I'm being transferred and . . ."

"In that case, nothing doing."

"What d'you mean?"

"That's the rule."

"Your rule?"

"My rule? The warden's rule! Why, d'you dare . . ."

He had risen, an angry tin god. Olgi advanced with the heavy, decisive step of a fighter, an old fighter but a fighter still . . .

"Yes, I dare. You cunning little cur, you. Outside you steal and cheat, maybe rape little girls, and the minute you're inside you crawl and bootlick and spy, and get cushy jobs, to torment and keep down the rest of us. You louse . . ."

"But, but . . ."

"Shut up, you insect, or I'll knock you down."

The man was trembling with abject terror.

"I didn't know . . . I didn't think . . . look, don't be angry, if you really want to read I'll lend you my own books, they're good books, books that . . ."

"Keep your books, they must be lousy if they're like you."

But as soon as he was outside his anger vanished, and a teasing gaiety took over.

"How I scared that puffed up little bed-bug!"

The surgery was on the first floor, he went up an ugly, almost dark staircase, and on the landing found a ragged dwarf, with a horribly beaten-up face. One eye was bandaged. He had bare feet.

Olgi knocked timidly. No one answered. Inside he could hear loud talk and laughter. He knocked hard. The door opened slightly, an eye looked out, a voice asked:

"What is it? This isn't the time to come knocking. The doctor's here."

"I need a little sticking plaster," Olgi said decisively. "I've got a bad toe."

"Wait."

He waited about ten minutes. At last the door opened again, not completely, but just enough to let out an arm.

"Take this, it's better than sticking plaster."

It was a piece of gauze. Olgi smiled, but he wanted to laugh. Laugh noisily. Everything was laughable. He looked at the dwarf's injured face, and at his thin chest with its bruises showing through the torn, filthy shirt; and the dwarf looked at Olgi with the eye that was still open, and with his red swollen one as well.

"You've been badly knocked about, mate," said Olgi.

"Fifteen or twenty of them set on me," said the dwarf. "Swine! They said I'd interfered with a little girl, but it's not true. They didn't want me around, that's all. I'm from Naples, and I haven't hurt a soul. I went rag-picking, what's wrong with that? I used to get drunk, that's true, but I've never bothered kids. How they bashed me, the hogs. And then they shut me up here. Finished and done with, as we say in Naples."

126

"Goodbye, mate," said Olgi.

He went thoughtfully down the long passage again, with all its doors in a row, shut, mute, implacable.

"I'm going out to exercise," he said to the guard, who had settled down to a crossword puzzle.

"Go along, then," said the guard.

There were several courtyards in a semicircle round a kind of raised sentry-box, in which was a sentinel. But he wasn't armed, and leaning against the wall, in the shade, he was dozing. The courtyards had gates, but they were open, except for two, where the solitaries took their exercise. Olgi went into the first courtyard. It was steeped in sunshine. He blinked. He had become like a mole and couldn't bear the light.

There were only four men in that courtyard, taking the sun. One of them who caught Olgi's eye was very dark, with a black moustache and wavy hair, and looked like a Spaniard or a Mexican. Lying on a large Turkish towel, he was basking like an iguana in the baking sun. Although young he was already fat, especially his belly, which gleamed like a Buddha's.

Olgi noticed tufts of grass growing out of cracks in the wall. Yellow grass, dry and dead. How did it ever get a hold there . . .

He went out of that courtyard, and into the second one. Part of it was in sunlight, part in shadow. There were more people there. Some of them were walking up and down, some were proudly or timidly alone, some were talking in a group, generally about sport or women, or their crimes, or their hopes of managing, not perfectly perhaps, but at least not too badly, and so on.

The man from Agrigento, who was walking with a man from Palermo, who years ago had chosen to live at Marassi, shouted to Olgi:

"Look out for that looney, at Pisa he pissed under my bed."

He laughed noisily, and the man from Palermo laughed with him.

Olgi left the second courtyard and went into the third. It was a gambling courtyard. The men sat or squatted on the ground like Arabs, carefully or angrily playing with filthy packs of cards. Olgi saw the handsome fair boy who had been on the train with him. He wasn't playing but was watching the game. He was bare-chested and wore shorts. And, in his glowing untouched youth, he seemed to have landed by chance in the midst of those human cast-offs. Olgi was now looking only at him, the heedless god who watched those lousy Moslems playing, those wretched criminals . . . But he soon grew bored, and moved aside into the sun from the shade where the players were. He did an Indian dance; and suddenly, capriciously, went through the gate and vanished.

There was one more courtyard to see. There too, shade and sunshine fought for the small amount of space. There he found the previous day's newcomer, washing a handkerchief at the fountain.

"Alors, mon vieux, ça va?" said Olgi.

"Ça va," answered the man, and shrugged.

Olgi saw the man from Bolzano as well. He was waiting for a man in the toilet to finish before going himself, and was standing with legs apart, thumbs tucked into his belt, and the same pitiless face under his SS cap.

Olgi passed the time looking at the others in the courtyard. They were new faces but Olgi had a feeling he had seen them before. That wiry little fellow with a leather strap on his right wrist; that flabby fat man who amused himself spitting through the holes in the wire netting that divided the courtyard from a piece of wild garden; that big, badly-dressed man, covered in tattoos; and that old man with the gloomy stare; or that ambiguously handsome young man, who spoke like a Florentine, and girlishly wiggled his seat.

He had a frightful headache and went to sit down in a strip of shade against the wall.

128

XXIV

THAT DAY THERE WAS PASTA TO EAT, AND THE GREAT handsome man who sought the love of all women got two heaped-up plates down; and a roll. Yet he was still hungry.

"I'm never satisfied," he complained.

His was an old hunger. It had settled in his guts for good, just as, in some hovels, dirt can be found in layers. Olgi too had known such a hunger himself. In the terrible war and post-war years. But for some people life is always war, or post-war.

Abruptly he started singing again.

"What were you doing in Sicily?" asked Olgi.

"Nothing. I wandered about. You know."

"Who have you got at Asti?"

"No one."

"There's good wine at Asti," said Olgi. "Why didn't you stay there?"

"But I'm not from Asti. I was born in London."

Olgi dropped the conversation. He'd met loonies before, half-crazy ones, fake crazy ones, and wholly crazy ones!

What should he do? He dropped on the bed. The loudspeaker began to crackle. It was putting out dance music. A raging cacophony. Olgi's nerves were on edge. The tall man with the insatiable appetite had gone to sleep.

The music went on for an hour and when the radio was switched off Olgi sighed with relief. He had no musical culture, or perhaps even musical taste. He was indifferent to Beethoven. But he liked pop songs, as a rule. In this he was typically Italian. He knew everything of Nilla Pizzi, and of Mina, and Milva. He was crazy about Milva, although his real love, consecrated by time, was for Liz. In fact it was this marvellous actress, this beautiful, unfortunate woman, who came to see him at night. But not every night, because it took a suitable atmosphere to evoke her, a special preparatory rite. It was Olgi's sweet madness.

"Exercise," said the guard.

He wondered whether to go. How dreary all those ugly faces were, all looking alike, and all that talk that oozed crime and prison. But what could he do inside, in that stinking hole of a cell? If he could have used his spy-glass things would have been different. Looking out he would have forgotten, and been happy. Happiness, which was close at hand, had become out of reach because one hog refused him a bit of cardboard, and another refused him a little sticking-plaster. But wasn't nearly all human destiny like that? Olgi knew that it was.

He went out to exercise. He wandered from one courtyard to the next, hoping to see the fair youngster, but saw him nowhere. Then he became interested in a young, very tall German, who had horrible feet – he was barefoot – and a tiny, rosy face as sweet as a girl's. What events could have finally landed him, or shipwrecked him, at Marassi!

He was sitting on the ground clasping his knees and smilingly answering the offers of a pervert. There was also the Florentine with the girlish walk. His features were strangely flawless. But at one point, while he was laughing at the jokes of a man who was courting him, he revealed a ruined mouth, as repulsive as an old whore's.

Olgi left that courtyard. In the next one he found something to distract him: some young Spaniards, who looked like sailors, and might have mutinied, or even organized some resistance to Franco's régime. (Olgi, who hated tyranny, liked to imagine this, romantically.) Knowing Spanish, he might have questioned them, and heard something new and first-hand about the real conditions in Franco's Spain. (Although Olgi thought he knew enough about Franco's Spain to give a dry, incontrovertible verdict on it.) But how could he get away from all those nosy, stupid, curious people?

"Sing, hombre," said a jolly fellow from Liguria, who was as hairy as a monkey. "Sing, and por Dios don't refuse, we know you sing. Come on mate."

The man thus praised and pleaded with was a man of middle height, who looked serious and modestly proud. His companions were dressed like him in bluish trousers and dark shirts; they were the same height, and had the same look of modest pride.

"Sing, Pablo," said one of his friends with a thin moustache. "Es malo no hacerlo por los otros."

"Pero las guardias . . ." objected Pablo.

The other man shrugged, as if to say that the guards – guards of the kind they had there – meant absolutely nothing.

And Pablo sang. He sang really well. Everyone applauded, including Olgi. Feeling someone touch his shoulder he turned.

"You old brigand!"

"Pasquale!"

They hugged one another, moved. Five years before they had met at Procida. They were the same age, in some ways alike in character, and had equally long sentences to get through – though Pasquale had remained intellectually rough and untutored; and they had liked each other, and then grown friendly.

"You old brigand, what are you doing here?"

"I was listening to a song."

"I mean, why are you at Marassi?"

"I'm being transferred, I'm going to Saluzzo. And how is it you're at Marassi?"

"Well, mate, I'd a job to get transferred to Genoa, I can tell you. In the end, thanks to two MP's, a senator, a contessa, and a tycoon related to a cardinal, we managed it.

"They say gaol's the same everywhere, but that's balls. There's gaol and gaol, as you know better than me. The air's quite different here. And then I'm in the town where my family is, and I can see my wife and kids every week."

He laughed indulgently.

"Kids, did I say ... Titina's seventeen and looks like Marilyn Monroe, and Bruno's eighteen and better than Mr Universe. But of course, when the parents are handsome the kids are bound to be handsome too."

This was no vain boast: for Pasquale from Catania was in fact a tall handsome man, with an athletic build, splendid curly hair and fiery eyes; and Olgi knew his wife was a very beautiful Genoese.

They were making for the exit, meantime.

"Where are you taking me?" said Olgi. "I'd like to have a word with these young Spaniards. They must be communists, or anarchists."

"Oh, forget them, they're fascists. They refused to pay in a restaurant, grabbed the waitresses, and smashed some mirrors. I'll take you to my cell, I want to show you my kids' photos. But what's up, what are you thinking about? Still the same old clam, you've got to drag the words out of your mouth with pincers."

"Well, other people have so much to say ..."

As they were walking towards section four, almost everyone they met greeted Pasquale. Respectfully, too.

"You're an important person," Olgi remarked.

Pasquale smiled.

"I'm still Pasquale from Catania, even though I've retired and live on a private income."

"Open the door," he told the guard, as if giving an order.

"Straightaway," said the guard.

Pasquale's cell was like a drawing-room. At the head of the bed, draped with a curtain like a royal catafalque, was a kind of canopied altar, on which, between mystic artificial flowers, several photographs were artistically displayed: Pasquale's holy family.

"What did I say?" said Pasquale. "Don't they look like Marilyn and Mr Universe?"

Olgi saw two youngsters who were well set up, because they'd been well fed, and no more; but of course, parents are biased . . .

"And this is my Aurelia. That's a recent photograph. Would you think she was over thirty? Of course not! She's as firm and fresh as the day I married her."

He kissed the photograph noisily.

"Gorgeous! I'm as much in love with her as I was in the early days. So's she. You should see the letters we write each other . . . And on visiting days . . . She can't bring the kids any more because they disturb us."

He sighed and put the photograph of his lovely, ardent wife back in its place. He had grown gloomy again. Jealousy reached him too, inevitably.

"You're lucky, Pasquale," Olgi said.

"Lucky my eye," said Pasquale. "I'm doing twenty years, and you call me lucky."

"There are plenty of people with as many years to do who are far worse off than you are."

"True enough. I've no material worries. Aurelia manages pretty well with her draper's shop. Her brother Alceste sees to the kids' education. They'll go to university, their future's secure. When I think of what I had to do from the time I was fifteen just to avoid being hungry . . . Alceste's done well. He wants to open a night-club, you know. But sit down," and he cleared a stool. "Now I'll give you something special to drink."

"Don't worry, Pasquale, you know I don't drink."

"It's not wine, it's a liqueur, the nectar of the gods," said Pasquale absurdly. "I'll never understand what sort of a fellow you are. You don't drink, you don't smoke, and you don't even want decent food. So what's the point of living?"

He had dug out a bottle from under the bed as he spoke.

"It's Strega. I shan't tell you what it cost me to get it in. My right arm."

And, rather meanly, he poured it out. It was years since Olgi had tasted anything so delicious. His chest swelled with its strong sweetness. He clicked his tongue.

"Just as well you don't like drinking," said Pasquale. "You'd swallow the lot, if I'd let you."

And he prudently put it away. Olgi remembered what he needed, and had been unable to get; Pasquale could quite easily get it for him.

"Pasquale, I need a little cardboard and a bit of sticking plaster."

"Just as well you're not asking for the moon."

He called the sweeper.

"Hey, you thief."

The man arrived quickly, servile as well as serviceable.

"At your orders, Signor Pasquale."

"There are some cardboard boxes in the cupboard. Bring me the biggest."

"Right away."

A little later he came back with a fine big box.

"Will that do?" asked Pasquale.

"It's fine," answered Olgi.

"And now let's see about the sticking plaster. Go to Amedeo and tell him to give you two yards of sticking plaster. Say it's for me."

They looked at each other, not knowing what else to say. Now that Olgi had got these precious things he was in a hurry to leave. Pasquale wanted him to go, too. The 'commendator' went by twice, winking: a sign that some advantageous deal was in the air.

"Goodbye, Pasquale," said Olgi.

"Goodbye, Olgi," said Pasquale.

XXV

IT WOULD SOON BE THE FIVE O'CLOCK CHECK-UP, and overcoming the impatience that urged him to action, Olgi decided to wait. The second meal had already been brought round, so he knew that when the check-up was over the door would not be opened until nine in the evening.

The check-up took place: with their usual diligence they banged on the bars, counted, shut up again.

"Good night," Olgi said sarcastically. He was glad to be able to break the rules, and give himself a forbidden pleasure.

As he unrolled the tubes of cardboard, fixing them at the ends with strips of sticking plaster, he asked the tall man:

"D'you know who Galileo Galilei is?"

"I think I've heard of him," said the tall man.

"He was that pig-headed fellow who invented the telescope, an instrument that, with successive improvements, made possible the progress of astronomy."

The tall man shrugged.

"Galileo Galilei is me," Olgi declared.

The tall man went and sat down on the toilet.

"Don't you believe me?" Olgi went on facetiously. "Soon I'll show you the moon."

"Give me a roll," said the man from Asti.

"I haven't got one."

"Give me a fag."

"I haven't got one, and besides, I don't smoke. D'you know, or don't you, that it's harmful to smoke?"

"Why don't you hang yourself?" said the lunatic. "If you don't give me a roll I'll piss under your bed."

"You just try it, and I'll wallop that great ugly nose of yours so hard that it'll turn east instead of west. I've cut up a woman and eaten the best bits of her as mincemeat, so don't you joke with me."

He knew how to deal with madmen; but then he was slightly mad himself.

As he finished off the work he whistled: easy tunes that, in that pleasant job, flowered spontaneously. He slid the tubes inside each other and held them up to the light: they made a good straight line. All that was needed was to put in the lenses, setting them along the dioptrical axis. So then he took the lenses out of their hairy, intimate hiding-place. He had had them for five years, guarded with jealous care, like a treasure. To get them to pay off what they cost, he had had to work for a whole year making straw covers for wine bottles in a damp prison cellar.

He got up on to the bed and looked out. The world of the living was no longer a distant, mysterious reality, a forbidden Eden. Heaven or hell, who cared? It was the world. Only this mattered: that the world was in fact there. And that Olgi could in a way get inside it, inside the world.

First, because it was facing him, and was the most striking thing there, he looked at the new building. It was five storeys high, but the first two floors, hidden behind the prison wall, he couldn't see. Each flat had its balcony. Each balcony was hidden by awnings. Awnings that could be raised or lowered by working a handle. Each window had a blind. Hermetic blinds, as hateful as the prison windows.

In spite of this the building emitted gaiety – through its fresh paint on the outside, and its architectural decorations, but also through a certain aura as well, a feeling of humanity it gave off, as invisible as breathing, but alive. As much alive as the people who lived in the building, even though Olgi couldn't see them just then, since they were afraid of the hot sun, or busy inside the house, or out at the sea, in the shady parks, or in factory, office, and so on.

But soon there would be signs of life – he could already see hints of them – those hateful blinds would be raised, the awnings, now useless, would be rolled up, women would look out, children would play on the balconies; and Olgi would greet them and say, "Welcome back, Signora Life."

He shifted the spy-glass to the right, on to the old houses, but, with their oblique windows, they seemed to be trying to avert their faces, as if ashamed, and Olgi would have found it hard to cull any of their secrets. The world on that side died suddenly, cut off by the hard edge of the window. As it suddenly died overhead as well. Overhead was the sky.

He turned the glass to the left. He couldn't see the builder's yard very well, because of the distance, and because it was sheltered by a mound in front, on which grew a bushy hedge. But this didn't matter. It was just a builder's yard. Olgi knew what it was like, what a builder's yard was used for. It was hard work, like carrying sacks on the docks, or parcels at the station. Maybe even harder. Hands peeled, cement and lime seeped into the lungs, backs tended to curve, like those of peasants who work the land. And occasionally a man would fall from high up on the scaffolding.

He felt no greater interest in the hill, either. It was merely a hill, which meant a natural accident. And not even a beautiful hill. The colour of beaten straw merging into grey. With occasional rows of stunted vines and darker patches that meant olives. On one side was a winding hedge or ditch, almost entirely in shadow. Olgi's experience of human affairs told him that the shadow might make a comfortable refuge for couples who needed solitude.

He turned the spy-glass on to the new buildings again. It was beginning to wake from its afternoon torpor. One wing was already completely in shadow. On the top-floor balcony someone had rolled up the blind. Part of the balcony was taken up with vases and boxes of flowers, some just sprouting and others already well grown. Nice people, thought Olgi. There was washing on the line as well.

A woman came out from a room, leant on the railing, and looked down. Olgi was disappointed. He had hoped to see a healthy wife full of the joy of life, like the broad-beamed woman drawing water at the station at Orbetello, whereas this was a woman who might be any age, and might be married or single – tall, rather thin, with an old-fashioned hair-style and a sad, wasted face. She was no longer leaning on the railing, but had clasped her hands, as if seized by a sudden desperate wish to jump down, and the instinct of self-preservation was opposing it. Finally she moved away from the railing, took a few steps, touched some of the washing, went back into the room, and came back a little later with a cigarette in her mouth.

Olgi cheered up. No sorrow, no tragedy in the world. He liked this mixture of old and new, of modesty and open-mindedness. This woman interested him. He was sorry to have thought her plain. Her face, with its worn features, and its deep-set eyes, had a fascination of its own. He examined her body carefully. She wasn't fat, or repulsively thin; he guessed that under the shirt her breasts were neither too large nor too small, her hips had a pleasant line, even though a little thin, and her legs were definitely good. In fact he was beginning to like her more than the woman at Orbetello. "I'll call you Signorina Felicita." But his love of real life, the life of flesh and blood, rose against this bookish idea. "No, I'll call you Delia."

Suddenly Delia sat down on the terrace floor, for a moment Olgi saw her thighs right up to the triangle of her knickers. A flash of flame. He reacted like a boy of twenty. His eyes misted, the spy-glass trembled in his hand.

"Please, please show me again. Just once more, for a little bit longer. Oh, your thighs. Oh woman, your thighs. Come on Delia darling, get up my love, my sweet, why don't you do what I say? Don't you feel the urgency of my desire? I'm so unhappy.

138

Only you can make me happy. My sweet love I beg you – oh Delia girl, I implore you to get up, get up, oh hell and damnation."

But the telepathic order was lost in the lazy summer air and never reached her, and she kept her legs down and went on smoking, entirely absorbed in the pleasure of doing so, or in her particular thoughts.

Olgi was scornful, furious. "You stupid ugly bitch! Insensitive creature! Scraggy as a pin! And what d'you think you've got under there, anyway, you hypocrite!"

He moved down to the floor below, and life was appearing there too. A plump child of four or five was banging on a small drum, marching at the head of an army. He saw a dishevelled woman, clearly the child's mother, with a duster in her hand. She was big bottomed and big breasted, with thick black hair in her armpits. But Olgi, though in a state of acute amorous sensibility, wasn't excited. She wasn't his favourite type.

He moved the glass farther down, and saw a young man playing with a kitten. He was a handsome boy, with dark, delicately cut features, and a strong, harmonious body. An athlete, Olgi imagined, with those long loose muscles. Javelin thrower or runner or oarsman. His neat, practical clothes, too, were those of an athlete. With a piece of blue ribbon, the kind that girls still sometimes use to tie up their hair, he was making a grey kitten play; the kitten tirelessly grabbed it, dropped it, picked it up again, lay in wait for it, twirled and jumped; the whole repertory of pretty, comical feline agility. Suddenly the young man put out a hand, made the cat lie on its back, and caressed its tummy, and the little creature answered with tiny affectionate bites.

On to the terrace came a plump, matronly woman of over forty, well contained inside her modest dressing-gown. She must have been the handsome boy's mother, because they looked alike, and she too must once have been very beautiful;

now she was just an old mother and sensibly resigned to it. She looked at her wrist-watch and said something to the boy, who got up at once and went inside.

The woman sat down on a deck-chair, so decorous that not a fold of her dressing-gown was out of line, took the cat on her knees, played with him a little but straight away tired of it, and sat motionless, lost in her imaginings, or memories, or simply without thinking. The boy reappeared again, dressed in white. His mother looked at him delightedly, adjusted his tie and gave him money. The boy hurried out and the mother's face grew melancholy again.

With his mental telescope Olgi followed the handsome boy, saw him walking casually and composedly through the city streets, which were as welcoming as his own home, looking trustfully around him and looked at with trust by others, liking and liked; then he gave him a beautiful girl-friend, blonde, since he was dark, and sent them walking, close together, along a flowery avenue. It was a charming strip cartoon.

Why can't everyone be like that? thought Olgi. Young, handsome, trusting, happy and in love?

His ear, ever on the alert, warned him that danger was approaching. He was just in time to bend down and hide the spy-glass under the pillow when the spy-hole opened in the door. In the small square he saw the visor of a cap, and under it a swollen nose between two porkish eyes that peered suspiciously at him.

"What are you doing up there?" said the warder's harsh voice.

"I'm looking at the clouds," said Olgi. "Is it forbidden to look at the clouds?"

Swollen nose and cap withdrew with a grunt, and the spy-hole jerked shut, like a trap.

PART V

XXVI

WITH A LITTLE PATIENCE, AND EVEN WITHOUT IT, everything passes. Those three transit days in the Genoa goal passed too, as the four had passed at Pisa. Three and four make seven, that's simple arithmetic, but add them to those seven thousand one hundred or seven thousand two hundred or seven thousand three hundred already passed, and the bill of suffering, privation, humiliation, and despair, grows infinite.

"The man who's off," shouted the guard, "what's he waiting for?"

Olgi went down.

"What have you left in the store?"

"A haversack."

"Is this it?"

"Yes."

Door, gate, passage, gate, door.

"In here," said the guard.

And with professional diligence he locked the door.

It was a bare room, etc. Olgi went and sat down on the bench. He was drained of strength. Delia, and the hairy woman on the floor below as well, had shown him their most intimate, truest, most essential selves. In those three days Olgi's sensuality had been unleashed. When he had finished with one he began on the other, erotically exasperated till he was nearly mad. Afterwards he was depressed, and fighting himself. To think of wasting his energy and excitement in such an ugly way, instead of turning it into creative spiritual vitality! He said to himself: It's my duty to carry on and finish my work, it's the only fine thing that will come out of this life of mine, like a flower on a dung-hill. But this good resolution was immediately spoilt by another consideration: What, do you really delude yourself that your book's going to contribute to the spiritual enrichment of mankind? Even supposing it's really got something to say, and manages to express a sorrow that may have something to teach others, how many people are going to notice? And why deprive myself of the only joy I have? The only way I have of feeling alive still? Cold darkness will come soon.

Travelling with him were the squat man with the moustache and dark glasses, the half-wit from Asti, and the braggart from Agrigento who was going to the prison at Alessandri; there was also the healthy fair youngster and the snarling man from Bolzano, but these were going on a different train to another destination; and there were others, new faces with more or less similar destinies.

One stood out for his oddity, distinction, and agreeableness. He wore a white silk shirt, blue shorts, and sandals like a monk, his pepper-and-salt hair was cut short, and he was smoking Dutch tobacco in a pipe from Basutoland.

But, for the moment, the person who attracted everyone's attention, even more than this original man, was a smallish, thin, dark young man in blue jeans who seemed to be highly agitated. His suffering was so frantic and so naked that clearly his trouble must be quite irremediable.

Olgi listened. This young man's tragedy came down to the fact that he didn't want to leave. He was horrified at having to go to Bra to finish a sentence of a few months. The order for his transfer had come unexpectedly. His mother and wife knew nothing.

"Can I leave like this?" he said desperately, appealing to the solidarity of the onlookers. "Without embracing my mother and my wife? Like a dog?"

Olgi looked at him with slightly incredulous surprise, as if he were an inhabitant of another world, a Martian. But he wasn't a Martian, he was just a young man on earth, who, according to the natural and civil laws of this world, had a mother and a wife.

Olgi too had had a mother. He had, hadn't he? The fact that she had died last year, in the winter, proved that she had lived. She had lived for seventy years, a long life strewn with sacrifices and privations and then, since we must all die, she died.

And, although he had never legally had a wife, Olgi had had experiences that were like those of marriage. A woman or a girl who comes to bed with you, prepares your food and mends your clothes is almost a wife. Sometimes more loving and faithful than a real wife. And even that sweet way of being two together, of facing life as a pair, was outside him, years away from him, and he now lived in a limbo of ashen loneliness.

This was why Olgi looked with surprise, perhaps even with envy, at that small dark young man who had a mother and a wife. Some people were giving him advice, showing how to get feverish and ill, but there was no longer time for it.

"I swallowed two cigarettes," said the boy, "it was a bit upsetting but my temperature didn't go up much. The doctor said: 'He can leave, he's fit to travel'."

"You should soak a packet or two of strong tobacco in water," said a man with a heavy pockmarked face and a pair of whiskers as thin as rats' tails. "You get a soup that gives you setticaemia if you drink it."

Obviously he meant septicaemia, but Olgi either failed to notice the mistake or, noticing it, didn't laugh, although to a man like him, who had seen almost everything, the whole business might seem ridiculous; just then he was thinking of the engineer he had known during those four transit days at Pisa. He too had soaked some packets of strong tobacco in water, but not to prevent his departure – on the contrary, to speed it and make it definite. Olgi knew there were quicker and more certain ways of killing oneself, hanging oneself from the bars, for instance, as Pinzi and Morandini had done, but very likely the engineer, being full of complexes and strange ideas, had decided to copy a schoolboy model. Hadn't Socrates died drinking hemlock?

The first escort arrived, and the fair boy, the man from Bolzano, the pockmarked fellow with rats' tail whiskers and three others left. The dark young man in blue jeans wrung his hands.

"Now the escort will come for us too. What can I do? Bang my head against the wall?"

"Not a good idea," said the original fellow with the pipe from Basutoland. He spoke without taking the pipe from his mouth and his words might have been ironic or serious. "The wall's made of hard atoms, harder than the heart of a prison doctor."

At last he took the pipe from his mouth and fiddled with it. His light, slightly misty, absent-minded eyes were now staring at the frenzied dark boy with faintly ironical benevolence.

"D'you really not want to go? Does it really matter so much to you? Then don't go. There's no need to ruin your stomach, let alone dash your forehead to bits. When the escort comes say firmly to the head of it: 'I'm not going because I'm not in a condition to leave.' It's so easy."

"But . . ." said the dark boy. He was attracted by the ease of this solution, but just because it was easy he doubted it.

"But, suppose they won't listen to reason and make me go just the same?"

The original fellow with the pipe laughed politely.

"And how can they make you leave if you won't? You're not a parcel of goods, a bundle that can be humped on their backs, but a human creature with reason and will."

He had stuck the pipe between his teeth again, and it was impossible to make out if he was talking seriously or joking. He was looking insistently at Olgi, but Olgi hesitated.

"Don't you think I'm right?" he asked at last, half seriously; and Olgi, entering into the game exclaimed:

146

"You certainly are."

"Then I can refuse to go?" said the dark boy fearfully. "Will it be all right?"

"It will," said Olgi, deliberately terse. "All you need do is hold firm, and don't be scared of the consequences."

"Consequences?"

"Trifles, a few days in the punishment cell, that's their way and you should know it."

"But I've never been punished, it's the first time I've been in prison. Smuggling cigarettes. I'm an honest man, and I'm married."

Olgi smiled, and so did the man with the pipe. The escort came, politely but firmly the dark young man refused to have handcuffs put on. And there was half an hour of argument and excited consultation: the head of the department called the sergeant, the sergeant called the first maresciallo, the first maresciallo called the second maresciallo.

"You must leave."

"I'm not well."

"That's not true, the doctor said you were fit to leave."

"But he hasn't even looked at me . . ."

"You must leave."

"I'm not well."

"Settle it yourselves," said the head of the escort, losing patience. "I can't wait, the train'll be off. This luggage, whose is this luggage?"

"It's mine," said the man with the Basutoland pipe.

"Then pick it up. Or do you want a porter?"

"I pay porter," said the man, who when he wanted to spoke Italian perfectly well. In fact he was born in Italy, at Milan, but of American parents, and his name sounded German.

"No carry luggage with handcuffs."

All the same he picked up a small bag; a larger one had to be carried by a carabiniere, and a third was taken by another carabiniere, and a bulging kind of duffle-bag with a shoulder-strap was left.

"You've got only a half-empty haversack," the head of the escort said gently to Olgi, "why not carry this fellow's bag?"

Olgi carried the bag. It was fiendishly heavy. He was about to drop it but pride in his old strength spurred him on.

"What have you got in it? Bricks?" he said, making an effort to joke. "Horseshoes?"

"Books," answered the American born in Italy and with a German name, "just books. After all, wisdom is weighty . . ."

XXVII

THE TRAIN WHICH THE HEAD OF THE ESCORT HAD said was just about to leave had in fact not even arrived and they had to wait patiently shut up in the van, handcuffed and chained, until the blessed train arrived; and no one talked, no one felt like joking; until the Sicilian burst out:

"But at least open the window, you dog of a . . ."

And the squat man with moustache and sun-glasses exclaimed, in the wake of the other's indignation:

"Christ, at least open the window!"

"The window," echoed the man from Asti stupidly.

"Are we men or aren't we?" a rosy-faced man with the top of his head quite hairless, like an attractive tonsure, asked Hamlet-fashion.

"Men," said the American, as if waking up suddenly, "always men. Irreducibly men."

"Mice and men," said Olgi.

"That's a good quotation," said the American. "What d'you think of Steinbeck?"

"Men or not," said Olgi.

"That's Vittorini."

"Man is the measure of all things."

"Anaxagoras, or Heraclitus."

"Men should talk less and think more."

"Confucius, I'm sure that's Confucius. Or I'm not a sino-logue...."

"Man is the masterpiece in which the divine artificer was pleased. Man is spit. Man is pithecanthropus civilized. Man is an eternal prometheus. A fallen angel. A clown. Pooh," said Olgi, "what a lot of things man wants to be."

At last, for fear of a mutiny, the head of the escort opened the window. It was blazing high noon, Olgi stretched out his neck, to peer at life. They were in a yard where goods were unloaded, and at the end of it there was a plane-tree. In the plane-tree's shade stood a luxurious car.

"Look at that great shining car," Olgi said to the American. "Travelling in that you must feel distantly related to God."

"It's a Vauxhall," said the American "I've had one. The Porsche Super Roadster's better."

A self-possessed young chauffeur was fiddling with the radiator; and, wobbling as if she were walking on stilts, done up like a Madonna, her face a rainbow, a lady turned up. She stood in the sun for a minute, two gloved fingers pressed to her veiled brow, as if trying hard to remember something or work something out; then she let her gaze wander, and noticed that dark, ugly, severe, armoured object. She said something to the chauffeur, and the chauffeur said something to her. The lady said something else, and the young chauffeur hurried away. Then he came back with a few packets of cigarettes and went up to the van.

"It's forbidden to approach the prisoners," said a carabiniere, stopping him.

"The lady would like to give them these packets of cigarettes," said the chauffeur.

"The public is forbidden to give anything to prisoners during transfers."

"The princess will be sorry if you refuse," said the young chauffeur.

"Excuse us, we're just carabinieri," said another of them, "carrying out orders. But if the head of the escort will allow it . . ."

"Fair enough," said the chauffeur. "Where is he?"

But the head of the escort wasn't there, he'd gone to check the tickets or something of the kind.

"Well, let's do this," said the van-driver, a knowing middle-aged fellow, who seemed to have three faces in one: a thief's, a screw's, and a receiver's. "Give me the cigarettes, and I'll see they get distributed. The head of the escort's sure to allow it, he's the father of a family, like me."

(A profitable day, for that particular father of a family.) The young chauffeur handed over the cigarettes, thanked them, saluted militarily, and went back to his noble boss; and the rich car drove silently away.

The train arrived at last. It made complicated manœuvres, after which they were able to get on. The chains were removed but not the handcuffs.

"Why don't you take off our handcuffs?" asked moustache and sun-glasses.

"Later," said the head of the escort.

"What d'you mean later! Aren't we in our cell already?"

"I said later. When the train's left the station. Young man, you'd better be patient and polite to me, otherwise I'll make you wear handcuffs till you arrive."

Olgi tugged at the man's shirt.

"Drop it, mate," he advised him.

Everybody was busy arranging the American's luggage.

"If wisdom's weighty, then your authors are certainly wise," Olgi joked.

"The very wisest," said the American.

He wore his handcuffs as if carrying a bunch of flowers to offer a lady.

There were four in the cell: Olgi, the American, moustache, and the rosy man with the tonsure. Opposite Olgi was the American, beside him the rosy man with the tonsure. Olgi now remembered exactly where he had met this man: at Aversa. In the criminal lunatic asylum at Aversa. He even remembered the man's nickname: The Reverend. He turned a little to look at him. The other man was looking at him too, showing he had recognized him.

"You and I have met before."

"Yes," said the Reverend.

"At Aversa."

"At Aversa."

"You're the Reverend."

The man grew rosier than ever.

"They called me the Reverend but I'm not. I did just a year in the seminary. I gave it up because although I loved the priesthood I didn't feel pure enough. A priest must be pure."

He glanced fleetingly at the American.

"Did you recognize me at once?" asked Olgi.

"Not right away, but when I saw that eagle's head poke out from under your shirt I recognized you at once."

"This old hen makes everyone recognize me," said Olgi gloomily.

"It's very ingenuous to be tattooed," said the American. "All it does is let the police recognize you."

"When I had it done," said Olgi, "I never thought of that disadvantage. I was as proud as . . . as a Red Indian."

The American was looking at him with eyes that were slightly clouded. He smiled.

"Does that mean that in those days you had the mentality of . . . a Red Indian?"

"Just so."

"And now?"

"I'm a civilized paleface," answered Olgi. "Almost perfectly civilized."

The American stopped playing with his handcuffs; he was no longer smiling. Olgi took up the conversation with the Reverend again.

"How are things with you?"

"Twenty-four years," said the Reverend. "They even refused to recognize some mental illness."

"Twenty-four years is a long time," said Olgi.

"You don't say!" said the Reverend. "It's death to a man. They've killed me. Twenty-four years for a sexual crime!"

Another fleeting glance from the American, who then looked back at Olgi. He seemed to enjoy looking at Olgi. Again he smiled faintly. Olgi smiled too.

"They'll pass," said Olgi.

"But how, how!" said the Reverend desperately. "I've only done four so far. God, twenty more!"

"I've already done twenty," said Olgi consolingly.

"But you've done them. Whereas I've still got them to do."

"Where are you going?" the American asked Olgi gently.

"To Saluzzo. But I'm stopping at the prison at Alessandria."

"I'm going to the penitentiary at Alessandria," said the American. "But soon I'll be free. I mean I'll be leaving prison. Because I'm free now. Even if I'd had a life sentence I'd be free. You're free too."

His voice had become a murmur.

"Yes," said Olgi.

"I shall have Christmas at home," said the American, and his voice was normal again. "With my wife Shirley. The most gorgeous wife a man ever had the luck to get."

"Lucky you," said Olgi sincerely. "Is she American?"

"Yes, but she's lived in Italy for years. She's a model."

"I suppose she must be lovely."

"Lovely and frigid."

"A nuisance, but it may be an advantage too," said Olgi, alluding to unfaithfulness. "And . . . d'you love each other?"

"We adore each other."

"You upset my ideas," said Olgi. "I thought people could adore each other only in bed."

"The sensual dazzle," said the American. "L'amour c'est une autre chose."

Meanwhile the engine was jerking and puffing.

"Hell," said the man with the moustache, and worse things besides. In spite of the heat he was wearing a dark shirt, buttoned up to the neck. He had huge jaws, a big broken nose, a large, lumpy brow. His mouth was like a longing to bite hidden in a bush of whiskers.

"Where are you going, dear sir?" the American asked this brute.

"To Turin."

"D'you live at Turin?"

"I'm from Brindisi. I am going to Turin for trial. A tart was strangled in Turin and they blame me, from Brindisi."

He laughed.

"What can they do to me?"

He stopped laughing and repeated:

"What can they do to me?"

The American was looking at Olgi. Olgi's eyes were saying: With that face, and those hands, if there's the slightest suspicion, chum, you've had it.

As he was communicating this to the American Olgi thought: Suppose he really is guilty? Suppose he's innocent? If one could only read into the human heart! But who can do so?

"What can they do to me?" repeated the man. His voice quivered with anger and impatience, and he clenched his jaws, seeming to demand an immediate answer.

"If you're innocent they won't do anything," the American answered optimistically.

"I was at Brindisi when this tart was strangled," said the man dully. "I can prove I was at Brindisi. But they can't prove I was at Turin when she was strangled. That's why I'm laughing. I'm quite calm."

Olgi thought: He didn't say: I'm innocent. He arms himself with alibis and quibbles. But the law's got more quibbles than you. And in his heart he condemned him. That rough, almost ferocious man was very dislikeable, anyway.

At last the train moved, unrolled its long coil of carriages, and ran like a great noisy beast through the heedless happiness of the sunshine.

XXVIII

THE HEAD OF THE ESCORT KEPT HIS WORD.

"It's better without handcuffs," said the Reverend, delicately rubbing his wrists. He had fat, feminine hands.

"You don't say," said Moustache.

The American held his hand politely out to Olgi.

"Richard B," he introduced himself. "How d'you do."

"Olgi Valnisi," said Olgi. "But are you German?"

"That's the greatest insult you can give me, supposing I'm a German," said the American. "I was born at Milan, of an American father and an American mother. From Minnesota."

"Your name sounds German," said Olgi.

"Baltic," said the American.

"Then you're descended from the old Baltic barons," said Olgi jokingly.

"And fine old brigands they were," said the American. "If

I'm descended from them it means that I've come down in the
world, because I'm inside for conning."

"I didn't ask you," said Olgi.

"But I wanted to tell you."

He lit his pipe.

"That's a fine pipe," said Olgi.

"It's from Basutoland."

"Ba . . . ?"

"Basutoland."

"Forgive me, I'm rather ignorant, and not only in geography.
Where is it ?"

"In the part of Africa that belongs to the English. But I
haven't got just this one, I've got ninety-nine."

"Ninety-nine pipes?" exclaimed Olgi. And he laughed, as
spontaneously as a child. "But why ninety-nine, and not a
hundred ?"

"I hate round numbers, they suggest a thing's finished,
whereas nothing's ever finished."

The train had been running half an hour and already there
was a different smell in the air, a smell of sea and countryside,
sometimes only of the sea, and sometimes only of the country.
It was a land of vines and olives, mainly, with large untilled
spaces, all stones and gorse, and lichens in their primordial
stage. But Olgi took no notice of the landscape, he was more
interested in the personality of the American. (He had already
laid bare the elementary mechanism of the other two, and they
didn't interest him.)

The American took out some sweets and offered them
round.

"Perugina sweets," said the Reverend. "Delicious."

Moustache grinned, they were delicacies to savour slowly,
but he stuffed four at once into his oven of a mouth.

"They're delicious," said Olgi.

"It's Shirley who sends them," said the American.

"Sometimes I have a feeling I'm her son instead of her husband. A son of forty-six."

"You're my age," said Olgi.

"What month are you?" asked the American.

"March."

"I'm in April. We were born under the same sign of the Zodiac."

He said this gladly, and in this expressed gladness there was an underlying feeling of brotherliness, which cut out the other two.

"Have you been married long?" asked Olgi.

"Eight years. Shirley's thirty-two, but she's like a child, a big child woman. I'll show you what she's like."

He opened his case and took out some photographs. One, which was large but unframed, showed Shirley just getting out of the driving seat of a car. She had very long legs, long gloved hands, and a tiny white hat worn obliquely on her short curly hair. She was showing all her teeth, in the model's rather empty, stereotyped smile.

"She must be remarkably tall," said Olgi.

"Five foot eleven, without heels."

"An Amazon," said Olgi.

"And she's aggressive," said the American. "Anyone who tries to get up to anything with her had better look out! Once she knocked a tooth out of a creep who was peeping at her while she was sunbathing naked on a rock."

"That shows she's a hundred per cent American," said Olgi.

"Of course," explained the American, "she likes being admired and courted tactfully, like anyone else. But she can't stand vulgarity. And the poor girl sees vulgarity everywhere. Even now, when she's in Venice on holiday with her parents and her sister, she wrote and said: 'Dear Richard, there are faces of a terrifying vulgarity around.'"

Olgi made no comment, but just smiled. The other two men were peering forward.

"Might I . . . ?" said the Reverend. "What a beautiful lady! Is she American?"

Moustache took it out of his hand. He said nothing, but through the bristles his mouth exhaled; his eyes, as usual, could not be seen. The photograph came back to Olgi, who asked:

"Does she drive the car herself?"

"Of course," said the American. "Driving's one of her passions. Her other passions are eating well, having a fine house, and visiting museums and art galleries."

"Is this car the famous Polca?" asked Olgi.

The American smiled.

"No, it's not the Porsche, it's a Bentley. In those days we had a Bentley."

"Is that better than the Porsche?"

"Of course. It costs ten million."

"Christ," said Olgi. "But what are you, Rockefeller, Onassis, an oil tycoon, a coffee king, a director of a San Francisco syndicate, or Anastasia's partner?"

"I'm just a citizen of the world who, realizing he's in the world for just a short while, tries to make his stay here as pleasant as possible."

"So much so that you end up in gaol," said Olgi. "Didn't you foresee this?"

The American made a broad gesture.

"How long have you been inside?"

"Twenty-two months."

"It's not much, but it's quite enough," said Olgi. "It's not much in which to suffer all you can suffer, but quite enough to learn something in."

"I think I've learnt something," the American said softly.

"What do you do, as a profession?"

"Journalist. I'm a translator too. And I paint. Unprofessionally. For industrial advertising, in particular."

"What d'you translate?"

"I'm now translating Ezra Pound, and Confucius from Chinese."

"Is that all!" laughed Olgi. "D'you know Chinese well?"

"Ezra Pound taught me."

They talked of Ezra Pound, of how difficult his poetry was, of his political views, of his imprisonment in the lunatic asylum, and so on. Fragments of the life of this Italianized American appeared as they talked. He had started as an advertising man on Curzio Malaparte's *Prospettive* and Mino Maccari and Leo Longanesi's *Il Selvaggio*. He had never been a fascist. When the war broke out he fled to Switzerland. He came back to Italy to take part in the liberation movement. In val d'Ossola he was wounded. He hated the Germans. He despised the Americans. He was a communist.

One by one he opened the drawers of his own life, of his soul, and spread the contents out before Olgi's eyes, with the extrovert's easy-going expansiveness, but with trust and liking as well. Shirley was a model and sometimes had small parts in films. Her family had been understanding, affectionate and loyal in the 'unfortunate occurrence'.

"And what about you?" said the American, touching his knees familiarly. "Aren't you going to tell me anything?"

The words were ordinary but spoken so sweetly that they seemed like a caress.

Olgi shrugged.

"What is there to tell? My life is summed up and exhausted in four words: twenty years in prison."

"I think I can understand what twenty years in prison may mean," said the American. "But before this long, dark parenthesis there must have been something in your life."

"I don't know if there was anything," said Olgi. "I started work when I was twelve. At twenty my country remembered me, and put me on a boat that was like a floating prison. My father was an anarchist, I'd inherited his ideas, so you can imagine how much I enjoyed yelling: Long live the King, Long live the Duce, when the flag was ceremoniously raised. I stuck it for two years, till one day, provoked by a pompous naval guard who thought himself an unbeatable champion, because he'd had a few boxing lessons, I vented my long-standing anger on him. I was a docker and I hit him like a docker. The result was the phony boxer went to hospital and I was sent before a military tribunal. I got five years."

The train stopped, it must have reached Mignanego or Ranco. The Reverend was reading a magazine full of half-naked girls. Moustache, actual or alleged strangler of whores, was dozing, cheek on hand.

It was clear that Olgi was unwilling to speak of his past, he wished to be free of it, to destroy it, to put a weighty tombstone on top of it. He felt the American looking at him, willing him on in a friendly way.

"I was at Gradisca, in the military gaol at Gradisca," Olgi went on. "After the secret armistice and the king's escape the officers there were very uncertain and bewildered. Not Colonel P, though, a Sicilian, who'd already decided to hand us over to the Germans for deportation to Germany. We mutinied. The guards used machine-guns. They'd have killed the lot of us if we hadn't heard from Gorizia near by that Tito's partisans were defeating the Germans. The Colonel bolted in an armoured car. And we ran like hares. At Palmanova I got on a goods train that took me somewhere or other. Partly on foot, partly by train, I got to Pisa exhausted. After the last raid on Livorno my family'd packed up for Capannoli. I walked the whole night, and when I got to Pontedera the carabinieri arrested me. From Pontedera to Pisa, from Pisa to San Miniato, from San Miniato to Volterra. That really was prison. A handful of beans in a blackish soup and two small rolls weighing fifty grams each. I was twenty-five and could have eaten an ox. We slept on the ground on sacks of straw. Good and quiet, too, because at the slightest protest, at the slightest infringement of the rules, there were ferocious reprisals, punishment cells on bread and water. Every day someone died. They'd start to swell up and after a few days they'd die. Or else the SS and the Black Brigade would turn up and carry off ten, twenty or thirty to shoot at the Balze or on the bastions. I wasn't lucky."

Mechanically he put a sweet in his mouth, as if to sweeten the horror of those years.

"And then?" said the American.

XXIX

THE TRAIN HAD BEGUN MOVING AGAIN AND THERE was no longer the smell of the sea or the sky or the earth, only the stink of heat and the stink of sweating human flesh.

"The hell at Volterra lasted a year. My usual weight is about thirteen stone, and I went down to eight, like the living skeletons of Belsen and Dachau. I shared a cell with a very young soldier from Piedmont, who in the evenings, about five o'clock, at the time when he was used to having supper, would start crying softly. I had enough strength of mind to save up a roll for the evening, and I'd divide it in half, very carefully so as not to waste a crumb, and I'd give half to that big baby, whom I hated even more than I hated the gaolers. Every day he took pieces of my flesh, in that half roll. Well, let's get to the end of it: one Sunday, in June '44, shots fired by the American artillery hit the prison. Those eighty men, who'd borne wretchedness and tyranny in silence, turned from lice into lions when the fear of death toughened them. They hurled down doors and gates and overcame the few German guards, and everyone was unexpectedly free, those who'd stolen and killed and those who'd been imprisoned unjustly.

"I won't go into my adventures. When I reached Livorno, I found a heap of ruins instead of my home. A woman who knew my mother put me up, and with her husband I set to distilling alcohol for the allied troops. Then that source dried up. My partner said: 'What'll we do now?' I said: 'I'll wait till the port's rebuilt and then go back to humping sacks'. But he'd already been in prison for theft, and said that with the chaos around us he wasn't going to hang about with his hands in his pockets, when even small boys went in for stealing. He said he was meeting some good fellows at midnight to raid a US store; and if I liked I could come along. I went. And so I became a thief.

"It was less tiring than humping sacks, or digging sand, or mixing lime and so on, and very much better paid. I liked it, too, because of the risk, it made me feel a man. I took a pretty, capricious blonde as my mistress, who sent me mad with jealousy and desire, and I heaped her with furs and jewels. I wore a gold wrist-watch and a flashy diamond ring, and carried a loaded gun in my pocket. In a few months I'd got the outlook of a professional gangster. I drank, gambled, and lived in a state of constant cold, cruel excitement. Then it ended as it had to. I was arrested for theft, escaped after a few months, got caught again, escaped again, and caught again. This time the charge was more serious: stealing from a jeweller's. Some of the evidence was circumstantial, and I hoped to get off through insufficient proof. They tried me for escaping twice: two years. Never mind, I said to myself, two years'll go pretty fast. Those months in gaol had sobered me and calmed me down. I'd decided to change my life, and to be satisfied with my wretched hard work on the docks. My girl came to see me. I'd never managed to understand what sort of a creature she was, but now, when I no longer felt that bold, wicked excitement and began to reflect, I felt I was beginning to understand her. And to love her, still with desire, but with something more besides, a brotherly tenderness.

"They tried me for the theft: eight years. It was stiff, but not enough to finish me completely. I still felt young, and full of life and strength and hope. I wouldn't do the full ten years, Italy was changing its institutions, it had become a free, democratic nation, there'd be amnesties and pardons . . . And I had her love. 'Don't feel too bad,' she'd told me. 'I'll wait for you. Whatever happens I'll wait for you.' Then there was another trial at the Court of Assizes: twelve years. Added to the others that made twenty-two. Twenty-two years in prison. It seemed to me too harsh a punishment, I couldn't accept it with resignation. For five years I lived with the thought of escape. But every time I tried and failed only meant I was more closely guarded and made my already hard conditions worse. Whenever there was a dark, stinking, narrow cell, with double and triple bars, it was kept for me. From one strict penitentiary to another. And so the years went by. My girl grew tired of waiting for a man who never came back, and one by one my relations died. My hair fell out, my muscles stiffened, I got rheumatism and heart trouble; a thousand, thousand times I've repented; we're in 1961 and I'm still in prison and I'll stay here until death comes and ends the whole business."

The train had stopped but continued whistling, shuddering and jerking as if impatient to go on. Olgi got up and went to look out of the crack. It was a small country station. Peevish hens scratched greedily in a patch of garden, a lean dog went by, wagging his tail. There was a sound that suggested water falling between steep, stony banks.

Olgi had a pain high up in his chest and throat, as from a prolonged burning thirst.

"These sweets are very good," he said, "but they've certainly made me thirsty . . ."

And as the train was moving again he knocked to go to the toilet. At his heels came a stout carabiniere and two others were watching from the end of the corridor. He slammed the door abruptly, almost angrily. The stout carabiniere seemed not to mind at all. He stayed on guard at the toilet door, ears cocked, tense as a pointer.

Olgi drank from the tap at the basin encrusted with yellow dirt, and the water was tepid, revolting. Above the basin hung a mirror. He lingered there looking at himself. First with amused curiosity, as if finding he was someone else, or unlike himself, then with disapproval, and finally with anger. He shook his fist at that fat man, with an absurd bull-neck, bundled up in anonymous prison clothes, at that pale, sickly face showing a weary, almost inert d spair, "You hog," he cursed himself, "you bastard, you bundle ɔf shit, it's your fault . . ."

He spat on his owɪ image, his face twisted in a spasm of pain that had cut off the flow of tears and the yell, his eyes wild, mad. When he went out he wore his usual face, stamped with a good-natured, if faintly ironical expression of ability to stand anything.

From the corridor windows he could see the distant hills, where peaks and crests alternated, harmoniously, appearing soft against the background of a clean, sun-filled sky.

The American was still smoking scented Dutch tobacco in his Basutoland pipe. Olgi thought: At Christmas he'll be home, in the arms of that gigantic Venus made in USA lucky man. He says she's frigid but no woman's frigid, it's him, this paradoxical communist who travels in a Bentley, runs up debts and cheats his neighbour to get holidays in Capri, who hasn't got what it takes.

He tried to push away every trace of petty envy, but in the depths of him, as a living man cut off from the enjoyment of life, he envied the American for all the good things he would soon be enjoying again, and from which, even in prison, he still got a certain vitality, refreshment and warmth.

And pitilessly, no longer looking objectively at him, he thought of the calculated eccentricity of his clothes, the equally deliberate extravagance of owning ninety-nine pipes, and so on. An intellectual poseur.

The American took the pipe out of his mouth and smiled.

"Better now?"

This solicitude, expressed so conventionally and banally, crowned Olgi's irritation.

"I don't see why I should be better or worse," he replied abruptly. "With me it's always the same."

The American calmly put his pipe back in his mouth. Olgi started talking to the Reverend.

"Is it long since you left Aversa?"

"Last year. They'd sent me to Santa Teresa in Florence but I didn't like the atmosphere. So I asked to be transferred to Procida. But instead of sending me there they sent me to Alessandria. They do just the opposite of what you want and ask for."

"But Alessandria's a good place, you know. As a rule only deserving cases get sent there."

"Yes, it's true, it's a good place, but I'd have preferred Procida. Because of the mild climate, and the sea. I love the sea."

"I love the sea too, but we're in prison."

The Reverend stopped fanning himself with his newspaper. He had folded it in four. Of the delicious girl on the cover only a strip of thigh with suspenders and half her buttocks showed.

The Reverend gave a bewildered moan.

"Twenty years! How shall I ever get through it?"

"It'll pass. Everything passes, wears out, and is forgotten, said Olgi, joking gloomily.

The Reverend glanced at the plump buttocks once more. Suddenly he asked:

"D'you remember C . . . ?"

"I don't remember his name," said Olgi. "I don't often remember names."

"That shopkeeper from Nocera Inferiore, who played chess with you . . . Can you possibly not remember?"

"Yes, I remember now. He used to lose and get angry. When I let him win he invited me to lunch."

"He got out. Last year."

"Good for him," said Olgi.

"His was a sexual crime too, didn't you know?"

"I played chess with him, I didn't bother about what he'd done."

"They gave him five years remission. He did three and then they sent him home for good conduct. Whereas they gave me twenty-four years for the same crime."

With any encouragement he would have continued moaning and pleading for the whole journey.

"And what about Salvatori?" asked Olgi. "Is he still there?"

"What Salvatori?"

"That bicycle thief who said he was a 'giant's mask'. And he always sang that song about 'Zampampero'."

"He's gone really nuts."

"And the captain who drilled his troops in the courtyard – is he still there?"

"They sent him to Barcellona."

"And how about that Sardinian peasant who killed his son for finding some treasure?"

"He's still there."

"And Ciccio Scudieri?"

"Dead."

"And what about the crippled man from Calabria who said he was Napoleon?"

"I didn't know him."

The Reverend fanned himself with his newspaper. He was sweating. He moaned:

"I'll get out in 1981!"

And Olgi said:

"Just think of the wonderful inventions and new things there'll be by 1981!"

XXX

THE TRAIN HAD STOPPED ONCE MORE. AND OLGI took the opportunity to interrupt this pointless conversation, and to get away from that foul nonsensical uproar, from those crazy, ugly creatures, who no longer aroused pity or terror in him, since he was so used to them that they seemed to him normally human. He went to the crack to look out.

On the wall of a hut painted yellow he read, printed in black, the letters: Arquata Scrivia. They had arrived at Arquata Scrivia. So they were still in Liguria. That hut, only a wing of which was in sight, two trees that were elms – and Olgi childishly enjoyed recognizing them and giving them their right name – was all that could be seen of the town. But he could hear voices calling, and greetings, and the sound of vehicles and creaking trolleys. And a young shrill voice shouting enthusiastically: "Orangeade, beer, fresh tangerines . . ."

He stayed there watching the city's unexciting image until the train moved, and concrete images followed one another fast: a nuns' nursery school, an electric power-house, clumps of small white houses, gardens; and then again the open, silent, hard-working countryside steeped in sunshine. Olgi sat down again. Moustache had taken off his dark glasses, and was wiping his eyes with his handkerchief as if he had been weeping. But it wasn't tears, it was pus. So he wore dark glasses to protect his illness, not to hide.

"What's wrong, trachoma?" asked Olgi.

"It's a present from working in the mines in Belgium," said Moustache. "I got the illness there, but they wouldn't admit it,

166

and wouldn't give me a cent. If it doesn't stop soon I'll be completely blind."

"Have you been to a good oculist?" asked the American anxiously.

"Yes, I've been to a professor in Turin. It's because I was in Turin to see about my eyes that they accused me of having strangled that tart."

He didn't say: that poor woman, Olgi reflected. Does this way of referring to her constitute what's called the psychological proof of guilt? But how many ferocious murderers, speaking of their victims before they've been found out, have used the most tearful, pitiful adjectives! He's not moved at the thought of going blind, so how could you expect him to be moved because an unknown whore's been strangled? He may very well be innocent. And yet that won't stop them giving him a life sentence if there's a single shaky clue that points to him.

Moustache put his glasses on again. He creaked his formidable hands (but could a miner's hand be otherwise?)

"I shouldn't care if they condemned me," he said, "so long as they recognized my innocence within two or three years. So I'd get compensation. I'm told there's compensation for judicial errors now. I'd be quite happy with a million. Then I could set up a little business and earn my bread. Because, being half-blind, I can't go on being a miner. With the best will in the world, I couldn't. I couldn't be a labourer of any sort."

The Reverend went on fanning himself with the newspaper. And the girl's buttocks swayed, first to the right, then to the left, ironically, incongruously . . .

Olgi's eyes met the American's.

"What books have you got in your bag?" asked Olgi. "D'you carry around your own small library?"

He thought of the engineer so keen on his theory of the superman and death. The American told him what books he had in his bag: books on the history of art, political economy,

167

the philosophy of history. A single poet: Pound, in the original edition. No fiction.

"Don't you like fiction?" asked Olgi. "I like it best."

The American said there were several kinds of fiction writers, but only one kind interested him.

"Which kind?" asked Olgi.

"The one that shows man's condition truthfully."

"That's a definition they all use," said Olgi.

"Agreed, but phoneys abound in literature. You write yourself, don't you?"

"What makes you think that?"

"Your eyes, friend, your eyes."

Olgi remembered the man from the Marche and laughed.

"But I don't write with my eyes."

"The writer uses his eyes, though, his eyes above all."

"There are writers who are called visual and are pretty superficial."

"I mean the special eyes that let you look inside things, into the intimate mechanism of things."

"I haven't got those special eyes," said Olgi mournfully. "I've just got ordinary ones."

But then he admitted that he wrote. For twelve years he'd been writing. But he didn't add: 'It's hard' or 'It's terribly hard,' because he was talking to someone who knew the job.

"I'd like to read something of yours," said the American. "Have you got what you've written with you, or have you sent it home?"

"I'm like a snail, I carry my home with me."

He indicated the haversack.

"The exercise book is there."

"May I?" insisted the American. "Will you let me?"

Olgi hesitated.

"But we're nearly there."

"We're not at Tortona yet. Or are you afraid?"

"What of?"

"Of my judgement, the judgement of someone who does the same job."

Olgi opened the haversack and took out a big black exercise book. It wasn't a single exercise book, but several sewn together. The sewing, which was pretty clumsy, was Olgi's own work.

"Nicely done, isn't it," he grinned. "Compared with me Bodoni was a craftsman. And then this nice funereal colour. The chief *poète maudit* would have envied it."

The American shrugged. Olgi held out the exercise book ungraciously.

"Laugh away: solecisms, barbarisms, nonsense galore."

The American didn't answer, but started reading at once. He read with concentration. Olgi started looking at the countryside. Plains and hills alternated pleasantly, the land seemed more fertile, better irrigated.

The train whistled, stopped, and reached Tortona. After a quarter of an hour it left, and the American was still reading. This might be flattering to Olgi's self-esteem, but he knew how dangerous self-esteem was and refused to pay sop to it. He put out a hand to take back the exercise book, but the American, with unexpected rudeness, pushed him off.

"For God's sake let me read in peace."

This surliness pleased Olgi more than any praise. The American read for an hour on end, and then he looked forward to the last page, where the novel was unfinished.

"When will you finish it?"

"In a couple of months. I'd rather not give it an end, because life never ends, but every literary work has a beginning and an end, so I must keep to the rules."

"Hurry up and finish it and send it to a publisher."

Olgi put the exercise book in the haversack.

"I'm . . . afraid of publishers."

"Leave it to me," said the American. "I'll talk to my publisher. An intelligent publisher certainly wouldn't let a book like yours slip away."

"But . . ." said Olgi.

"You may make money, become famous, have great success," said the American.

He took out a page of white paper from his bag and wrote something on it.

"This is my home address. For anything you may need."

He folded the sheet and slipped it into the pocket of Olgi's jacket.

"Get ready, put on your irons," sang out the head of the escort.

They had at last arrived at Alessandria.

"First those who are going to the prison," said the head of the escort.

The American held his hand out to Olgi, then suddenly hugged and kissed him. Olgi stayed still, slightly embarrassed by this effusion. All he said was:

"Goodbye."

Then it was Olgi's turn. He was taken over by a gigantic carabiniere. The prison van wasn't beside the prison coach, nor close by, as was nearly always the case during transfers, so that the prisoners could be passed from one to the other immediately and safely. Like a large dog on a lead, Olgi pattered behind that human Eiffel Tower. They crossed two lots of tracks, then a strip of empty pavement almost entirely in shadow, turned into a kind of little piazza where there were two lime-trees and a public urinal; on a bench a woman who was still young and pretty sat reading a book while a few yards away two happy children ran round in a circle shouting and laughing uninhibitedly. The attractive woman appeared surprised – afraid? – at those symbols which walked past, severe justice and chained crime, and looked apprehensively at the two children, but they went on shouting and laughing, for perhaps to them it seemed like a grown-ups' game. The ugly vision had already disappeared – had it been a kind of dream? – and with a touch of her finger the mother tucked back a curl, smoothed her blouse tenderly over her breast and, reassured, returned to reading her delicate love story.

"When will we go on to Saluzzo?" asked Olgi.

"I don't know," replied the colossus.

His voice fell from above impersonally, and the words seemed strangely thin in comparison with his bulk.

The prison van was there, at the opening of an alleyway. Inside were the carabinieri who had already taken the permanent prisoners to the gaol. Olgi went silently to the far end. The carabinieri were nearly all young and strong, and their assured faces harmonized perfectly with their weapons and uniforms. One, taller and handsomer than the others, was delicately carrying an envelope. His face showed irritation.

"He gives me all the dirty jobs," he burst out at last. "I asked him to take me to the barracks straight away, but no, he wanted to go to the prison first, then to the courthouse, then, when it suits the general, to the barracks. I know Sergeant Ascione's got it in for me. But it's not me he's insulting, it's the lieutenant. And I'll tell the lieutenant so."

The others were prudently silent and took no sides. A lieutenant is a lieutenant, but a mere sergeant may sometimes have more power to hurt than a lieutenant . . .

They reached the courthouse. From outside it looked quiet and domestic. They went up a modest staircase, no different from that of an ordinary house, walked along an airy passage with a seat-locker for two ferns in round-bellied pots. They went into the office. A plain-clothes clerk, bald, and rather bent, rather sad, was typing slowly; and a jolly, fat, scented sergeant, with a Neapolitan accent.

They took the chain and handcuffs of Olgi, who answered the ritual questions.

"Valnisi, Olgi, son of Pietro?"

"Yes."

"Age forty-six?"

"Yes."

"Where are you going?"

"To Saluzzo."

"Special characteristics?"

"Tattoos."

"You've got 857 lire, right?"

"Yes."

"Sign."

"When will I be transferred to Saluzzo?"

"Tuesday."

"Tuesday. But it's Tuesday today."

"Well, it means next Tuesday, obviously."

"A whole week here!" said Olgi.

The scented sergeant looked at him severely.

"We don't beat the prisoners here, you know, we don't tie them up in medieval chains, we don't let them die of hunger."

"I know you're humane," said Olgi, "but a transfer's always uncomfortable."

"You've got to be patient," said the Neapolitan. "Last week my mother-in-law died, and what was I to do? Blame God or the government? You've got to be patient. Pick up your things and follow me. But where's your luggage?"

"I left it at the Danieli Hotel," said Olgi.

There was a gate at the end of the passage. After it came another, longer, passage, narrow and dark. A second gate opened, with thicker bars than the first, and the sergeant called:

"Bossone."

From the lower depths came a hoarse voice.

"Ready, sergeant."

"Here's a man being transferred. Search him and settle him in."

Olgi went down a long narrow gut, turned, and by a window found a lazy, sweating guard. The guard looked at the prisoner, the prisoner looked at the guard.

"I think we've met," said the guard, who spoke with a Calabrian or Sicilian accent.

"Yes," said Olgi. "At Porto Azzurro. In 1949. I even remember your name. You were on duty permanently in the punishment cells."

The guard looked at him with suspicion and fear; but Olgi's big face looked stupidly good-natured.

"And now where are you going?" the man said, reassured.

"To Saluzzo."

"Come in here."

He searched Olgi minutely. He even made him take down his underpants.

"Give him his things," he told the sweeper.

He whistled, blowing through the key.

"Man being transferred," he shouted.

"Send him down," answered a voice from the depths.

"Go down," the guard Bossone told Olgi.

He went down and stopped at a gate. A keen young guard opened it and said:

"This way."

They went half-way down a passage and down four slippery steps, and the keen young guard opened a door about four inches thick, then a rusty gate, and said:

"In here."

Olgi went in, laid his bundle of supplies down in a corner and said:

"Good evening," since the hovel was inhabited.

"Good evening," answered two different voices.

Although it was barely six o'clock, and the sun was shining

vigorously outside, the light in there was already on. He felt the need to urinate, as he always did when something worried and oppressed him. The latrine was separated from the room by a partition. In his pocket he felt the piece of paper the American had put there. He took it out and looked at it. It was finely made paper, and on its smooth whiteness the American's expert hand had traced elegant whirls. Olgi made a ball of it, threw it into the toilet, and pulled the chain. It worked.

PART VI

XXXI

INSTEAD OF ORDINARY BEDS THERE WERE BUNKS, three in each set. Two sets along the wall, by the door, another tucked behind the toilet. The one behind the toilet was free.

"You could do what we've done," said the man with a hearing-aid. "Take out the second and third bunks and stick them up against the wall with the others we're not using, so at least you can breathe."

"There's plenty of air here," muttered Olgi.

"What?" shouted the deaf man. In spite of his hearing-aid he caught only snatches of words. He was already in bed in a bunk about a foot off the floor. The other man was in bed too. He was reading *Bolero Film*.

"I'll leave them as they are," said Olgi. "They're like a sort of esplanade, this way."

They were like an army gaol, too. But it wasn't memories of the kind that prevented Olgi from taking down the bunks. He could use them as a basis for something he wanted to do.

"If you'd arrived an hour earlier," said the deaf man, "they'd have given you beans like us. There were beans this evening. Peppers tomorrow, and tomato and potato salad the next day. The grub's not half bad here. The pasta's good, and so's the bread. Where are you on the way to?"

"Saluzzo," said Olgi, laying the straw mattress out on the wire base of the middle bunk. He smoothed the rough straw down with the palm of his hand and spread out the first sheet. It had a large patch in the middle, and in spite of washing still bore obvious stains of anonymous masturbations. Olgi pretended not to see them. He spread out the second sheet, then folded the blanket and put it on the wire base above, so that it

M   177

was like having a cover, a roof. The light would not hurt his eyes. The pillow was as flat as a pancake, but that was just as well, as a high one would have made his neck worse. He grabbed the iron edge of the top bunk and heaved himself up with youthful carelessness, but instead of dropping on to the middle of the bunk he banged the base of his spine on the outer bar. In just the one blasted spot where his rheumatism had got a hold. He made a face and glanced at the two men, but they hadn't noticed his discomfiture. Then he lay down to try out the softness of the bed. The rusty wire netting creaked lugubriously, and so did all its joints. As he stretched out Olgi realized how clumsy and obscene it was, and got out again, not cautiously and slowly, as, with his age and aches, he should have, but in a rush as if he were twenty and as lively as a cricket. Something went wrong again, and he wrenched himself slightly, and clenched his fists, as if he had been insulted. He looked at the deaf man, whose face had the evil gaiety of an elderly child.

"I've been at Saluzzo myself," said the deaf man.

"When?" asked Olgi, now without curiosity.

"Thirty-five or forty years ago."

Olgi laughed, then looked more carefully at him. He had thought the man his own age, but he must have been much older, if he had been inside since prehistoric times.

"How old are you?"

The deaf man heard, or guessed the question's meaning.

"Seventy."

"You're pretty spry, grandpa."

"What?" yelled the deaf man.

"You seem young, Amenofi," Olgi shouted in his ear.

"Younger than you," said the old man joyfully. "Where have you come from?"

"Civitavecchia."

The other man, who had only said good evening, stopped

reading *Bolero Film*. He was about thirty-five, short and hairy and with a very low forehead.

"Did you know Di Stefano?" he asked, speaking correct Italian with difficulty.

"Yes," said Olgi, jokingly. "I knew him when I played back for Real Madrid."

"Di Stefano, he came from the same town as me," said the simpleton. "He's been at Civitavecchia seven years."

"Yes, I know him," said Olgi. (Not that he remembered him in the least.) "We were friends. He's a bright chap."

"He's from Comiso too," said the man, proud and pleased. "He's been inside seventeen years. He must have another sixteen or seventeen months to go."

"Eighteen," said Olgi.

"His wife's a cousin of the brother of a girl friend of mine," explained the man from Comiso.

"Glad to hear it," said Olgi.

The other man smiled and, in an effort of love, went on reading *Bolero Film*.

The window was high and rectangular, with double bars. Olgi measured the thickness of the wall by eye and said cheerfully:

"How wasteful architects were fifty years ago!"

He was glad no breath, no ray of light from outside penetrated the hovel: this was just what he needed, in order to work. The more they took life away from him, the more he felt the need to recreate it within himself. But if any scrap of reality from outside distracted him, if a piece of real life gripped him, he was no longer capable of straining over words, in fact he loathed them, for always falling short, and being haphazard, and quite failing to express reality, cunning and deceptive and flattering though they were.

He thought of the seven days he had to stay there, and now he wished they could have been thirty, fifty, seventy. Then he would have been able to finish the book he had been working

on for years, with long gaps due to illness, his difficult circumstances, the mistrust and hostility of those in charge, transfers,
and even, to the disgust merely that he occasionally felt at the
mad vanity of trying to build something solid and lasting with
bricks as ephemeral as words.

But he hadn't got even a pencil stub. This time he couldn't
reproach himself for carelessness or lack of cunning: the way
that keen screw had searched him, even a needle wouldn't have
got through. All he had allowed him to take into the cell was
his pocket dictionary – and a fat lot of use that was! – because
he thought it was a missal! But he had enough toilet paper.

"Have you got a pencil?" he asked the deaf man. (He had to
shout the question three times in his ear.)

"No," the deaf man finally answered. "If you need to write
to your family, tell the sergeant at tomorrow's check-up and
he'll let you write in the head warder's office."

Olgi shrugged.

"Comiso, have you got a pencil, or maybe a pen?"

"No," said the man from Comiso, and went on laboriously
reading.

It was sultry and hot in that cellar. In winter it must have
been freezing. Olgi took off his worn jacket, and turned back
the sleeves of his striped shirt, which needed a wash. And so,
with the small amount of hair he had left cut down to his skull,
and his thick arms and chest tattooed, he looked like a hardened
criminal wallowing in the prison mire.

"How long have you been inside?" the deaf man asked him.

"Twenty years."

"I've done forty. Not all together, of course, once four, once
six, once seven, once three, once twelve, and so on. I've still
got another three of this sentence to go. What d'you think,
shall I finish it or shall I die first?"

"You'll live as long as a tortoise," Olgi yelled in his ear.

The other man nodded gaily.

"I'm healthy. If I wasn't deaf I'd have nothing to complain of. I wasn't born deaf either, you know. They broke my ear drums at the police station in '32. I can't hear a thing with the right ear, even with the hearing-aid, it's an old one and out of date, they've got electronic gadgets now, but they cost a packet and where'll I get that from? With the left ear I can hear a bit. A while ago I wrote to the Minister of the Interior to try and get compensation. They said they weren't responsible for methods used by the police under fascism. Then I wrote to a lawyer and he said 'I advise you to drop it or you might get another sentence for calumny'."

He looked up and moved his thumb and first finger round in a circle which meant: you've got to be pretty wretched to hope for any help from him.

"D'you smoke?"

"The doctor's forbidden it. But now and then I allow myself a Muratti's Ariston."

"D'you know you can get beer as well as wine in the shop?"

"I loathe spirits."

"There's fruit, too, pears and apples, all sorts."

"I only eat cooked fruit."

He could have gone on chattering until eight o'clock, because he didn't want to go to bed before that, and wasn't in the habit of doing so.

"D'you know the broadcasts start at eight here? The opposite of other gaols. The broadcasts are tied up with the ones at the penitentiary, and as they all work or study during the day, they have the radio on in the evening. From eight to ten. Want to read this?"

He held out a thick volume bound in black leather.

"It's the Bible. The priest gave it to me. It cost five thousand lire. If you give me two packets of strong tobacco and two of cigarette papers I'll give it to you."

Olgi shook his head.

"Two packets of strong tobacco without the papers."

Another denial.

"One packet."

"No."

"There's the whole history of the world in here," said the deaf man. "If you read it you can learn a lot of things."

He tapped it, opened it at random and pretended to read. Olgi started walking up and down. He always did this before going to bed. Not to digest what he hadn't eaten, just out of habit. The deaf man shut the book peevishly, took off his hearing-aid, put a handkerchief on his face. With his feet sticking out at the end of the mattress, he looked like a corpse.

XXXII

HE WALKED UNTIL THE FIRST BELL RANG. THEN HE went to the toilet, cleaned his teeth, swallowed some water – instead of supper – and this time got carefully into the bunk. The other two were already asleep. The man from Comiso was snoring. Amenofi, the deaf man, had turned over on his side and was showing his withered buttocks. He ate, he slept, he calmly carried out the other functions of life; what effect had forty years of prison had on him? What had they taught him? What had they changed? How long does shale take to change its structure? Sometimes Olgi felt he had lived not through a single age, but through all the earth's ages.

Beyond the door was the gate, but not the usual kind; it was like a cage, with bars thicker than they would put on at the zoo.

Above it was a small crucifix, covered in cobwebs. Beside the Christian symbol of suffering and redemption was a small box that broadcast inexhaustible human rubbish.

Olgi took off his underpants, and then his shirt as well. He shut his eyes, thinking of what he would write tomorrow. But he soon tired of planning it cold like that – his creative work took place on the page itself.

He looked at his belly, his thighs, and his arms. He was still a good-looking man. His face was lined, but his body, at least externally, was still young.

He glanced at the other two, lost in sleep, as if they didn't exist. Sheltered from the glare of the light, naked in bed, he was alone in the world. Too much alone in a world made to be lived in with others.

There was a bellow from the box, and crazy sounds danced and spun wildly in that dreary enclosed space. The usual wretched dance music. Sooner have the tom-tom, Olgi thought, the living excitement of wild black men, than this insipid dance of civilized paralytics.

Then the proper programme began. They were broadcasting from Riccione. Local singers were competing on the stage with winners from other towns. The trilling, sophisticated voice of the master of ceremonies sounded as folksy as an official tourist pamphlet while he described the elegance and attractiveness of the mostly very young girl competitors, fished with amiable irony for the secrets of their love life, and tried to discover what their admissible tastes and ambitions were. A bold girl of seventeen, asked "Why did you take up singing, signorina?" answered candidly: "Because I wanted to become a famous singer." "And why d'you want to become a famous singer?" "Because I can make lots of money that way." "So you're not thinking of the glory?" "What's the good of glory to me? I'm thinking of all that lovely lolly" (applause from the "elegant audience in the hall"). Another, to the question: "Signorina, are you thinking of getting married?" said: "At present I'm thinking only of my career." A man who had been at the university and had three times failed his exams had formed a group with three other idiots like him that called itself The

Breakers. "Why d'you call yourselves that?" they asked and he replied: "Because we want to break into success."

The youngsters' 'sound' attitudes were suitably appreciated by the 'elegant audience in the hall'.

If they'd at least been able to sing and play! Talent, when it really exists, makes all kinds of weaknesses and absurdities forgivable. "Call these simpering apes and stuck-up parrots singers and musicians?" Olgi sneered. "Oh, Milva, console us. You're like the deep sea, like a field of hay in springtime, like the swallow whirling wildly in space, like the murmuring waterfall, like fire under the earth: your voice is a girl of twenty running in the sunshine to meet her lover."

He felt a nip in his back, put out a hand and caught the bed-bug. With his thumb he squashed it against the wall, and a broken shell was left in a smudge of blood. Ten minutes after the broadcast had stopped, the men came round for the counting.

How long had this been going on?

But another day started.

"Exercise," said the guard.

It was a cloister surrounded by four high walls. There was a toilet and a wash-basin. Two stone seats. Olgi looked round for someone who might help him. There were some gay, lively youngsters, one in shorts and wooden-soled shoes was giving boxing lessons; a few old beggars; a ruined businessman. Olgi went to sit down on a bench, the only corner of shade. A man moved up to make room for him.

"Thanks," said Olgi.

"You being transferred?" the man asked. With grizzled hair that hung over his forehead, and a pepper and salt moustache like Clark Gable's he did in fact look rather like Gable, in both features and expression. Though he wasn't so robust-looking. He wore the official striped shirt, and his own shabby trousers. One of his shoes gaped at the sole.

"Yes," said Olgi. "I'm being transferred. I'm going to Saluzzo.'

"Where have you come from?"

"From Civitavecchia."

"Were you always there?"

"I've been in practically every gaol in Italy."

"Including Portolongone?"

"Certainly."

The man like Clark Gable looked respectful and admiring.

"Are you here waiting for trial?" asked Olgi.

"Yes. Insult to and resisting of the police. But it's true. They stopped me getting the train and I didn't want to miss it, because they were waiting for me in Rome to make a film. Clark Gable had died and I had to stand in for him."

"Did you tell the judge all this?"

"Of course. So they'll have to let me out."

"And what did the judge say?"

"Nothing."

You'll be lucky if they sentence you, Olgi thought. Because if they send you to some criminal lunatic asylum, and you're really the poor devil you seem, with no money, no support and no protection, you'll never get out.

He looked at the man's likeable face, like the famous star's, trying to solve the mystery. Was he really mad, or was he pretending? Had he thought up this dangerous idea to avoid prison, without realizing it would be far worse for him? And if he was mad, how was he mad, and how far? But Olgi no longer sought to unravel human mysteries. It took a great deal of pride and certainty to do so. Or a great love of one's neighbour. And Olgi was no longer sure of anything. And his neighbour . . . was his enemy.

"What was your job?"

"Barber. For years I was at sea. Then I got a short sentence for theft and they took away my seaman's ticket. I had a small

185

shop with a partner, but my partner's taken advantage of my being inside now, and has made off with the lot."

"You should have got one of your family to act for you."

"I'd only got a sister, and she died on Christmas Eve, so now I've no one else."

He got up, and moved his right foot, which had pins and needles.

"Shall we walk?" he suggested.

"The sun's too hot. Have you got a pencil or a pen you could lend me?"

"I've got nothing. They don't let us keep a thing in this gaol. On writing days they give us pens and inkwells, then take them away."

"I know that," said Olgi. "I didn't come inside yesterday. But pencils get around just the same. And even fountain-pens."

"That's true. I'll see if I can get you a pencil now." He called the young man who was giving boxing lessons.

"Germano."

The young man trotted over, bare-chested. His wooden-soled shoes made a gay rhythm on the crumbling paved yard. He was rather good looking, with eyes that touched people and objects very lightly, like restless butterflies.

"What d'you want, Clark Gable? A fight?"

"Have you a pencil to give this friend of mine from Porto-longone?"

The young man's glance rested on Olgi's face for a moment. "No."

And he jumped back among the other young men, flung two of them down in a moment and lifted another across his neck.

"Let's see if Paolino has one," said Clark Gable, indicating one of four cell windows that gave on to the courtyard. "Paolino's studying French. He killed his father, poor soul."

He called Paolino, who was sitting on the bed with a book in his hand.

"He never comes outside. He's shy. He's ashamed, but his father was a wicked brute, a drunkard."

Paolino approached the bars.

"What is it, Riccardo?"

"Here's this friend of mine who's come from Portolongone," said Riccardo-Clark Gable.

"Good morning, Paolino," said Olgi. "Are you studying French?"

"Yes," said Paolino timidly. He had turned red.

"Je connais le français," said Olgi. "Have you got good books?"

Paolino showed him the book he was reading.

"Good," said Olgi.

"I've got a dictionary and a grammar as well. But it's hard work without a teacher."

"You must stick to it," said Olgi, "and not be put off at the start. Good lad."

And he looked at Clark Gable, who said:

"Paolino, have you got a pencil you could give him?"

"I haven't, I'm sorry," said Paolino. "I do my translation exercises when they give me a pen and ink on writing days. I'd like a pencil myself, but it's against the rules."

Olgi smiled.

"Now I'll try Marcello," said Clark Gable.

He was a young man who was bawling rather less than the others, with a heavy dark chin and the eyes of a faithful dog.

"Marcello, this friend of mine who's come from Portolong-one needs a pencil. Have you got one?"

"Yes," said Marcello. He held his hand out to Olgi. "But it's in my cell. This afternoon we'll be out for exercise . . . So you're from Portolongene. Hard, eh?"

"Things have changed even there."

One of the group of young men called Marcello.

"Come and try your strength with Germano. He beats every-one. Maybe you can stand up to him."

But Marcello said:

"He beats me too. When I worked at the cement factory my arms were strong, but now . . ."

With Olgi he went up to the bench where Germano was beating all his adversaries, one after the other.

"May I?" said Olgi.

"With you?" said Germano.

"I've got arms."

"But you're old . . ."

In fact Germano was estimating the strength of Olgi's thick wrists, and the still powerful set of his shoulders.

Olgi put his elbow beside Germano's and twisted his thick fingers in his young rival's longer ones. They looked into each other's eyes. Twenty-five years ago, in Triero's inn . . . He and Attao, nicknamed Drifter: six feet of muscle as tough as wood. The contest had lasted an hour: after which Triero called quits.

Germano put his whole strength into the first attack: he always succeeded, but his arm was like a stump nailed into the bench. His face already showing the shame of defeat, he waited resignedly for the old man to lower his arm. But suddenly Olgi's arm yielded.

"You've won," he said, smiling.

XXXIII

WHEN THEY CAME BACK TO EXERCISE IN THE afternoon Marcello had kept his word. It was a fine long pencil.

"But it's indelible," said Marcello. "Does that matter?"

"All the better," said Olgi. "But I shan't be able to give it back at once. I've got a lot to write."

"It's yours, I've a chance of getting another."

"Thank you."

"Shall we go and sit down?"

The two benches were filled, and they sat down on the ground against the wall. It was obvious that the young man wanted to talk, but had no idea how to begin. Olgi himself felt no need to talk. He was perfectly well as he was: he had that treasure of a pencil in his pocket, and was out in the open air with a likeable loyal-looking youngster.

"Did you like last night's broadcast?" asked the boy.

"No. Nonsense, rubbish. If only those idiots could sing."

"They're students, mostly," said Marcello. "They don't have to worry about making a living."

He stared ahead of him, towards the toilet; the door was open, and a man could be seen crouching on the edge of the hole. But Marcello, intent on developing his thought, didn't see him.

"I'm a workman," he said softly. "That is, I was one before . . . before I started stealing."

He looked at Olgi's tattooed arms.

"Please, don't judge me by my tattoos," said Olgi. "I'm not . . . what I seem."

He rolled down his shirt-sleeves, and buttoned them at the wrist.

"That's better. The old, bad, cynical fellow's disappeared. You were saying you were a workman. I like workmen, not thieves."

Marcello told his story. He had worked in a cement factory, and on Sunday mornings he went to the café to play billiards. There he met Cavaldo.

"He's that half-bald fellow over there, who drags his left leg," said Marcello. "He's a professional thief, at least he'd been stealing for years. What could he do with a leg like that?"

Cavaldo had a scooter, and could play around with girls and so on. Marcello was engaged, his girl was called Mara, and she worked as well. On Sundays they used to meet and go to the cinema, it was all rather monotonous. Marcello hated the rich. The rich had everything, the poor nothing. And when Cavaldo suggested a profitable deal, he accepted. Once you gather speed downhill, there's no stopping you. The only time you stop is when you smash your face against the prison wall.

"Now we've got three thefts to pay for. I don't know the law well, but Cavaldo does. They'll put it all into one trial, luckily Cavaldo thinks the sentence will be four to six years for me, as I'm a first offender, and eight to ten for him since he's been convicted before. I've been inside ten months. While I've been here I've realized all kinds of things, first that you can't change your fate as a workman by an individual revolt, even if by setting out to become a thief. Property is theft, admittedly, but you can't get rid of its injustice by stealing again. In these months I've been reading a great deal, books my elder brother Nino, who belongs to the Party, brings me. He's forgiven me. Mara has forgiven me too. But I've broken off the engagement."

"Why?" asked Olgi.

"Because I don't deserve a girl like Mara. And because six years is a long time. I don't want her to sacrifice herself for so long."

"And how has Mara taken this decision of yours?"

"She still writes to me and sends me parcels."

Olgi was moved. More than his old convict's rough exterior could allow to show.

"Girls called Mara are loyal, brave and faithful," he said. He had in mind a certain kind of girl called Mara, but she was more than a literary memory: she was a living Mara who walked through the streets of the world, full of awareness, and of the seriousness of life.

"Tell me, sincerely: do you love Mara?"

"As much as I love my mother, and sometimes, I feel, more. Especially now, when I haven't got her near me. Our meetings at the cinema seemed to me so wretched, but if at this minute I was offered a million lire or the chance of sitting beside her, holding hands in an ordinary suburban cinema, I'd give up the million."

Olgi suddenly grabbed his neck and shook him, gay and violent.

"You great idiot, you're stupider than those dolts on the radio last night. D'you want to lose a girl like Mara, d'you want to give up a happiness you can build up with your own hands? You've fallen, but you've fallen on your feet, lad, so cheer up. There's talk of an amnesty pretty soon, you know. You may be inside another five or six months, and what's that to a couple who really love each other? Write to her. Why make her suffer more than she has already?"

"I think I will," said Marcello.

"You'll get married and be happy, with lots of fine children," said Olgi.

On other occasions he had used these words as a joke, or even ironically, but now, with the passionate faith of a child, he wanted to believe in the story's happy ending.

Germano came up, looking half mortified and half hostile.

"You . . ." he said.

Olgi disliked his tone. He now regretted having allowed him to win. If he bothers me I'll hit him. I'll knock him out for half an hour. That'll stop him playing cock of the roost.

He got up.

"What d'you want?"

Germano took his arm.

"Walk up and down with me?"

"Well, in the shade, along this strip of shade."

"Why did you let me win?" asked Germano.

"Because at your age it's painful to accept defeat, whereas at mine you're used to it. One defeat more or less . . ."

He had freed himself from Germano's arm, but softened the ungraciousness of the gesture by pretending to blow his nose.

"You're still as strong as an ox," said Germano, completely won over.

"I don't like the comparison," said Olgi.

"What's a comparison?" asked Germano. "I'm very ignorant."

Olgi smiled.

"Comparing a man to an ox is a comparison. I don't like being compared to an ox. I don't think anybody'd like being compared to an ox. If only because of the horns."

"Well, what I meant to say was, you were still very strong. At my age you must have been terrific."

"At your age I was already in prison."

"I'm inside for living off a prostitute," Germano told him. "They gave me two years and eight months, confirmed at the court of appeal. I've appealed again but there's not much hope, even though Rosina said I was her fiancé. And in actual fact we were engaged . . ."

"What are you telling me?"

"Rosina's from Calabria, we became engaged when I was in the army there. Then she came to Cuneo. I told her: 'Well my girl, get busy, because I'm unemployed. It's the factory or the street.' She chose the street. She didn't earn much, because she's nothing much to look at, and not too good at it either. What she handed over only just about paid for my bad habits."

"I shouldn't have given you two years and eight months," said Olgi scornfully, "I'd have given you thirty. To think you'd sink to living off a country bumpkin like that! With your splendid natural talents! With your outstanding gifts of courage and intelligence and independence! A man as brave and shrewd as you! Why, it's really high-class tarts you should be living off, call girls at half a million a go who tinkle as sweetly as cash-registers. Then you'd be properly set up, decked out like a Prince, with a flat at Parioli, a villa on the Riviera, and a Maserati or an Alfa Romeo."

"My mother and sister work from morning till night, sewing," Germano muttered. "There's no Maseratis about it."

"Because they're stupid," said Olgi. "If your sister, who must be pretty, was as bright as her brother, she'd know how to make money. A poor man's a man who wants to be poor. Rake it in, you bungler."

And he banged him in the chest. But Germano didn't want to box. He was thinking of the wretched poverty at home, and of poor Rosina too. But as Olgi went on prodding him, he started leaping around him. He was a good dancer, but not much use at hitting. His blows all came up against Olgi's defensive forearm.

"But your guard's hopeless," said Germano. "You're too shut up."

"Shut up, shut up, I'm always shut up," Olgi sang to a hit tune.

His rather aggressive and teasing good temper was still with him when he was back in the cell.

"Hey, Amenofi, got anything good to tell me?" he yelled in the deaf man's ear.

"Anyone with lolly can get along, even in prison, but if you haven't got it you may as well hang yourself," said the deaf man.

Echoing this droll idea, Olgi recited some verses of Heine:

> Hat man viel, so wird man bald
> Noch viel mehr dazu bekommen.
> Wer nur wenig hat, dem wird
> Auch das Wenige genommen.

Wenn Du aber gar nichts hast,
Ach, so lasse Dich begraben—
Denn ein Recht zum Leben, Lump,
Haben nur, die etwas haben.*

The deaf man unfortunately didn't understand, and even the man from Comiso gathered little of it.

"When are you leaving?" asked Comiso.

"Next Tuesday," answered Olgi.

"I'm off tomorrow," said Comiso happily. "I'm going to Augusta. In Sicily. That way I can be nearer my family. I don't like being inside on the mainland. I've been away from Sicily nine years."

It turned out that he had killed as well, not to avenge the honour of some relation, but because of a quarrel which had arisen through sharing a stable. Rancorous feelings long brooded over, and then satisfied, perhaps with Dutch courage from an extra glass of wine, with a shot in the back.

By eight o'clock Amenofi and Comiso were sleeping placidly.

"Innocent happy souls," said Olgi ironically, envying them. "Insomnia, the casuist explains, is the pricking of a bad conscience, which torments sinners and reprobates. In fact L'Innominato† used to come out with his dramatic rigmaroles at night. In prison, where there are so many rogues, conscience ought to work overtime. But I can count on my fingers those who really feel remorse. Judging by my own insomnia, of

* Literally: "If anyone possesses much, he will soon obtain much more. Whoever has only a little, from him will even that little be taken. If, however, you possess nothing, then get yourself buried – for only those who possess something, you wretch, have the right to exist." The title of Heine's poem is *Weltlauf* – "The Way of the World". It is the first of his *Lazarus* poems in the *Romanzero* collection.

†One of the main characters in *I Promessi Sposi* (*The Betrothed*) by Alessandro Manzoni (1785–1873).

course, my sins must have been so bad that in comparison the sins of Manzoni's notorious character were trifles."

He got into the bunk, taking great care, and his mind was full of vital impulses, like a pregnant woman about to give birth. But he waited till the loud cackle on the radio was finished. In the silence he found his voice again. He had cut up the lavatory paper to the size of book pages. It was rough and yellowish, and he had to press hard with the pencil. He wrote slowly, choosing the words with meticulous care, but rarely consulting the dictionary. Like all writers with living matter to communicate, he didn't let himself be distracted by the beauty of words. He didn't worry about 'style', but worried constantly, immensely, about being sincere, determined never to be satisfied with an inexact expression.

At dawn he was still writing.

XXXIV

HE WENT OUT TO EXERCISE, ABOVE ALL TO SEE Marcello, and talk to him. Here was a youngster greedy to learn, and to know. They talked about books, and Marcello was ingenuously surprised that a man with so little schooling – Olgi had told him he had had only four years' primary schooling – possessed such a wide, confident knowledge of several literatures.

"But how have you managed to read so much?" exclaimed Marcello. "And even to learn languages, English, French, Spanish . . ."

"Twenty years in prison's a long time, son," said Olgi, "and you must use it somehow, if you're not content to live at the level of a beast in a cage."

But Olgi knew about more than literature, he amazed

Marcello further by talking competently of football, cycling, boxing, light music, the cinema and the theatre, and then of labour matters, trade unionism, Taylorism, etc.

"You're an encyclopaedia," Marcello said admiringly.

"I'm not an encyclopaedia," said Olgi, "I'm just a man who's interested in all aspects of life. We've chatted and chatted but tell me: what about Mara?"

"I've written to her, if that's what you wanted to know."

"Good," said Olgi.

He was glad. They walked in the sun, without it bothering him. In fact he enjoyed its warmth and brightness. He felt he was twenty years younger, and that this boy he had only just met, this Marcello, had the eyes and the smile of the brother he had never met.

"In my letter to Mara . . . I talked about you."

"About me? Oh no," protested Olgi. "You mustn't do that. Your lovers' quarrels are no one else's business."

"I tried to make her see the sort of man you are."

"We've known each other one day. What d'you think you know about me?"

He looked put out, but was pleased. So much so that he teased poor Clark Gable.

"When you get to Hollywood, Clark, see if you can get them to give me a small part. As a gangster who's an alcoholic and a drug addict I'd do fine."

"Paolino would like you to give him a few lessons in pronunciation," said Clark, who enjoyed doing things for other people.

Olgi looked up at the window of Paolino's cell. He was there by the bars, with his book in his hand.

"I'm coming."

Germano held him up on the way.

"Hey, old rock, I've got something to show you."

It was a photograph of Rosina. Short and plump, with a

flower in her hair, and a sweet resigned smile, she was every soldier's ideal girl. Olgi turned over the photograph and read what she had written in her uncertain handwriting:

To my eternal love
Rosina

"When did she send it?"

"It's a recent one, about three weeks ago."

"Then go on being her eternal love," said Olgi in a neutral voice. "Does she send you money?"

"What she can, poor girl. As you can see, she's nothing special. Fit for rutting soldiers and peasants."

He laughed. He had neat shining teeth; he had a twig in his hair. Olgi looked at the face of that handsome, irresponsible youth, who was neither good nor bad, and measured how weary he was, how very weary – not wise – he was, since he couldn't even work up any indignation.

"Marry her," he said "and you're set up for life."

"Good morning, sir," said Paolino.

"Good morning, Paolino," said Olgi. "But don't call me sir. My name's Olgi, call me that if you like. Or better still nothing."

He gave Paolino a lesson until the bell rang for the end of exercise.

"I've learnt more in this half hour," Paolino said gratefully, "than in the six months I've been working on my own."

"That's too much," said Olgi. "Of course you do better with a teacher. Everyone should have one."

He looked gloomily at the dreariness of the yard.

"Wait," said Paolino.

He came back with a fine apple.

"Take it," he said, blushing again.

"I'm not used to being paid for lessons," said Olgi, smiling. "I'm . . . a disinterested teacher."

"It's fruit my mother brought me," said Paolino.

"D'you love your mother?" asked Olgi.

"Yes," answered Paolino in a breath.

"Exercise over," shouted the guard.

Olgi took the apple.

"Thanks, Paolino. We'll have more lessons this afternoon. But don't give me any more apples."

The man from Comiso had already left. The deaf man had collected a few cigarette ends and was opening them on to a sheet of newspaper.

"I could die of bubonic plague and those swinish sons of mine wouldn't send me a lira," he said, shaking his fist, a wretched and furious prophet of ill-will.

"But you're always in prison," said Olgi. "You go in and out, in and out. D'you expect your children to help you?"

"Nobody, nobody loves me," croaked the old man.

And he began to cry.

"Stop it, Amenofi," said Olgi. "You're incoherent and . . . revolting."

He stopped whimpering when the soup arrived.

"How can one bear it?" he went on complaining childishly, with his mouth full. "Just soup, and nothing to go with it."

"Here's something to go with it," said Olgi and gave him half the apple. "Smile, now."

"But those bloody nobs eat all they want," the hardened rogue said aggressively. "And they want me to stop pinching, do they? Why, I'll still be pinching when I'm hobbling on a stick."

Then, after lunch, while the deaf kleptomaniac was dozing, Olgi read and re-read the pages he had written the previous night. He kept correcting and changing, and wondering: Have I said all I wanted to say? Have I left out anything that needed saying, have I added too much? He read on, doubtful, discontented, cursing the 'lousy job', saying "But who's making me do it, why do I do it?" etc., envying the bricklayer, the miner, anyone who produced something with the effort of his muscles, and envying the animals, the birds above all, who needed no articulate language to communicate, no such complicated art.

That evening he didn't write, but read a fictionalized biography of Amedeo Modigliani, which Marcello had lent him. Modigliani's personality as an artist, and that short intense life that seemed so disordered and anarchical, had always fascinated him. Knowing he was ill, he hadn't put a woollen cap and slippers on his vital energy, he hadn't used it wisely and prudently, like a capital he must exploit, but had answered every call and every stimulus avidly, with his whole person. Greedy hands had robbed him: evil dealers who had taken his immortal paintings for a few francs, to pay for a modest supper and a few glasses of absinthe; and women – which is another name for the amorous – who were attracted and made lustful by the remarkable beauty of that melancholy, dark young man, and by the small amount of virile strength that still palpitated in his feverish, exhausted body.

From attic to attic, from filthy eating house to dubious bistros, growing ever poorer and more alone, sicker, purer. At Livorno his mother wept for the 'madness' of her beautiful exiled son; and at Montecitorio his bearded brother the deputy, harangued the people whose tribune he was, was applauded, and drove home in a landau.

He had fornicated with whores like La Golue, and discussed art with geniuses like Apollinaire and Picasso. He had taken part in every pictorial experience of his time, and no technique, no school had muffled him. In forms and in the arrangement of colour he not only wanted to express his own special, personal way of 'seeing' reality, but tried passionately to grasp, transfuse and immobilize on the canvas the mysterious, because ever fugitive, essence of life.

His pictures were masterpieces (later they were worth millions), and he flung them under his rude bed, discouraged and disgusted, or else exchanged them for a little absinthe or hashish.

Then death came to solve and pacify all. And while Amedeo Modigliani was dying in a cheerless hospital bed, one of the girls he had loved, crazily in love with him to the point of martyrdom, flung herself from a fifth floor window.

Olgi finished the book as dawn was breaking: another whole day to live through, with love or patience and obscure weariness, just as the carpenter planes his wood.

XXXV

DURING THE MORNING EXERCISE HE DIDN'T SEE Marcello, and asked about him.

"He's had a visitor," Clark Gable told him.

Olgi didn't walk about; he sent Germano, who wanted to play the fool packing (he'd had a money-order from Rosina and was noisily happy), and gave Paolino a lesson. Paolino was not particularly intelligent and had been taught very little, but he had a touching willingness to learn. Then why had he decided to study French, the language of literary men and diplomats, instead of improving his own imperfect Italian? But Olgi knew that French or Chinese or Sanskrit or a thousand other ways of keeping busy were simply ways of fleeing from a reality that, if accepted without correctives, led straight to madness or suicide.

He could read into the unmysterious soul of this boy. What was harder was to foresee what he would become after fifteen or twenty years in prison. (Because presumably he had this much to do.) What sort of man would he be when he left? Now he was just a poor boy who, in a world without love or charity, had killed his father to protect his mother. A boy who behind bars sang his ingenuous love of life by doing exercises that were hard to read. He read:

"Les ténèbres étaient profondes. Je ne voyais rien devant moi, ni autour de moi, et toute la branchure des arbres entre-choqués emplissait la nuit d'une rumeur incessante. Enfin, j'aperçus une lumière . . ."

It was a passage of Guy de Maupassant.

"Enfin, j'aperçus une lumière," repeated Olgi.

"Didn't I pronounce it right?" asked Paolino, worried and upset.

Olgi smiled and finished the lesson.

He walked absorbed in that desert enclosure full of strange people, in the fierce shameless sunshine. He was alone again, alone and without hope, in a world that was wholly wrong.

He leant against the wall. The expression on his face was grotesque and desperate, but his eyes were hard as a clenched fist. Germano prudently kept away. The black mood lasted even in his cell. Sometimes it lasted whole days.

They opened the door and the gate to serve soup. An old sweeper was dragging a pot, followed by a guard carrying a ladle.

"Soup," said the guard.

Amenofi had his bowl filled.

"Beetroot soup," he laughed scornfully. "Fine!"

And to the old sweeper:

"Arturo, bring me a newspaper to read."

Olgi went on walking up and down.

"Why aren't you getting your soup?" said the guard. He was a lance-corporal, and under his nose, which looked as if it were made of cardboard, the curved whiskers bristled petulantly.

"What is it, soup?" asked Olgi, walking over to him. "Is this soup?"

"What else?" said the lance-corporal.

"It's slops scarcely fit for pigs," said Olgi.

"I see," said the man. "You've got the blues and you're taking it out on me. Well, d'you want it or don't you?"

"No," said Olgi. "I don't want it, I'm not a pig, I'm a man."

"As if I care," retorted the lance-corporal.

And he slammed the gate, and the door. They heard him saying to the old sweeper:

"If you only knew what a bastard he is . . ."

He was qualified to do so, was cardboard-nose and he could judge him exactly . . . The anger that wasn't even anger but a gloomy disgust with everything, turned into crazy hilarity.

"If you only knew what a bastard I am," he yelled into Amenofi's ear.

The deaf man, chewing pasta and beetroot like a goat, touched his forehead.

"You're daft," he said.

He swallowed.

"So what'll you eat?"

"Ambrosia."

"What?"

"Ambrosia, the food of the gods."

A bastard, and daft: this was what he was, and this only: a bastard, and daft.

They had hung other suitable labels on him, but always the same kind of thing as bastard, and daft: irredeemable element, socially dangerous, crafty pretender, lucid paranoic, and so on.

An upsurge of black poison, and a longing to be out of the world. He lay down on the bunk, and draped the blanket over himself. It was his slightly childish way of refusing the world's reality. He was alone, with his pointless suffering, in a shapeless dark world made of suffering. "Now no eye can see me. No one judges me. God? But God's a human invention. God doesn't exist." And he contradicted himself at once. "God must exist. He sees me."

The door opened, but not the gate. The guard looked anxiously at his shape.

"Take off that blanket," he ordered. "I must see you, I want to see what you are doing."

Olgi obediently took off the blanket. He was in the world. Someone was watching him.

At exercise he met Marcello again at last. He looked, if not happy, at least content.

"I had a visit. It was my brother Nino and . . . her."

"The kisses there must have been," said Olgi.

"Mara asked me to remember her to you."

"Thanks. She's kind and good. All working girls, in proletarian novels, are kind and good."

"But what's that you're saying? What's the matter?"

Olgi kicked a melon skin and sent it flying.

"Why don't they sweep this yard out?"

Marcello lit a cigarette.

"Why not have one? It helps to get rid of the blues."

"It's bad for coronaries, too."

"Is that why you don't smoke?"

Olgi smiled and accepted the cigarette.

"No, it's not. It's that . . . smoking's pointless."

"Lots of things are pointless, but they help you live."

"That's true," said Olgi.

He felt the young man's searching eyes upon him, but they were good eyes, loving and loyal. Yet instinctively he drew back, frowning.

"Tell me Olgi, haven't you got anyone?"

"Anyone how?"

"Relations."

"I've got two sisters. A widow and an unmarried mother."

"And do they write to you?"

"Twice a year. At Easter and Christmas."

"No help, of course."

"None, of course. But I don't need anything. Excuse me, I'm going to give Paolino a lesson. It's flattering to feel I'm a teacher."

That night he wrote. He felt he had to finish this book of his, and at the same time he was sorry to finish it. It was like using up a store of good logs that might have warmed him during the long winter; like exhausting a reason for living. He wrote until three o'clock; then he slept. And he dreamt – he nearly always dreamt the same dream, with variations of place and detail, but with the same central bio-psychological meaning – that he was walking along roads he knew well, light, happy, unsinister roads, when suddenly a wall barred his way; he climbed it, and found another even higher wall, then a gate, then another gate, and then doors made of iron, with spy-holes that were jaws, and bolts that were sharp-edged swords.

These were Olgi's dreams.

Next morning during exercise Marcello took up their previous day's interrupted conversation, which clearly he was anxious to finish, with his natural bluntness, he came straight to the point.

"We're a family of workmen," he said. "We haven't any money in the bank, but if five of us eat six can eat just as well. We want to help you."

"What?" said Olgi. "You want to help me? Why? I've struck it lucky, everyone wants to help me. But I don't need help. I'm . . . self-sufficient."

It occurred to him that this was the answer he might have given the engineer and the American. He put his hands on Marcello's shoulders. He wasn't smiling or joking. He was serious.

"Thank you, Marcello. This is the help that matters: feeling that there are brothers in the world."

XXXVI

AMENOFI LEFT ON FRIDAY AND SOMETHING HAPPENED
that upset the prison a little. Clark Gable had tried to kill
himself. He had stuck a needle in his chest and banged it with
the heel of his shoe till it was right inside, though not at the
heart. He was rushed to hospital.

This produced a chain of troubles, strict searches, etc.
And it supplied food for discussion for at least a couple of
days.

"Crazy thing to do," Germano remarked and thought no
more about it.

"Why did he do it?" Marcello asked Olgi.

Olgi didn't answer. The question was superfluous, and the
answer would have been superfluous too. They talked a while
of various seemingly unconnected things; then Olgi gave
Paolino a lesson. He got no intellectual pleasure out of it, it was
something he had to do, a duty he had imposed on himself.
That evening he didn't write, didn't feel like it, and read a
book: Antelme's *The Human Species*. It wasn't a gay book, but
nothing in Olgi's world was gay.

He read till the midnight check-up, then forced himself to
sleep. He felt somehow unwell, both physically and spiritually,
and tried to free himself by escaping into sleep. Briefly, he
dozed; then suffering pierced him, soaked his whole being. He
was used to these crises, as he was used to the prison bars and
the rest of it; they no longer frightened him, and he bore the
pain with humility and dignity.

The violence of this attack made him see that it might be the
final one, and he hoped it was. His heart seemed to roll round
in his chest, stopping at the epigastrium, his lower limbs were
already cold, his forehead sweating, his consciousness clouding
over. But in the breathless darkness that hung over him, a ray

of clear thought persisted, the consoling thought of death that would at last solve everything, pacify everything.

The crisis lasted several hours; then the pain diminished, his blood flowed in a calm rhythm again, his heart settled down in the casket of his chest, the grip on his diaphragm relaxed, his lungs started working normally, and even his brain began to weave again the mysterious thread of thought.

He murmured: "This is what a human being must suffer before death."

In spite of everything his organism, impelled by an inscrutable law, wanted to live, wanted to go on living; but Olgi did not share its relief, all he felt was sorrow and a frightened weariness, as if he had undergone an appalling hardship, and had to do so again.

That morning he didn't get up, didn't go out for exercise; not to recover his strength, and help his body in its efforts at renewal, but because he was afraid of standing up again, and carrying out the few elementary operations that enclosed a living creature's entire activity.

Nor did he take the soup that day. Cardboard-nose wasn't doling it out, but a keen, suspicious young warder.

"Why have you refused the soup?"

"I haven't refused it, I just don't feel like it."

"I'll have to report it, you know."

"Report away," said Olgi.

After half an hour the head warder came into his cell. With him was the scented sergeant and behind him were three stout warders. The head warder was a short, dark man between forty five and fifty, definitely a southerner, and possibly Sardinian.

"Why are you still in bed?" he asked.

"Because I like being in bed," answered Olgi.

The head warder suddenly pulled off the bedclothes. He saw a naked man who was anatomically correct. Nothing specially suspicious, no infringement of the Rules.

He covered Olgi again.

"Why won't you eat?"

"I do eat."

"That's twice you've refused the soup."

"I don't take it because I've got something better."

"Yesterday you told Lance-Corporal Perticone that you wouldn't have soup because you weren't a pig, and he could give it to the pigs. This sort of talk can be reported, you know that?"

"I know, but I don't give a damn."

"You don't? Why, of course not, when you think of all the punishment you've taken! You're being transferred, but we know all about you. Your biographical details follow you wherever you go, as you must know after all these years inside . . ."

"I know, but I don't give a damn for my biographical details. Excuse me, but is not giving a damn liable to be reported?"

"We've some good punishment cells for cooling off hot-heads."

"I've lost my hair and my head's stone cold."

"We know you all right."

"Who am I? A man. A man. Un homme. The Spaniards say hombre. And, excuse me, but – who are you?"

"I'm head warder with twenty-five years service, and no one makes a monkey out of me."

"Please, d'you mind stopping?"

"I've stopped. And you've been warned."

He went out, melodramatically, and took the scented sergeant by the arm.

"Giaccone, keep a very good eye on this scoundrel. He's getting on, and he's done years inside, but I still don't trust him. You won't find the leopard changing his spots. In all my years of service, I've not had a single black mark. No one has ever escaped, and this one's not going to ruin my career."

"You're a cunning old fox, sir," said Sergeant Giaccone, persuaded.

Olgi stayed in his bunk until two in the afternoon, the argument with the head warder not having angered him in the least. The man was doing his job. With a sense of duty. It was all Olgi's fault, for twice refusing soup. Soup that was neither good nor bad, because prison soup should be swallowed without any fuss or stubbornness.

"I might have explained that I sometimes like fasting. As Rabindranath Tagore says: 'The lighter the body the better the spirit rises.' Or less metaphysically, I might have convinced him that my fast had no polemical quarrel with his digestion."

Thinking this way – shrewdly, sharp-wittedly, genially – meant being a part of life again. Accepting the whole of life again, good and bad, trouble and enjoyment.

"I'll stay in bed till a few minutes before we leave. Today's Saturday, then there's Sunday and Monday. Two days and a bit in bed. What's that? When you had that stroke, you didn't get up for six months on end. You can live in bed. You can live perfectly well in bed."

But as soon as he heard the bell for exercise he got up quickly and dressed. He was longing to be outside, among men. Ugly, limited, full of faults, but men. And among them a favourite. Someone who is or seems finer, nobler, than the rest.

"Why didn't you come to exercise this morning?" asked Marcello. "Were you ill?"

"Was I ill?" said Olgi jokingly. "Do I look the sickly type? Why, I've health and strength to spare."

He puffed out his chest and thumped it with his great proud fist, and then gave a rasping, valetudinarian's cough and wheezed.

"Any news?"

"My lawyer came to see me yesterday. I'll be tried before Christmas. He thinks I won't get more than three years."

"Never trust lawyers," Olgi advised him gloomily. "Remember Dostoievsky defined them as 'Conscience for sale'."

"But this is a really good fellow. He's a socialist."

"Socialist nobs of any sort," continued Olgi jokingly. "I don't trust socialists who try to get ahead."

"He's not like that, he's just a socialist. He wouldn't take anything for defending me, just his office expenses. Don't you call that a good fellow?"

"A benefactor. Even when you get into a lawyer's clutches you need luck. My defence pinched the small amount I'd got left from my days as a second-rate outlaw and got me the maximum sentence as well."

"There'll be an amnesty soon, the lawyer told me so. The law they're hoping to get through will mean three years' remission for first offenders. If it goes through right away I may spend Christmas at home."

"Christmas really is something," said Olgi. "Hugs and goodwill all round, sins forgiven, charitable ladies visiting hovels, and even prisoners getting a pinch of good from it. Ah, Christian piety's a fine thing."

Marcello's eyes were serious, sorrowful.

"You mustn't despair, Olgi."

"Me despair? What d'you think I am – a greenhorn innocent? Why, I'm a hardened criminal."

He went up to the bars, behind which Paolino was smiling shyly.

"Hallo, Paolino."

"Hallo, sir. Not seeing you I was afraid you'd left."

"I'm leaving on Tuesday, you know."

Paolino swallowed before speaking.

"Tuesday will be a sad day for me."

XXXVII

IT WAS A LARGE CELL, AND, USED AS HE WAS TO A
nine-foot cubicle, it seemed immense; about thirty feet by
thirty-six, with a cone-shaped ceiling and beams that would
have held up a cathedral, its corners dark and murky with dark
hairy spiders lurking in them, and as silent as the tomb. But
from outside, as it was still day-time, came the plaintive cheep
of sparrows in search of food.

The sparrow! The prisoner's friend! Olgi had never raised
one, but one day, at Portolongone, the mason had brought
along a sparrow that had fallen out of its nest. The mason, a
snub-nosed murderer, had the tiny creature wrapped in a little
cotton wool in his cupped hand. The bird had no feathers, his
eyes were still shut, and he made no sound.

"Here," said the mason, "try and get it to live."

"I don't like raising birds," said Olgi.

"You can do it for once. He's an orphan. He fell out of the
nest. His mother must have been a scatter-brain, making her
nest in the gutter just where it catches the wind. He was blown
right out."

"Poor soul, it's obvious she hadn't studied meteorology,"
said Olgi.

"Take it."

"But suppose he's dead."

"He's not dead, he's alive."

"He's not even cheeping."

"He'll cheep, you try and get him to live, and when he's
grown send him off."

Olgi put the bird into his round convicts' cap, carefully
making a warm nest round him with the cotton wool. He wondered about food. What, though? A grown sparrow will eat
anything but a new-born one needs delicate little worms, Olgi

thought. He called the sweeper Spaccamonti, who knew as much as an ornithologist about birds.

"You should give him chopped-up millet mixed with egg yolk," Spaccamonti said.

"But where'll I find millet? I haven't even got an egg. This orphan's life depends on you."

Spaccamonti had been sentenced eighteen times, and prison was his home. He wouldn't have given one of his fellows a breath of air on his deathbed; but that tiny sparrow fallen out of its nest sent him upstairs and down, knocking at twenty cell doors like a beggar. With his pitiless thief's hands he made the nourishing meal and, in order to show Olgi how to do it, put it in the creature's mouth as delicately as a mother.

"Little and often, because if he swallows too much when he's small he may die."

"I see," said Olgi. "A meal about every hour. And how about at night?"

"Nothing at night."

"But women suckle their babies at night."

"Sparrows sleep at night."

"This chap sleeps all the time, I've got a feeling, all day and all night."

"What the hell, he's small. When you were small you slept all the time, didn't you?"

"That's true," said Olgi, "when I was small . . ."

He fed the bird for the last time before going to bed. He slept a couple of hours, perhaps more (in those days he was only thirty-five, and healthy, and sleep was the best cure for misery), then a feeling of maternal responsibility prodded him awake. He got up, uncovered him a little, stroked him with a finger: the tiny, unaware thing was alive. Reassured, he fell asleep again. The midnight check-up woke him, and he dashed to the baby's cot. He was alive. Olgi slept deeply all night, and cockcrow awoke him.

He took the bird from his cotton wool nest, and held him delicately in his great fist, to feed him: naked, blind, one of nature's timid efforts, an instinct that seemed to be starting from scratch.

Olgi was amazed to see how fast the little creature developed, and how he adapted himself to life's demands. From one day to the next he was dressed in a thick fluff, and learnt – but who taught him? – to throw out his waste matter, so as not to dirty the nest. His method of doing this was ingenious: he would go to the edge of the nest, which was Olgi's cap, and with his seat stuck out he would throw his own faeces far, with a force that was really remarkable in so small a creature. On account of this ballistic talent of his, Olgi named him the gunner. Before, he had to force open his beak in order to feed him, but now the gunner imperiously demanded to be fed. He stuck his neck out enormously and his mouth gaped till it looked like a trumpet. And he was no longer satisfied with scraps.

"Come on, gunner," Olgi would say gaily, "stoke up the ammunition dump. Life's fine and the world's yours."

Crop full, the gunner would settle down to sleep. And meanwhile he was growing bigger and stronger and putting on feathers. After a month he had strong feathers and bushy tail, and a gallant, tough nature revealed in treacherous pecks. To Olgi, his nurse, he was very much attached.

Another month went by, he was now full-grown, and ready to face the battle of life. Olgi opened the window. He was sorry to lose a comrade, but hated making him share his prison.

"Come on, gunner, get away, look how big and fine the world is. Go on, say hullo to the town and people for me, and everyone you meet."

But the gunner seemed unwilling to take off. He crouched on Olgi's shoulder, lovingly pecking the lobe of his ear. Olgi picked him up and put him on one of the bars.

"Look how fine the world is. This blue sunny sky's all yours.

And the mountains and the hills, and the fields, and the leafy trees, and the sparkling, murmuring river – it's all yours."

The gunner cheeped but refused to fly.

"And then think of the pretty females," Olgi went on. "Why, you'll be crazily in love!"

The gunner flew back on to his shoulder.

"I see," said Olgi, "you're a bit stupid. People are quite right to say 'He's got the brain of a sparrow' when they're talking about someone pretty dim."

He took the bird in his hand and flung him into space. The gunner cheeped, and then flew surely and swiftly into space, and vanished behind a large maple-tree. Olgi went and lay down on his bed, opened Tolstoy, his latest literary discovery, and in the great Russian novelist's pages sought to explain his little personal drama. He wanted to avoid thinking of the scrap of affection, the scrap of good he had lost. But the immortal pages gave him no comfort.

A flutter of wings and the gunner landed on his chest.

"Why, just look at that," said Olgi. "He's really fond of me. These creatures have a heart. He's given up his freedom to be with me."

He tickled the small head.

"I could keep him with me, and feel a little less alone."

But he got up again and flung him into space. Again the bird came back to him. Then Olgi lost patience and shouted at him.

"Bugger off, you fool. Can't you see I don't want you? You give me the creeps, wanting to stay inside. If I only had your wings . . ."

He pushed him off, but the bird flew on to his thigh, and Olgi slapped him away again, but without realizing his own strength; the sparrow struck the wall and fell dead on the floor.

"You're a murderer," cried Olgi, despising himself, "you scum."

More than ten years had passed and he still remembered this evil deed, and suffered.

A ray of sunshine fell sidelong from a tall rectangular window, and made a strip of light on the old rough skin of the wall. Like a child Olgi held out his hands to it. Then quickly the ray disappeared.

XXXVIII

THE WARDEN OPENED THE DOOR BUT NOT THE GATE.

"Mass is on," he said. "Want to go?"

"Yes," said Olgi.

Then the warder opened the gate.

"Where is it?" Olgi asked.

"The chapel's on the left, down the passage."

It was a large cage, and at the end of it was a kind of small room where the priest was to say Mass. The door and walls of the small room had been knocked down to make room for the altar. Behind the altar was a partition, behind which the priest put on his vestments. Instead of the usual pews in rows there were benches, because on days when it wasn't used for church-going the cage was used as a school.

Olgi found about ten others there. There was the failed shopkeeper; an old farmer who had killed his daughter-in-law; others whose crime Olgi didn't know; a fair youngish boy with long hair that curled on his neck, who kept turning round to the others, winking and grinning.

The priest was old and white haired, but thin and upstanding. He wore hefty black shoes that poked out from under his surplice (which made an odd impression on Olgi), and he looked at once sharp-eyed and tolerant. He got through the Mass fairly fast, not preaching on the Gospel, which was the parable of the servant in debt who had asked his master for pity, and then refused pity to a debtor of his own. The allusion was so clear that everyone must have understood it. The priest's hasty Latin had an attractive Piedmontese accent, and there was a homely simplicity in his way of dealing with God.

"Ite, missa est."

The old farmer was weeping softly, the failed shopkeeper made the sign of the Cross ostentatiously three or four times, the grinning long-haired youngster dashed to the exit of the little room, meaning to wait outside for the patient priest and exploit him.

"You can go into the passage," said the warder.

Marcello was talking animatedly with Germano and some others about sport, but when he saw Olgi he moved away from them.

"Have you been to Mass?" he said, but there was no sneer in his question, only faint surprise.

"Yes," said Olgi, "I went to Mass."

"D'you believe in God?"

"I don't know," Olgi replied. "But I don't refuse anything. I leave the door open, and when you least expect it a welcome visitor may come in."

But Marcello couldn't follow what he meant.

"When I was a boy I believed myself," he said. "And I used to pray. Not to God but to Jesus. He was power, goodness, and love. I'd join my hands and say: 'Dear Jesus, let Father always have a job, don't let Mother ever get ill, let Grandma live to be a hundred. Send bad people to hell. And I'm your little friend Marcello, who really loves you.'"

"We've all prayed like that," said Olgi. "And then what happened?"

"When I was seventeen I went to work in a glass factory. When things went wrong the men cursed; when they were gay, they talked filth. My grandmother died when she was only sixty,

215

of kidney trouble that made her scream with pain. Every step I took in life denied what I'd believed as a boy. Instead of going straight to hell, the wicked did better than the good, and had big houses and cars. Lies and injustice triumphed everywhere. Where was dear Jesus? What was dear Jesus up to?"

"Not being able to answer these questions, you became a communist," said Olgi.

"Yes, I became a communist."

"And suppose communism were as impotent to cure the evils of the world as Jesus?" asked Olgi.

"It would mean our race was accursed."

Olgi smiled.

"Sometimes I really do believe that man is accursed, that he's inescapably accursed; but then I realize that in spite of everything there's greatness in man."

This time it was Marcello's turn to smile.

"Then what are we to do about it?"

"This is what I've concluded: that in any social régime, in any situation, from the moment we start living we must live as men. With all the courage and dignity we can muster."

But he realized that even this fine phrase changed nothing, solved nothing in man's destiny. It was valid only for some people who . . . believed you.

"What a lovely day," he said.

"Yes," said Marcello. "But soon it'll be September."

Olgi went to greet Paolino.

"Hullo, Paolino. How are you?"

"Fine, thank you, sir."

"Why don't you ever come down to the yard, and take a turn? Do you good."

The boy didn't answer. He looked at the book he was holding.

"We won't have a lesson today," said Olgi. "Sunday's a day of rest."

"Yes," said the boy.

"How did you spend Sundays, before?"

"At home?"

"Of course, at home."

"Behind the railway there was a space we called the sports-ground. The soldiers went there for drill and we went to play football."

"Did you like playing football?"

"Yes. I wasn't bad at centre forward. I could kick and put the ball where I wanted it. Our team's captain wanted me to take it up professionally. But I was working, and could only play on Sundays. So I dropped the idea."

"Had you a girl-friend?"

Paolino blushed.

"No."

Olgi put his hand through the bars and ruffled the boy's hair.

"Be brave, Paolino," he said, staring intensely into his eyes as if hoping to hand on his own capacity to fight and hold out, even if not to hope.

"Yes," murmured Paolino. "I must be."

Olgi went back to his cell feeling a gentle melancholy, as a man sometimes does who has suffered deeply and wishes to lighten the suffering of others, and cannot do so, since each man must, inevitably, take his ration of sorrow. But he wasn't sad. Physically he felt pretty well. Two days of fasting had refined and cleared his blood. His illness was like a lazy, cruel beast that lived on him. It sank its fangs into him, then settled down to sleep again. And then Olgi had peace.

A wide strip of light came in incongruously through the window.

The door opened and the guard said:

"Bread."

Olgi took the bread from the dirty hand of the old sweeper Arturo, who grinned.

"There's pasta and meat today," he said.

And he meant to imply: "Today, when the food's good, you won't refuse it."

"Got a cigarette?" asked the sweeper.

"No," said Olgi.

The warder shut the door again.

After an hour it opened again.

"Time for your meal," said the warder.

"What meal?" said Olgi.

"Your meal. Didn't you order a meal?"

"No, I didn't," said Olgi.

"Then someone sent it, someone from outside. Haven't you any relations?"

"Not in this town."

"But the meal's for you."

"Impossible, have a good look, it must be some mistake."

The warder read the card again.

"It says Olgi Valnisi. Aren't you Olgi Valnisi?"

"Yes, I'm Olgi Valnisi."

"Then the meal's yours."

"Impossible, I tell you."

The warder, though still polite, grew impatient.

"Now listen – you take the meal and stop wasting my time, there's a good chap. The meal's for Olgi Valnisi and you're Olgi Valnisi. And besides, it's signed by the person who sent it. We do everything as it should be done. We keep the rules, and everything's got to be done according to the rules," he said solemnly.

"Who sent it?" asked Olgi.

Once more the warder read the card.

"Mara Borghatto. D'you know her?"

"I should say so," said Olgi. "She's my girl-friend."

The warder looked rather surprised. He was young, and

reacted as a young man. But he was a warder too, and, concerned only with his warder's job, said: "The sweeper'll come and fetch the basket later."

Then he shut the gate and the door.

Olgi took out the contents of the bag: there was a small pot containing soup. The soup smelt of chicken. There was a fine piece of boiled meat, roast rabbit and chips, a piece of cheese, two pears and two apples. And there was half a litre of wine, a fine clear red wine.

He had laid it out on the bed, and with rather sorrowful tenderness looked at those things that expressed more than the physiological need of nourishment. This was how men ate. Food that cost sweat, and then meant gaiety.

I'm eating what they're eating, Olgi thought. And he saw them all gathered round the table, the eternal human family: Mara's father, the pensioned-off railwayman, his wife Ersilia, Duccio and Piero, Mara's brothers, Giovanna, Duccio's wife, their children Teresa and Giacomo; and Mara. Eating the food they were eating, it was if Olgi were sitting at the table with them, a member of the one inalienable family. The break was finally mended, the long expiation over. Beyond the law, in spite of the law. In the brotherhood of the human heart.

XXXIX

WHEN HE WENT OUT FOR EXERCISE HE GRABBED Marcello playfully by the neck.

"Ah, you communist who play at Good Samaritan . . ."

"What's all this about the Good Samaritan?" Marcello said, surprised.

"Pretend you don't know?"

"What are you talking about?" said Marcello. Then Olgi

realized from the expression of his face that the idea of the meal hadn't been his.

"Your girl brought me a meal. Aren't you jealous?"

"Good," said Marcello approvingly. "I hope you enjoyed it."

"The poor certainly eat well," said Olgi, since he wasn't the kind to confess that Mara's present had moved him to the point of tears.

"They're all at work in Mara's family," said Marcello, "and if they have rabbit or chicken on Sundays it's not extravagant."

"All citizens, at least on Sundays, should have a chicken in the pot," said Olgi, and thought of Henry IV.* Whereas Marcello was thinking of communism.

"You see, my dear Marcello," said Olgi who was in a mood to sweeten dialectic with humour, "the odd complications and unexpected injustices the course of history turns up. There's social progress, more widespread well-being, and the only ones badly done by are . . . the chickens."

He looked towards the window of Paolino's cell.

"He's not there any more," said Marcello.

"Why?"

"Well, you see, he's young, someone propositioned him, he resented it, and to avoid trouble they isolated him."

Olgi wasn't surprised; and didn't say: who's that swine, etc., etc. Even this was an effect, a result, a way of being in 'that' reality.

All he asked was:

"Where did they put him?"

"In one of the isolation cells underground."

Olgi didn't say: poor lad, and didn't even think it. He knew how appallingly that defenceless child, who was just at the dreadful beginning of it all, would be tried. He was like soft

*Henry IV of France, who said that every citizen ought to have a chicken in his pot on Sundays.

clay, and no one could tell what harsh shape he would be moulded into.

"Once I spent four years on end in an underground cell. And then . . . and then . . . And I'm still alive. I look at the sun and I'm not surprised. I talk to you and I'm not surprised. The way we can forget things in life is marvellous. Or terrible. I don't know."

"We should make sure such things don't happen," said Marcello. There was no pity in his eyes, only harsh decisiveness. Vengeful archangels might have looked like that. But he was only twenty-six, he had eaten all the pasta and meat he could, and he felt uneasy dwelling on what was sad and ugly. Olgi, too, didn't want to think of anything sad and ugly just then. He'd have time for that, oh, he'd certainly have time. . . . He couldn't bear to think he'd soon lose the friend he'd so recently found. And so he lived as if the moment would never end.

"There's a good programme this evening," said Marcello. "Festival of Song."

"Is Milva singing?"

"Yes. So's Mina."

"I prefer Milva," said Olgi.

"I prefer Mina," said Marcello.

For quite some time they carried on like this, then the time for exercise was over and they parted with a *ciao* and a slap on the back. Marcello went up, Olgi down. He was whistling the tune of one of Milva's songs.

"You're very gay," said the warder. "Lucky fellow!"

He was a man over forty, cadaverous, sunken-eyed, and with the muddy skin of a man with liver trouble. He was sitting on a small bench, head and keys dangling, and was in no hurry to shut the prisoner up. Alone underground there he was very likely bored. Or bewildered by gloomy thoughts.

"Why shouldn't I be gay?" answered Olgi. "I've eaten well, I'm feeling well, that's why I'm singing."

"You're healthy," said the warder. "Lucky fellow!"

"Disgustingly healthy," said Olgi, and laughed.

"Don't make too much row," said the warder. "The sergeant may hear and come down to see what's up. I'm ill, myself."

"What's wrong?"

"I'm all ballsed up inside: intestines, liver, spleen. I ought to have proper treatment, not just pills and diet, but give up my job. But with the pension I'd get we'd starve. I've got a wife who weighs ninety kilos and four daughters who suck the marrow from my bones. You married?"

"I'm single."

"Lucky man. How old are you?"

"Forty-seven."

"Two more than me. And I look like your father. If only I'd got your big handsome face. And those shoulders, that neck."

"I've been inside twenty years," said Olgi.

"We're all of us wretched, some for one reason, some for another."

He shook his head.

"Life's just one long misery!"

He looked at Olgi, neither liking nor disliking him, just as he might look at a wall or a chair.

"What have you done, to be so heavily guarded?"

"Nothing, as far as I know. I'm a quiet fellow."

"I can well believe it. Twelve or fifteen years ago you may have been dangerous, but you're calm enough now. And a good fellow, at that."

"Thank you for those few kind words," said Olgi.

The man who was 'all ballsed up inside' opened the door, sighing, opened the gate, sighing, closed the gate again, closed the door.

Olgi began writing. He wrote until the radio started crackling. Then he got into bed and sipped at the programme of songs. Milva was the last to sing, and Olgi was enraptured: the woman's beautiful, deep, passionate voice gave him sharp pleasure, like physical enjoyment. And even when the radio was silent, and within him, a living man, there was again a grave-like silence, a grave-like solitude, that voice continued to work on him, in fervid excitement.

The bed-clothes were a heavy shroud on his naked body, and he flung them off to the end of the mattress, joyfully touching his chest, his belly, his thighs.

He sighed: to have a woman. His whole being yearned to be united with a woman.

He pulled the bed-clothes up over him again, so that all was dark and intimate around him, and he could be alone with the amorous ghost of a woman; with the others, the fierce stupid others, outside.

And he began the hard exercise of concentration and evocation. A lifer at Porto Azzurro, half mad and half fakir, had shown him how. It took a powerful effort of concentration, to annul himself in the object of his thoughts. Then imagination created reality. Olgi sweated with pain and effort, but at last it came. And a great joy sang in Olgi's heart. She had eyes that were big and bright as stars: a small woman, who yet filled creation with herself.

She came forward slowly, swaying voluptuously, since she knew her lover liked her to walk in this provocative way. She was wearing a light dress with a very low neck, and under it so little that you could hold it in one hand. On her curly black hair she wore a diadem, because she was a queen.

They didn't speak, they embraced. He was naked, just out of Eden, strong and hairy, but touching as well, offered thus, like a child. Pressing him close, kissing him on the mouth, she murmured: "Oh, my man." With trembling hands he helped her undress. Naked she lay down on the bed (no longer the dirty convict's straw mattress but a princely marriage bed) and enjoyed being admired and desired. Like all women she was born a whore, and yet, tenderly modest, she held her hand over her sex. And he was sweetly surprised to see how small and delicate her hand was. A man could never be hurt by such a hand.

He bent down to kiss her hand, and urged like that she laughed and took the hand away. Trembling, she said again: "Oh, my man."

She held out her arms, wanting him on top of her. But although he was yearning, yearning infinitely to take her, he delayed, prolonging his visual pleasure. His adoration of her extended even to her clothes. He murmured: "How beautifully a woman dresses."

He looked, touched, kissed her dress, her vest, her bra, her panties.

Her face was radiant.

"You're so hungry, my poor man, but I will satisfy you. There are good things here," she exclaimed with whorish pride, "to still a man's hunger. But come to me now, kiss me, what are you doing with my clothes? Are you kissing my panties? Why, I'm better than my panties. I'm living flesh. If there were nothing else, well, I could understand it, but with all this waiting for you . . ."

Then he touched her beautiful hair.

"Woman's hair," he said.

"Woman's mouth, woman's breasts, woman's belly and hips. Woman's thighs . . ."

He touched her and kissed, until she cried:

"Stop! I can't wait any longer. Come."

PART VII

XL

"THE MAN WHO'S OFF," CALLED THE GUARD.

Olgi went up, and at the top of the stairs met the gay and scented Neapolitan sergeant. He looked happier than usual, perhaps because he was losing such a dangerous lodger . . .

"And how about shaving?" he said, worried and correct, "why haven't you shaved?"

Olgi touched his chin.

"It's not too bad."

"But it doesn't look right. D'you want to discredit the old firm? Go and shave, you old bandit."

"Incorrigible bandit," Olgi corrected him. "Treacherous bandit."

The scented sergeant gave him a cordial slap on his broad shoulder.

"But you're a nice old bugger."

Olgi went to get shaved. It was a small room with a rickety table, a wardrobe fixed to the wall, a basin. The barber was talking to a friend of his, a fellow-prisoner. He had erotic whiskers, thick, gleaming hair, cruel, cunning eyes. The other man too looked as if he'd turned up in prison by mistake, through a slip of fate, but that he'd manage pretty well under the circumstances.

"Well Gastone," the barber was saying, "you can see if I don't mean to take up with Liliana when I get out in November. But . . . just one last go. And at the best moment I'll spit in her face. That's the way to treat women."

Gastone grinned mischievously, agreeing.

"A slash on the cheek won't do because you get six or seven years. Your idea is better. To a sensitive woman that's worse than a slash."

"Think so?"

He looked malignantly at Olgi.

"What d'you want?" And he looked like an overweening swell turned to a beggar.

"I'm just leaving," said Olgi, very calmly. "You've got to shave me."

"Then soap yourself."

Above the basin was a fly-blown mirror. It made comical shapes of its images. Above the mirror was stuck a picture of the madonna with the divine child in her arms, among some dried olive sprigs.

Whiskers, a barber in happier days, thief and pimp by nature, had a pious soul. He'd tripped up, but he'd redeemed himself. The prison governor, the chaplain and the maresciallo were all convinced he'd sincerely reformed. And he was to be pardoned. Perhaps he might even throw Gastone a life-belt . . .

Good-humouredly Olgi saw his large satanic face being covered with white lather; it looked like the face of a poodle, with just the point of his nose visible, and the glitter of his mad eyes.

He sat down on the mended chair, and with four hasty strokes of the razor Whiskers took the hair off his face. Olgi washed his cheeks and thought of Marcello. A name, and yet. . . . And of Paolino too, and of poor deranged Clark Gable, who were something more than names for Olgi the traveller. Solidarity, pity, enrichment. A man gave and he received. Meantime his journey was approaching its end.

"Now you look really handsome," said the scented sergeant.

"I was always handsome," answered Olgi.

The sergeant opened the door of a small room, searched Olgi and checked the contents of his haversack again.

"What d'you want these rags for?" he asked disgustedly.

"I'm fond of them."

The sergeant looked into the book.

"What sort of a name's this? He's not Italian."

"He's a writer and poet, born at Swansea, died in New York in 1953, when he was just forty," said Olgi.

"Poets die like the rest of us," said the scented sergeant. "And what's this fat exercise book? What are you writing? *My Prisons*?"

"Maybe," said Olgi.

"Well, now I'll shut you up in here for a bit, till the carabinieri turn up."

"You do that," said Olgi.

In the small room there was a plank bed with grey bedclothes piled up on it. And a bench, but not fixed to the wall. No window, or opening. Olgi packed his 'rags' into the haversack and picked up the book. He looked at it and caressed it tenderly. Its cover was worn, the spine was broken in several places. Yet it still sent out warmth and life, and unimpaired beauty. He opened it at the last page and read aloud:

For a long time he waited on the stairs, though there was no love now to wait for and no bed but his own too many miles away to lie in, and only the approaching day to remember his discovery. All around him the disturbed inhabitants of the house were falling back into sleep. Then he walked out of the house on to the waste space and under the leaning cranes and ladders. The light of the one weak lamp in a rusty circle fell across the brick-heaps and the broken wood and the dust that had been houses once, where the small and hardly known and never-to-be-forgotten people of the dirty town had lived and loved and died and, always, lost.*

He lay down on the bench and repeated, looking at the ceiling: "had lived and loved and died and, always, lost." He wondered: Why am I not dead too? What does this living of mine mean? How much more do I have to suffer? Or will the end come soon? Will it really be the end? Of course, for me it will be. I may fall while I'm getting off the train or crossing the

* The concluding paragraph of *Portrait of an Artist as a Young Dog* by Dylan Thomas.

tracks, fall face downwards without a cry, lose consciousness and die. Then perhaps, I'd be happy.

The carabinieri came, two of them: a sergeant and a lance-corporal. The sergeant had recently got married. He oozed self-importance and policemanly correctness. The lance-corporal had mocking eyes, a straight nose and a mouth that was never still.

"Congratulations," said the scented sergeant. "I heard yesterday you'd got married."

The other man smiled faintly, which prevented any familiarity.

"When did you get back?"

"Yesterday."

"Has your wife joined you here?"

"We've got a small flat in via Crispi. Three rooms, and the rent's twenty thousand. It's a problem, this business of where to live."

"It's a disgrace," said the scented sergeant. "Why doesn't the state provide free houses for its employees, at least those who are most useful and loyal? Things weren't as crooked in the Duce's time; everyone had to be honest, including landlords."

"That's the holy truth," grinned Olgi.

"I didn't ask your opinion. You criminals are all hand in glove with the communists."

The married man took no sides, he too was a fascist at heart, but the government was now in other hands and his duty was to serve the government.

"Put his irons on," he said to the lance-corporal.

"You'll have a quiet transfer," said the scented sergeant. "Just the one man to watch."

"One man may be worse than ten at times," said the married man.

Olgi looked at him. He had the smooth, austere face of a clergyman.

"Chain me up tight," Olgi said to the lance-corporal. "I'm a dangerous criminal."

"You're all dangerous," said the lance-corporal. He put on the chain.

"So long," said the scented sergeant.

"So long."

"So long."

XLI

IT MUST HAVE BEEN NEARLY MIDDAY, AND THE TRAIN was still standing with its engine silent, and seemed unlikely to be leaving soon. But Olgi knew that the last stretch of the journey was short; about an hour from Alessandria to Cavallermaggiore, and from there, on the train that came from Turin, less than half an hour to reach Saluzzo.

He was alone in the prison coach, which he had all to himself, yet he took up the smallest amount of space, a single section; it was quite large enough for him, though, being intended to hold and guard four people; and it was safe, solid, and unbreakable, though the lock allowed thieving eyes to steal a look from outside, now and then.

What he saw was a bare patch of grass and stones, a marvellous island to play in, and he was surprised there were no children there, and was suddenly frightened of living in a world without children. The bare patch ended in a wall beyond which were shapeless huddles of houses, but far away, and now out of reach.

A workman went by with a small flag under his arm, he was whistling, and when he came near the prison coach he glanced up at the barred window, his workman's face contented, his overalls almost new. Perhaps he'd been taken on quite recently, and he was whistling, he had a flag, and his cowhide shoes squeaked as he moved away.

Olgi looked at the desert of grass and stones again; the sun illumined it, like naked truth.

Then a train arrived, and stopped. Olgi managed to see a window, two windows, three windows. The people were sitting on plush seats, well dressed, clean, polite, well behaved. They talked to each other, and smiled. Olgi was enchanted by a marvellous girl. Rubies glittered on her finger-tips when she moved her hands, her hair was blonde, and clung like a cap to her tiny head, a jewel glittered on her slim wrist, her painted face had a rather enigmatic, Byzantine softness, but from her neck down she was all living carnality, a fount of joy.

Opposite her sat a middle-aged man, with a businessman's self-confident, dominant air. He must have had some relationship with the beautiful girl, because they looked at each other, and smiled.

Then the train left and Olgi sat down again. He sat twisted, shrunken, as if trying to avoid violence or because of some inner convulsion; and kept shaking his head obsessively. Then he clenched his fist and started banging on the bare wooden seat.

Startled by the noise, the sergeant went to peer in at him.

"He's mad," he told the lance-corporal, "that man's mad."

"They're all more or less mad," said the lance-corporal. And he began talking again about his girl at home.

"I love her, but I don't yet know if I'm going to marry her. She's got no dowry, her people have nothing, and I've only got my pay."

"That man worries me," declared the sergeant.

"You take your work too seriously," said the lance-corporal. "In another ten years you'll have an ulcer and you won't even have got to be maresciallo."

"I can't relax, that man worries me," repeated the sergeant.

"As soon as I saw his face I felt something odd inside me, like a voice saying: 'Look out, this transfer may give you trouble'."

"What sort of trouble? Balls. He won't escape, you can count on that."

"That's not what I'm afraid of."

"Then what?"

"I don't know how to put it, but I just don't feel easy."

He went to peep again, and this time the prisoner had his face in his hands.

"Did you knock?" he said, as he wanted to see Olgi's face.

"No, I didn't," said Olgi, but without taking his hands from his face.

"I thought you knocked, I thought you needed something."

"I didn't knock, I don't need anything."

The man went and sat down again beside the picked carabiniere, who had started reading a satirical newspaper. He wanted to say: reading on duty's not allowed, but, cautious, duty-dogged, forelock tugging fellow that he was, he was basically irresolute and timid as well. His father had made him join the carabinieri, his mother had made him marry. Gratefully he acknowledged that their choice was right. Serving in a military organization that kept order and maintained the peace gave him a pure, religious happiness. Marriage, too, was an institution that satisfied him completely.

He tried hard to think of his wife, in order to avoid his irrational, motiveless anxiety, but she now seemed to him a gentle, beautiful ghost who was powerless to help him. Just as the system of ideas that had sustained him was powerless to help him.

He got up and pretended to look out of the window, then tiptoed over to peer greedily into the prisoner's cell. He was now surprised to see Olgi sitting up serenely. The twisting pain, the raging indecency of unwatched despair, were superseded by calm, resigned, perhaps hidden suffering, which aroused no anxiety or shock. He was alone, yet he looked like a man travelling with others, all polite, all with a sense of proportion.

Suddenly Olgi turned his head and his eyes met the sergeant's through the hole in the middle of the iron door. Olgi smiled and the sergeant unexpectedly blushed. Again he went to the window, and the increasing number of people now arriving cheered him – some with handbags and suitcases, some with nothing, ordinary people with a job, a suit to wear, a mediocre destiny.

Olgi lay down on the seat, the back of his neck on the haversack. The seat was short so he kept his knees up; and, incorrigible egoist that he was, still kept smiling. He thought he had reached ataraxy, whereas in fact he was still a slave to that 'stupid lustful flesh' of his. He had only to see a sophisticated girl for his whole scaffolding of wisdom to come tumbling down, and within him all that was irrational, all that was a part of his flesh and blood screamed no, no, no, every one of the thousand times he had told himself there was nothing to be done, that this was his destiny, and so on.

"To punish you," he told himself humorously, "you won't get up from this seat till Cavallermaggiore."

He forced himself to think of nothing, but his will was powerless to stop the flow of images and memories, as it was powerless to stop the peristaltic movement, the kidneys secreting, and all the other organic functions, so long as he was alive.

The coach jerked, the long animal woke, the engine started puffing and blowing, and whistled to hurry late-comers. Then the great wheels turned relentlessly, and with them the carriage wheels till the whole train was running in the wake of the great peaceful sun; and even Olgi's marvellous heart ran with the train, in the sun.

With a lover's fidelity he stared at the strip of light that came in through the crack and gave form and substance to the sounds, to the uproar that reached him. Till he couldn't hold out any longer, and, like a happy child who enjoys defying his father's orders, he went to the crack to look out. Never had the sight of the world seemed to him so interesting, so delightful.

He felt that everything he saw, hills and mountains, vines and olives, houses and gardens and streets, the people he saw at every brief stop, and the animals, even the invisible birds in the sky, had all, all been created expressly for him. All of it was him, and he was all of it, intertwined, inseparably linked.

That hour, one of his last, passed very quickly.

XLII

THIS HAPPY COUNTRYSIDE HAD NO PRISON IN IT – Olgi liked imagining that – and besides, he would have to wait hours, not days, for the train from Turin, so there was no need for him to break the journey at a prison. They took him into a small room in the small station, and he was glad there wasn't a guarded room there, otherwise they would have shut him up in it. He was rather less glad when, having asked for the irons to be removed, he was kindly but firmly refused.

"When does the train from Turin come?" he asked.

"At a quarter to six."

"It's now a bit after one. I've been wearing handcuffs for over three hours. Do I have to wear these till six? What am I an ox? A human being can hardly be expected to hold out as long as an ox, can he?"

The sergeant didn't answer, nor did the lance-corporal, who was sitting in the doorway, his long legs crossed, his big feet in big strong boots, his mouth working continuously like a ruminant's. The sergeant was sitting down too, pretending to be absorbed in deep thinking although in fact a single thought possessed him: that of handing over this disquieting prisoner to the escort which was to come from Turin, before . . . In his consolingly foggy mind this word floated, coloured black and red: before . . . But before what? He could have cried at the incomprehensible something that terrified him. He ventured to look at the prisoner. Well defined and catalogued in his prison clothes, yet mysterious, wickedly elusive, since he must be very wicked . . .

"Well now," said Olgi, "are you going to take off these irons?"

"Anywhere public and unguarded it's forbidden by the rules."

"Take me to a guard room, then."

"There's no guard room."

"Then take me to prison."

"I can't."

"Take me to the barracks. There must be a carabinieri's barracks. There's one everywhere."

"I can't."

"Even if you take off the irons you're not taking any risk. I shan't escape. Where could I escape to? I've been inside twenty years. I'm nearly fifty. And I've got a bad heart."

"I'm sorry," said the sergeant, not looking at him, "but I can't."

Olgi didn't press it. It was fair, after all, that is, it was the rule to trust no one, even if it would have consoled him to be trusted a little at last. A little trust, at least, from someone like himself, even if love was impossible . . .

At the end of the room there was a small table and a bench. Olgi began copying into his exercise book what he had written on the sheet of lavatory paper. Wearing handcuffs this wasn't easy. It took effort and pain, and still more effort and pain. Yet he had to do it, even if it was pointless. He was sweating with pain, and towards the end his vision clouded.

"What's the time?"

"Ten to four."

Olgi put the exercise book back in his haversack. He felt slightly odd, though not in pain, as if he were beginning to live in another dimension.

The lance-corporal yawned.

"I'm hungry. I'm going to get myself a sandwich roll. Anything for you, sergeant?"

"I never eat between meals."

"Hey boy," called the lance-corporal. It was a boy of about twelve, working for some shop in the station.

"Yessir," he said. He was a boy but already had an adult face. He didn't look at Olgi.

"Tell the girl at the buffet to bring me a roll and a beer."

The girl from the buffet arrived with the roll and the beer. She was a faded blonde, over thirty, with a silly giggle, and she swayed her broad hips.

"Well look who's here again," she said.

"I'm on duty, on a transfer," explained the lance-corporal.

"Good afternoon, sergeant," said the blonde. She didn't look at Olgi.

"Good afternoon, signorina," said the sergeant formally. The lance-corporal bit into the ham roll.

"And how are your marriage plans, signorina?"

"Well, I've advertised, but no one'll have me."

She put her hands on her hips. "Not that I deserve it."

"Certainly not," said the lance-corporal, chewing, "but you see, signorina, marriage is different."

"What do you mean, different," the disappointed woman protested, "It's that you men are all so foul. I'd make a good wife, I would."

"Your trouble is you want to marry a carabiniere or a

237

business man," said the lance-corporal with his mouth full. "Why don't you look for a workman or a peasant?"

"And starve? I want to marry someone with a safe pay-packet."

"Ah, then you're marrying the pay-packet, not the man," said the lance-corporal, jokingly. "That's worth knowing. And to think I had an eye on you myself . . ."

"You can tease away, but I certainly wouldn't marry you. You've got a roving eye. No, I don't go for you at all."

"But lots of girls have."

"Look who's swanking. . . . D'you know the proverb?"

"'He who's scornful wants to buy.'"

"Think I'd buy you? Who d'you think you are, Rudolf Valentino?"

"He's dead. I'm alive."

The blonde shrugged her shoulders. She was put out, and looked like a big, ingenuous, hurt little girl. The lance-corporal swallowed the last mouthful, and gulped down the bottle of beer. He paid.

"So long, sergeant," said the blonde.

"So long, signorina," the sergeant answered.

"Signorina, please," said Olgi.

She stopped uncertainly.

"Signorina, please," Olgi repeated.

She went timidly to the table behind which Olgi was. He had risen. The woman looked like a hen with a falcon towering over her.

"Signorina," said Olgi, "might I have something to eat?"

What a lovely voice, she thought, and it seemed to her incredible that he could have such a beautiful, warm, human voice.

"What d'you want to eat?" she said, and looking him in the face. All her fears vanished. He was a man without evil mysteries. He was smiling. Instinctively she had put her hands on the table, beside those of the man bound by handcuffs. They were almost touching.

"Something hot, if possible," said Olgi.

"There's nothing hot. Cheese, ham, salami?"

Olgi hesitated, ham was good, and so was salami. Suddenly he remembered Enrico the Calabrian, the lifer from the Marche, and the poor man's rare joy when he got chicken to eat.

"Have you got any picnic baskets?"

"D'you want one?"

"Yes, if possible."

"There's just one left."

"Then I'm lucky. Is there chicken in it?"

"Yes," replied the blonde, "if you like chicken you're really lucky."

She laughed delightedly, pleased at his luck.

"Thanks," said Olgi. "And how much is it?"

"Seven hundred."

"Right then, will you bring it?"

The blonde brought the basket, and Olgi said to the sergeant:

"Give her all the money I've got."

"All?" said the sergeant, visibly put out.

"Yes, all of it."

He took the money from a yellow envelope, on which was written the prisoner's full name and the sum belonging to him: 857 lire. He gave the girl the money, and she thanked Olgi.

"Thank you, sir."

"Thank you, signorina."

"So long, and, have a good journey."

"So long, signorina, and I hope you soon find a good husband."

"Oh, thank you."

As she went out she banged her hip against the door-frame.

"Ouch," she said, but smiled, and gave the smile to Olgi. It was the smile of a servant-girl, yet worth having, all the same.

"You've got no money at all now," said the sergeant in a tone of moralistic reproach.

"All the better," said Olgi. "When a man no longer owns anything, then only is he rich."

And he began to eat. The piece of chicken must have been delicious, but it gave him no pleasure. It was dead flesh, the flesh of a poor murdered winged creature. Olgi's stomach contracted, and diminished his retching.

A violent noise approached, it was the train coming from Turin.

"Hurry," said the sergeant. Olgi, dragged on the chain by the lance-corporal, swayed, scarcely able to distinguish the images of the world. But that woman who was also hurrying across the tracks was a woman, and that child the woman was holding lovingly by the hand was a child. He opened his eyes wide, but could hardly see anything. Yet he smiled at the woman, and at the little girl. Even in the appalling, definitive pain that seized him, he could smile. It was with this final image of beauty and innocence that he fell.

"A doctor," the sergeant started shouting, "please get a doctor."

They rolled him over on to his back and saw that he was dead. This time, gracious and desired, it had come. A smile was fixed on Olgi's pale face, which could now be troubled no longer. Those who had gathered round looked at him, and were surprised to see a dead man chained and handcuffed, and even more surprised to see a dead man chained and smiling.

THE END

Prison asylum of Reggio Emilia 1960 and Penitentiary of San Gimignano 1961.